MW01069829

HUNGERSTONE

HUNGERSTONE

KAT DUNN

NEW YORK

First published in the UK in 2025 by Manilla Press

Copyright © 2025 by Kat Dunn.

Epigraph from *The Witch* screenplay by Robert Eggers. Published in 2016 by A24 Films.

zandoprojects.com

First Edition: February 2025

Text design by IDSUK (Data Connection) Ltd
Cover design by Alicia Tatone

The publisher does not have control over and is not responsible for author or other third-party websites (or their content).

Library of Congress Control Number: 2024946686

978-1-63893-216-1 (Hardcover)
978-1-63893-217-8 (ebook)

10 9 8 7 6 5 4 3 2 1

Manufactured in the United States of America

*To Tim, Saskia, and Coco, who first brought me
to the Peaks with great patience*

Wouldst thou like to live deliciously?

The Witch

I

It is not the dead
you should fear

1

IT STARTS WITH BLOOD.

In the middle of the night, I wake, like a hound scenting the fox, and place a hand between my thighs. It comes away sticky and dark.

I used to feel grief about it, once. Now, I am numb. A task my body gives me to dispense with: a rag, the awkward fumble with the safety pins and the belt that will lie against my skin for five days, bringing up rashes around my unused belly and hips.

There is an echo of a dream in my mouth, a copper taste on my tongue, and the prickle of the skin of my throat. I cannot recall more.

Henry is sleeping in his room; I can hear his soft snoring through the dressing room that forms the connection between our two private spaces. I still think softly of him, too, though I have come to doubt the strength of his regard for me after so many years.

I squat over the chamber pot and arrange my business. The nightdress is not stained, nor are the sheets—such is my intuition at thirty, when as a girl of sixteen I ruined so many bedclothes that my Aunt Daphne made me sleep with the belt on for a week either side of my courses as a precaution. I am mistress of my own house now, and I have sympathy for her penny-pinching. If I had a daughter, perhaps I, too, would begrudge her any accidents, wish her to hasten into adult responsibility.

I have no daughter. I have no child at all.

Leaving a bloody splatter against the porcelain, I place the lid on the chamber pot and push it beneath the bed. This is no quiet loss; I have not lain with Henry in many months. There was no hope to lose.

As my head crests the bed, I see something.

So fleeting. Just a flicker of movement, and the soft creak of weight on the floorboards.

I go still.

What was it? Where?

There—the corner of the room, where the darkness seems deeper.

I hold myself as quiet as I can, waiting for it to come again. My heart is clenched tight.

On the mantel, the clock ticks out the dead seconds.

Nothing.

There is no movement, no sound of the boards.

Fear seeps away, and I feel foolish. This house makes noises; every house I have ever lived in has eased and groaned with the wind and the damp.

I will not sleep again; the pain woke with me, so instead I furl myself in the quilt like an oyster in its shell with no pearl to show for the grit that works through it. Pain and blood, grief and hunger.

To be a woman is a horror I can little comprehend.

Blood has marked much of my still young life. Bleeding at twelve— younger than my mother had expected, an advent into a new age of motherhood she had not anticipated so soon. The absence of blood on my wedding night—Henry searching for it on the sheets in the morning, and finding none, pricking my finger on a penknife to smear a bright stain for the servants to find and know he had done his husbandly duty.

The blood that came each month after. At first, a disappointment, then a fear, then a grief, then an inevitability.

I was good for nothing but blood.

*

It is high summer, and the London house will have no more glory. We will close her up for the summer and retreat to the edge of Derbyshire and the new estate Henry has acquired, away from the smog of Sheffield proper. With ten years of migration, I am well used to the ebb and flow of the nomadic season, but there is still much to do. There are clothes to be mended and brushed, silverware and china to be counted and packed, clocks to be wound, dust sheets to be hung across the Chesterfield and sideboard. My desk is cleared, menus stacked and correspondence filed. There are no more invitations to be sent, no more seating plans to be decided. This anxious work of mine that has driven me for ten years, the precise and unassailable positioning of Henry and myself both in the upper ranks of society, gives the meaning to my life, makes walls and floors and borders in a borderless, insecure land. But it exhausts me. Once we settle in the country, a new round of social obligations will commence, but until then I am granted a reprieve: for a few weeks, it is enough for me to be only what I am.

I rise, aching and sluggish, and add a wrapper over my nightdress. The weather teases summer in bouts of bold sunshine and heat that sours the milk before it arrives from the dairy, then retreats in a flurry of gray skies and a heavy humidity that lies across the city like a fog. Between my curtains, there is a slice of white stucco and green bough. Our house is a fine building in the square near Holland Park, which Henry purchased from a drawing shown to him in Sheffield. We are surrounded by artists, about whom Henry is occasionally ungenerous.

Molly puts a slug of laudanum in my tea without my asking, and I am glad of it. My body is my enemy, and I will use every weapon in my arsenal against it. I breakfast lightly on kedgeree and strong tea, and remain in my bedroom, tending to correspondence.

Molly returns sooner than expected, something in her hand. "Miss Lamb has given her calling card."

Cora. I should have known.

"I am out to all visitors today, Molly."

I return to my letter writing, but Molly lingers at the door. "Yes?"

"She's talking to Mr. Crowther in the hallway—he was coming in when she arrived."

Of course she is. Cora knows how to make herself at home anywhere. Though she is more than half a decade younger than I am, it is one of many talents she wears easily, which come at so high a cost to me. Pretty, accomplished, and reassuringly conventional, the world seems to rotate around her every whim and delight. Sometimes, I feel too aware of her friendship granting reflected glory.

I do not look up. "Let him deal with her. I am occupied."

Molly bobs and slips away.

I am riled at the intrusion, too much in pain to be generous to those who lay endless demands at my door. On my writing desk is a tin of pastilles, and I put three into my mouth at once, letting the overwhelming rush of sugar blunt my mind.

To business: Henry's secretary has arranged a first-class compartment on the Midland Railway, and our departure from St. Pancras is set for the morrow. I do not know what to think about Nethershaw, the moorland estate for which I am now responsible. I have seen but one smudged photograph of its exterior: a long, low stone edifice of medieval and Tudor foundation that, unlike its distant neighbors, Chatsworth and Lyme, has not been wrapped in a Palladian façade. Its arched windows and crenelations give rise to images of monks and knights, an England we have long fled. Its position on the rising bank of hillside, leading to what is called in those parts an "edge"—here, Hungerstone Edge, flanked by Stanage and Burbage Edge—seems a bleak, alien landscape to me.

Until now, we have summered in rented houses in fashionable areas, but Henry is not satisfied. He wants his name on deed and register: on the marriage banns that joined my ancient family to his, and on the contract leasing four thousand acres of Derbyshire.

If I can become a woman in no other way, then I shall make it this: I am an unerring general in the campaign for our social standing. No rule of etiquette is obscure to me, no occasion too difficult to host.

I ignore the scatter of calling cards that arrive throughout the morning and think instead of the shirts and petticoats that came back from the laundry with scorch marks, the new gown that the dressmaker has yet to deliver, and my summer hat that on second look seems a little out of style. Is there time to order a new one before we go? Or should I give instruction to a milliner in Sheffield? No, it must be London. The steel wives of Sheffield will all have hats from the same establishments in York and Harrogate. I must come with the London fashions of this year, 1888, and not a single thing that speaks of a moment earlier. That is what Henry bought in me: taste, refinement, high birth, and good blood.

I take a moment to write a letter to my hatmaker with my request: whatever is considered the appropriate fashion for a married woman of thirty to be made up in my size and sent north.

A little before the luncheon bell, I dress. I have kept a tea-gown apart from the rest of my wardrobe, which has already been packed into trunks. This one is striped pink Liberty silk over a light corset, with a train trimmed in black velvet and a boned collar that sits tight around my throat. I am a beauty. It is well-known My eyes are cornflower blue and my skin like spilt cream. When we were courting, Henry would take down my hair from its pins and wind its heavy locks around his fingers like honey around a knife.

I was pretty then; I am beautiful now. My waist has thickened and my figure filled in the decade since our wedding, but it has only flushed my looks further into delight. There are perhaps some graces to being unmothered. My body is as unused as a dress not yet worn, and so remains as crisp and fresh as the day it was bought.

When I descend, it is to the hushed tones of a voice seeking privacy. Henry is in his study, and I linger outside, straightening a vase of dried flowers.

"... grand gift ... no ... surprised."

I can picture him, mouth cupped close to the telephone receiver, teeth yellow-stained by coffee and port, glistening with spittle when he runs his tongue across them, as he does when he is addressing a matter of urgency or importance. The telephone itself was installed only a few weeks ago—the first on the street—and Henry was as delighted as a schoolboy with a new toy, delaying the workmen at every turn so their cart could be observed outside our house the whole day.

It is our ten-year wedding anniversary in three weeks. The tin wedding. Perhaps Henry is telephoning Cutlers' Hall to insist the year be renamed steel.

We have spoken of no plans, but the words *gift* and *surprise* linger with me as I pass from the sheet-covered house into the tranquility of the garden. The dining room was amongst the first to be prepared for our absence, so we must take our final meals at the iron table on the terrace, or else like breakfast, on a tray in our respective rooms. Or at least *I* must—Henry will dine at his club or at a chophouse no doubt.

I wait for Henry with my eyes closed, willing away the pain in my stomach, frustrated by my weakness. The table on the terrace has been laid with the worst china for luncheon, the gold leaf flaking from the rims, along with a set of Sheffield steel cutlery from Henry's Ajax Works, and a selection of dishes repurposed from dinner last night: a little pressed beef, a coil of tongue, a small pot of shrimp beneath the oily plug of butter that seals them in, a dish of mashed potatoes, a shining glass of jelly, stewed fruit, cheeses, and biscuits. It is proper; I am pleased. I think of Aunt Daphne and her swollen knuckles rapping the etiquette book. *An elegant disorder is perfectly distinct from a vulgar confusion.*

My plate is too empty, and there is so much I want, but I must not start without approval. There is a note of my half-remembered dream in the metallic taste in my mouth—perhaps a storm is coming, the low pressure bringing the blood to my tongue.

Instead, I consider the grass that will need trimming and the flower beds tending while we are away. It is difficult to maintain control of such wild things without constant vigilance. This table, too, needs work. The green enamel paint has begun to peel in the crook of a curlicue in the wrought iron, and beneath it, specks of rust have taken hold. I worry at it with a fingernail. I have given little thought to our anniversary, and it troubles me that, of the two of us, Henry is the one to hold it in mind. I had not expected him to wish to celebrate, for it has been well over a year since he last visited my bedroom of a night—but perhaps some new mood has seized him.

I am struck by a sudden idea, and while I await Henry, I return quickly to my room and fish amongst the contents of a small, engraved box I keep at the back of my clothes press. At last, I retrieve the letter, the paper soft with wear. The postmark is dated a little over ten years prior: our courtship. I write a quick note—*my darling, yours from the start*—and go back downstairs.

As I'd hoped, Henry has gone to the lunch table, and I slip into his study to leave the letter on his desk. It is nothing really, only a trinket, but I am glad to do it.

A piece of paper catches my eye, different from the others around it: the handwriting is tentative, the letters unevenly formed, as though the writer is unfamiliar with ink and nib.

. . . dangerous working conditions . . . care given to human life . . .

Several words are underlined: *demands, ultimatum. Violence.*

"Lenore?"

Henry's voice cuts through the house, and I startle, sliding from the study as noiselessly as I can. My husband is a man who values nothing if not his privacy.

A balmy July morning has brooded over with cloud, and it is not quite warm enough to eat outside, but luncheon is already laid. I arrive at the table as the first spot of rain hits my wrist.

I look to the skies. "Shall we move indoors?"

Henry is irritated, already loading slices of beef and a spoon of mashed potatoes onto his plate. "It will pass, and I am hungry."

Not even the thick cloud can dull the glossy shine of Henry's hair or wash the color from his cheeks. I have seen him look as handsome in a crumpled nightshirt and tousled hair as in a top hat and tailcoat. Sometimes, when we are seen together at an assembly or dinner party, I am struck wordless that *this* is my husband. To know myself so envied.

I take the potted shrimp and excavate them with the point of my knife. There is a trencher with fresh bread, and I take a slice upon which to smear the salty shellfish. Henry watches it disappear between my lips, and his mouth twitches in distaste. I slow my eating.

Henry demands fresh tea, for the pot on the table has gone cold, and as we wait for Molly to return, I look at the oak at the end of the garden; it must be a relic from before these houses were built, its canopy as high as the rooftops. While we are gone, a man will come and cut it down, for there have been complaints that it blocks the light.

Molly brings the tea.

As I reach to pour it, Henry says, "I am hosting a shooting party for my new investors."

I send a cup to shatter on the paving stones.

"A shooting party?" I ask, staring openly. "Do you speak seriously?"

He holds my gaze intently, daring me to speak of the past that hangs in the air between us.

"Why would I not?"

I cast down my eyes. "Of course. When can we expect our guests?"

"Don't be ridiculous. It's a shooting party, Lenore. When do you think?"

I hesitate. "The twelfth of August is very soon."

The Glorious Twelfth, the opening of the grouse shooting season, is but two and a half weeks away. I looked again this morning through the documents detailing the Nethershaw estate: an unspeakably large swath of moorland is tied up in the holdings, and a certain amount of it is the habitat of grouse and pheasant.

Henry laughs. "You will hardly be preparing all the food yourself—I am sure you can cope with giving a few instructions to the staff."

It will be a great deal of work and require the renovations to be redirected to the guest rooms. Very well. I am more than capable.

Molly has come with a dustpan and brush for the shattered cup. I take my napkin and kneel with her to gather the shards. Blood speckles the pale cloth—I have cut myself: a neat parting of skin on the tip of my index finger. I put it in my mouth, suckling the sting with my tongue.

Henry has poured the tea, and he watches me as I swap finger for cup for finger, as though I am a piece of artwork he is unsure he likes, having brought it home.

I am only a wife, but I hold more of Henry's reputation in my hands than he has ever been able to accept.

*

The dream comes like an oil slick.

It is night. I lie in bed fixed in place. I do not recall the moment moving from sleep to wakefulness, but I am here, eyes open and fixed on the soft velvet folds of the red canopy of my four-poster bed. Dust lies thick, and a spider climbs amongst it like a hermit in a wasteland.

I cannot move.

This is the first thing of which I am certain.

It is as though thought and action have been severed as cleanly as a knife through meat. My body is not my own.

The second is that there is a presence in the room.

I cannot quite say where. A sense of a shadow in the corner, just at the edge of my vision—and then it shifts, drifting towards me, changing from haze to a smoky form the height of a person.

That is when the fear begins.

As the shadow advances, I mean to edge away, wanting the safety of a solid wall against my back, but I cannot move. I am helpless. A cold rush floods my veins.

The shadow lingers at the foot of my bed, before, in an instant, it vanishes, as though sucked back into Hell.

I try to move a finger, to press my nail into my palm, but it is in vain. Instead, I strain for the noise of my clock or the strike of horseshoes against the cobblestones—but I cannot hear anything. The shadow has deadened the world, and I am alone in its grasp.

Then, so quickly and neatly I am too surprised to make a noise, a head appears at my bedside: the pretty head of a young woman, a sweet, heart-shaped face and eyes that glitter in the dark. She cocks her head and regards me curiously, her full red lips drawn into a pout.

She rises, and a weight settles on the counterpane beside me as she lies down. I try to scream, but only a muffled sound escapes me. The woman is alarmed, and she presses a finger to my mouth. Hush.

All I can move are my eyes, and I track her movements as she pets my arms and shoulders, my cheeks, my throat. She combs her fingers through my hair, making a noise like a purr. Her hands slide across my body, the soft plane of my stomach and the curve of my hip. She nuzzles into my neck, and then I feel a warm, wet tongue on my skin and two sharp pinpricks.

It is as though the spell is broken; life floods back into my body.

I spring up, scrambling away from the woman so violently I slip to the floor. The light has changed, the room somehow smaller and duller than before, and I am half tangled in a sheet, sweating. When I have the courage to look to my bed, she is gone.

I dart low, looking beneath it to see if she is splayed upon the floor, but there is nothing. No one.

On my knees, I look wide-eyed around my room.

A noise behind me—I turn, heart racing.

Molly is at the door. "Lady Lenore? Are you all right?"

I allow her to help me up.

"Did you fall?"

I swallow the tremor in my voice. "Yes. Thank you."

There is no one else here. I put a hand to my throat, but it is dry. There is no blood. "Molly . . ."

She looks to where I indicate, not comprehending. "Yes, my lady?"

"It's nothing."

Molly settles me back in bed. Gingerly, I touch my hand to the space where the woman lay. Perhaps it is only my imagination, but I think I can sense a dip, a warmth from her weight. I run my hand across it.

"There's a chill tonight, my lady—I'll close the window. Bad dreams come if you sleep beneath the full moon." A flat disc of silver hangs in the clear sky, so bright it casts shadows from the trees.

A dream? I make no comment and instead only give my thanks.

Molly pushes down the sash and draws the curtains, then she leaves me, the door clicking shut, and I am alone with one thought:

I never left the window open.

2

HENRY IS AWAKE AND in his study when I descend, tossing a stack of documents into the fire one by one. My hand clenches around the newel post. My letter.

"What are you doing?" I come to the doorway. "What are those?"

The papers in his hand go into the flames. The grate is full of curls of ash.

"Things I have no further need of."

Henry does not like me to enter his study, but the knot in my stomach drives me in, and I cast around his desk for the letter and my note. It is gone.

"I left something here for you. Did you find it?"

As though he doesn't hear me, he tosses another stack of papers onto the fire. I see the page with poor penmanship meet the flames. My letter must have already been destroyed.

"Henry."

He looks up, frowning. "Lenore. A man must have his private space."

"I wanted to do something nice for you." I feel my lip tremble and am ashamed.

"Unless it was a stack of banknotes, I am sure it can be replaced." He laughs at his own joke, but I do not join in. Sighing, he gets up from his desk to come to me and take my hands in his. They are smooth and cold, and hold mine painfully tight. "You're not getting emotional, are you?"

"No," I say reflexively.

"No. You are not some hysterical woman. That is your great strength: you are more like a man emotionally."

The bones grind together in my hand.

Henry is complimenting me. I should be happy.

Before he releases me, he draws me in closer and presses an almost tender kiss against my temple. It feels like a benediction; I close my eyes and drink it in.

When he goes, I am released to my fussing. I check and recheck which trunks will travel with us from Sheffield station and which to send on with a servant on a cart, which new bills can be delayed and which I must settle before we leave.

The hour of departure comes, and it is when I am standing before the hallway mirror, pinning my hat in place, that I find myself wondering what it was Henry felt compelled to destroy by fire.

*

I grew up in a fine house some distance from this ship I now steer. If there was ever something rotten festering behind gilt, it was that house. It gives me no pleasure to think on it now, but I am reminded every time our carriage turns left towards Hyde Park. We will pass the old house on our way to the station, and I pull down my window blind to shield myself from the view.

I need no reminder of its dark aspect.

My years in that house are alive within me every day.

I was orphaned when I was twelve years of age, in an unpleasant and mundane carriage accident near the Angel. A few head of cattle had escaped their drover in the Metropolitan Cattle Market near the Caledonian Road and fled in the hope of some pastoral refuge. Of course, London had little to offer in that way, and by the time they reached the Great North Road, the pleasantries of the Islington streets had driven them into such fervor that they trampled a hansom cab, two cress sellers, ten barrels of small beer, and my family's coach. I assume we must have been traveling somewhere to be so far from our villa in Richmond, but anyone who could have told me where we were going was dead in the cacophony of hoofs striking flagstones and splintering wood.

I am told I was extracted from the snapped panels and velvet, drenched head to toe in blood. This is the one detail I remember: a surgeon spoke at the coroner's court and explained that my mother's jugular had been severed by a passing shard of glass. She bled to death before the wreckage fell still.

They thought I was dead, too, at first, so bathed in bright red arterial blood. Then my eyes opened—two bright white points in a scarlet mask. I believe at least one passing woman fainted away.

This was my induction into a motherless world, alone and met with fear and horror.

*

The Midland station at St. Pancras is an eclipse on the Euston Road: a vast, gothic moon swelling in front of the modest brick and clock tower of King's Cross, blotting out the remains of Somers Town and the Old St. Pancras churchyard. I am told that when the earth was turned to build the railways, a plague pit was discovered. A slum that had been built on a bedrock of bones was demolished and ploughed back into the earth.

Our brougham has been snarled in traffic the entire way from Mayfair, and I have been anxious lest we do not have adequate time for the porters to transfer our trunks to the guard's van.

Henry leans out the window to wave a folded note at our driver, who hops down while we wait in the queue of carriages at the station entrance; he returns a moment later with two porters, who make quick work of the luggage stacked behind us. Finally, we are disgorged into the cacophony of travelers and porters, newspaper sellers and soldiers, train guards, groups of schoolchildren, entire families dragging their worldly possessions with them, and everywhere noise, noise, noise rising up to the barrel-arched ceiling of metal and glass.

I lift the hem of my gray wool traveling dress out of the dirt and follow Henry through the crowds to our train.

Henry advances to negotiate with a porter to have our trunks stowed in prime position, and I linger at the W. H. Smith & Son newsstand, looking over the magazines.

"Lady Lenore Crowther?"

A man has joined me, standing a little too near for comfort, with red whiskers and close-set eyes. He is well enough dressed, but wears a bowler hat, and his shirt collar has been poorly starched.

I take a small step to the side. "Yes?"

"My name is Laurence Gibson—please forgive me for taking the liberty of approaching you directly."

"Can I help you?" I clutch the book I have picked up tightly to me, as though a shield. I do not know what he wants and I do not like that I am alone to face him.

"I rather hope you might. I understand your husband's Ajax Works has taken a forward-thinking approach in compensation for injured workers—quite unique amongst the steel mills, it seems."

I take another step away. "I'm sorry—are you a friend of my husband's?"

Mr. Gibson smiles but does not answer. "I'm curious—such a generous offer, and yet there are rumors that safety at Ajax has declined precipitously during your husband's tenure. Can you address these rumors?"

My own smile falters. "I don't think I understand—"

"Lenore. Say nothing." Henry appears between us, his face twisted in anger and perhaps tinged with fear. "How dare you?" he snaps at Mr. Gibson.

"Henry? What is going on? He said he was a friend of yours."

"This is a journalist, not a friend." Henry pushes me behind him and bares down on Gibson. "It is an outrage that you accost my wife like this—you have made a terrible mistake. I will write to your editor and have you fired if you ever do this again, do you hear me?"

Gibson holds his hands up and backs away. "Excuse me, Mr. Crowther. No offense intended."

"You will regret this," snaps Henry, and with his hand clamped around my wrist, he pulls me towards our platform.

I am shaken. I want to ask Henry what this man meant when he said safety has declined at Ajax—but I know from my husband's expression that I must hold my tongue with him, too.

The North Express departs at 10 a.m. with a shriek of whistles and white steam billowing outside the carriage window to obscure the platform. We will arrive at 1:35 p.m., traveling up the Midland trunk line via Kettering and Nottingham. Shortly after our marriage, I would travel regularly to Sheffield with Henry, visiting his new steelworks under construction, seeing his father in the last months before his death since, and attending every occasion at which a new, aristocratic wife would be beneficial to display. Since then, though Henry has returned often on business, we have been elsewhere: in the houses we rented for the summer, or staying with the society women I have ingratiated myself with or the unpleasant men Henry feels should know him.

I am struck with curiosity for a summer in a place of my own. Perhaps this is the beginning of a new phase in our marriage, a gesture of his faith in our union.

As soon as we pull out of London, Henry leaves for the Pullman parlor car, and I am left alone in our compartment. It is newly fitted with plush upholstery in a busy print, and I have my traveling bag with a few paperbacks and my embroidery to occupy me. Gone are the days where a woman traveling alone was at the mercy of whatever man descended upon her carriage: a connecting corridor runs alongside all compartments, and a guard patrols the first-class carriages regularly.

All the same, I feel unexpectedly exposed on my own amongst seats for six, and I draw the blinds to conceal myself from passengers in the corridor.

A mistake: now all I can see is passing shadows cast against the stiff Panama cotton. We blur into a tunnel, only the pilot light of the gas lamp left in the darkness. The rattle of the rails is as loud as a hammer to the skull, and the carriage rocks; then we burst out into the smog-thick suburbs of West Hampstead and Cricklewood, coal-dark brick walls of the railway cutting towering on either side.

Anxiety burns bright within me like a night flare at sea. Not for the house I leave behind, but the one I am moving towards.

Nethershaw.

The management of an estate is the one area in which my skills have yet to be tested.

No, not the only one. Motherhood lies beyond me, too.

But the running of a grand country house and its attendant grounds, tenants, farms, and responsibilities is a role that only a handful of women must tilt their lance at, even within the echelons of high society. I do not know if it is within my capabilities.

A shadow lingers outside the compartment door, a stringy silhouette that reaches almost to the ceiling, distorted by the angle of the sun. I dig my fingers into my shawl, schooling every tense muscle in my body to stillness. I will not take fright.

Another joins it, and the figures resolve themselves into the conductor and a porter. They check my ticket and leave, and I quickly raise the blinds. Better to know what I am faced with than fear its specter.

*

From the chaos of my parents' death, I was plucked by a policeman and delivered to the Bow Street magistrates while my parents were shoveled onto a cart. From stained documents in my father's pocket, they ascertained my identity and word was sent to find some kith or kin who might receive a bereaved child. They discovered what I already knew but my shocked mind was too numb to explain: there was no one. My mother's people had always been few, and my father was the only child of his elderly parents, long since departed this world.

For a time, it was thought I might be consigned to an orphanage, though no one felt it entirely right that a child of my breeding be placed amongst the discarded chaff of the lower classes. I recall little of those hours spent wrapped in a blanket and sat, mute, at the side of the clerk in the entryway, watching lawyers and plaintiffs and criminals stream in from Covent Garden. I remember only the sense that the whole world passed before me, and yet I belonged nowhere in it.

As night fell and the issue of my existence became pressing, a telegram arrived from the police station at Whitehall. They had identified a relative still extant and conveniently residing near Berkley Square.

Aunt Daphne.

The clerk installed me in the back of a cab, unmindful of the horrors I had experienced only that morning, and paid the driver to ferry me on. I spent twenty minutes rigid with anxiety as the cab made its jostling way along the Strand and up St. James's into the quiet residential streets.

And then it was over. The door was opened, and I stepped down, trembling but whole, into the twilight. The lamplighter was working his way along the street and had yet to reach us; a trail of starlight prickled the gloom towards Oxford Street; around me, there was only shadow. The cab drove off before the door was opened.

Here, my memory is sharp: a portico stood clear of the Georgian brick front, black with coal smoke. Above the door was a fanlight that looked like the peacocks my mother had briefly kept until their noise had bothered her too much. On either side were oil lamps, unlit, and the windows were shuttered and dark all the way to the top of the building.

After a moment's indecision, I lifted the knocker and let it drop down once.

In the quiet, I heard footsteps on floorboards some way off, drawing closer and closer in a manner that made me suddenly feel alarmed at the idea of being confronted by who, or what, lay behind.

I recall the footsteps halting, the sound of a bolt being drawn, and then the door began to swing open.

And that is where my life ended.

*

As we move north, the weather worsens, and by Nottingham, the horizon is swollen with black thunderclouds. Henry returns to our compartment with ten minutes to our arrival, muttering and checking his pocket watch. He smells of brandy and cigarettes, but otherwise he looks very good in a dark-brown Chesterfield that is expensively tailored to his broad shoulders. His collar is neatly starched; his necktie is silk with a simple stripe and knotted in the English square style. I allow myself a small smile: I have returned him to his homeland a first-rate gentleman.

As the train slows, I stand first, take his top hat from the rack, and place it on his head, brushing a smut from the brim. He takes my hand in thanks, and for a moment I am back ten years past, a young bride who thought herself in love, whatever in love meant to me then. Henry's eyes I thought to be as green as sea-glass, that the curl of his forelock that always escaped, however carefully he oiled it back, made him look like an illustration: Robin Hood crouched in the forest, looking up at me with a wry smile.

The train lurches to a halt, and the guard is banging on our door. On the platform, a pall of rain slakes across the dirt, churning it into mud; the weather has turned wild and violent, wind gusting beside us to whip up leaves and newspapers. When I last traveled here, the station still had a sheen of newness to it. Built only in 1870, now it is nearly twenty years worn: two tracks beside a squat building, thick with smog and grime from the factories. Rain sluices between the rails, across the ground, falling in sheets from the roof of the station building.

A porter waits with an umbrella and helps me descend, my skirts bundled in one fist; nevertheless, I am soon wet, the wind catching raindrops and dashing them against my face.

A flash of lightning is followed too soon by the roll of thunder: the storm is almost here.

"Let us pass the night in a hotel." I press my hand to Henry's arm. "Nothing good will come of traveling in these conditions."

As our trunks are unloaded from the guard's van, Henry dismisses the porters who cluster about us in the livery of the Midland Station Hotel, a curved building a little way up the hill.

"Don't be ridiculous. There's no hotel in this primitive place worth the money." He marches towards the glass veranda at the front of the station and stamps the water from his boots. I follow him, wordless, my eye trained on the horizon and the roiling, dark cloud mass.

Sheffield lies before us, mounting the slope from the river valley, a tangle of overlapping stained brick and rooftops, as though the buildings are climbing over each other to escape to the still-green peaks. It is dirtier than I remember, the noise of the foundries and steelworks louder, though we are at least a mile from any industry. I can taste metal in the air. I think of all the hundreds of people at work under every roof and behind every wall, bent and stretched over a hoard of steel, hammering and scouring, filing and polishing, to send up a fog of filigree fragments to hang ever in the air.

I hook my hand into Henry's arm, wanting to feel something flesh and living. I think he will hail a cab driver foolish enough to go into the moors for enough money, but instead, a private carriage comes to a halt before us. An old-fashioned traveling chariot, a two-seater drawn by two horses with the driver sat above and behind the passengers—something I thought had gone entirely out of use, save for gentlemen traveling in more remote regions on their grand tour, had been hastily repainted, and a young groom sits in the driver's seat.

"Comes with the house," Henry says with a grimace. "Of course it will be replaced."

There is nothing I can do but take my seat and hold tight to the leather strap as we rattle over the cobbles away from the station. For a brief moment, I catch sight of the other major station: Sheffield Victoria, its solid bulk high upon its raised line, and beside it, the shining white edifice of the Royal Victoria Hotel. Why we cannot stay there, I do not understand. It seems pleasant enough to me.

We disappear into the warren of narrow streets, and it is gone. Rain makes the roads slick, and every approach is on an incline. Henry seems unbothered, but I draw the blind and try to think of anything but the crunch of my parents' carriage as it was crushed, the splinter of bone and sinew. I can still feel the thick slick of blood matting my hair, gluing my lashes together, coating my tongue and lips. I remember every physical sensation, but the emotion must be so great it lies beyond memory, beyond feeling. I thought myself unmarred by the memory, but perhaps I only run from it, and in a moment like this, the lies I tell myself become all too clear.

My only comfort is that I have no children of my own. If I die the way my parents did, there will be no child left to bear the pain.

Too soon we leave the city and pass first through farmland and then along the wooded valley of the Rivelin and the narrow road that snakes high above the banks below. Each time I wince when the carriage jolts over a rock or when thunder shakes the frame, Henry's lip curls, so I do my best to school my features into a pleasant, blank mask, and I draw steady, even breaths. I can control myself; I am not prey to the emotional whims and tantrums of other women. I am too competent at mastering myself.

I am interrupted by the carriage drawing to a sharp halt, and I bite back a yelp of fear.

"What is it? What has happened?" I peek behind the blind, wondering if we are beached in mud or have snapped a spoke, but the rain is too dense for me to comprehend much.

"Stay here," instructs Henry.

His door swings open and he jumps out into the mud and forest, then it shuts and all I can see through the glass are the ranks of moss-dressed trees. I hear him say something to the driver, and the coach shudders again as another body drops down. Then, footsteps in mud leading away from the carriage; they are soon swallowed by the drumming of raindrops on the roof.

I am alone once more, just as I was on the train, and I am struck by the awful idea that I will see a shadow again against the blinds. Quickly, I raise them on both sides and tuck my hands under my arms. My wool traveling suit had felt on the edge of too warm in London; now, I am freezing.

Too much time passes, and Henry does not return. I should stay inside; it is what he asked of me. But the longer I am left, the longer my mind conjures horrors trained perfectly to my own spirit. I must know what truly lies before us and the reason for our stop.

I dismount heavily, boots sinking into the mud, the hem of my skirt trailing through it. I lean against the coach, shielding my eyes from the rain with one hand, and edge forward, first to the driver's seat and then the two horses, who stamp and roll their eyes as I pass.

I do not at first understand what it is I see ahead: a curve of wood, something red, a bristling of white.

And then the picture comes together.

It is a carriage, a delicate phaeton unsuited to the rough hill roads and the foul weather, that has turned on its side at speed, snapping tracers and wheels, the crumpled wing of the hood collapsed over it all. The horse has long bolted, and Henry and the groom stand amongst the splintered wood.

My mind is a single note sung high and shrill. I can hear the screaming again, feel the sticky blood on my hand and the violence of being thrown.

Henry bends down and lifts the hood, gives a shout. The groom joins him. The whole wreck heaves, and then the two men are lifting something from within.

A body in white, soaked through with rainwater, her long chestnut hair streaming free from her limp head like a flag of a wrecked ship.

Darkness rises all around me, and I sink to the earth.

3

I COME TO NETHERSHAW in fits and starts.

At some point I have been placed into the carriage, waking briefly with my cheek stuck to the leather of the seat, soaking wet. I am dimly aware of a figure on the opposite bench, a flare of white cloth clinging to thigh and waist.

The woman from the carriage crash.

The rocking of the carriage lulls me under, and when I rise again, we have broken through the tree line, the conifer plantation falling away to expose bristling moorland of heather and gorse painted in muted colors by the lashing rain. I watch it through the misted window glass, a blasted heath that rolls on forever; in the distance, limestone crags rip through the landscape like a break in china, like torn paper.

Then, there, on a slope of nothing: a house. Low stone, turrets and crenelations, ivy smothering one side like mold growing across rotten fruit. The photographs gave nothing of its true nature. It is a mouth closed around a secret, a promise unspoken. Ancient, and unreal.

I remember nothing more but this: I dream of a woman crouched like a cat, licking her paw-hand clean of blood with a flickering pink tongue. I cannot see her face, but she is in white, and in the space when I think the white is her fur—

I wake.

The storm has passed.

Outside the diamond-paned window, a too-bright morning sun turns the glass opaque. My mouth is dry; I fumble a hand towards the side of the bed in search of water and find none. Working spit into my coarse tongue, I struggle up. The room around me is so green, I think in my sleep-addled state that I am still in that dreadful forest with the carriage crash before me.

The memory clarifies my mind like a lens.

The crash. The woman draped in white. Did she survive?

I am in a bedroom, and my trunk has been placed in one corner but not yet unpacked. The green I understand now: wallpaper freshly hung, showing a close pattern of interlocking vines. I riffle through the trunk for a pair of soft slippers and a loose cotton housedress that I can throw over my nightgown. Henry's things are not here.

My room opens onto a corridor running in both directions; it has been fitted with carpet, but it cannot conceal the way the floor slopes and twists. The ceiling is so low I can almost reach up my hand and touch it. I hear voices and follow them to a staircase that turns back on itself; at the half landing hangs a great portrait twice the size of life but so damaged by centuries of tallow smoke and dirt that the face is unrecognizable.

I bring to mind the plan of Nethershaw and deduce that this must be the central tower, and below the entrance hall. I am proved correct when I descend to more dark paneling and cold flagstones beneath my feet. The voices come from a cadre of workmen I spy through the open doors, wrestling wooden scaffolding from their cart. Outside, the hounds work themselves to a frenzy, a cacophony of inhuman noise that hurts my ears.

"Lenore." Henry surprises me, emerging from a side door. He casts a worried eye over me, putting his fingers to my chin to turn my face this way and that to see if I am damaged. Softly, unexpectedly, he tucks a stray lock of hair behind my ear. "You are well. Good."

I feel suddenly underdressed with workmen a matter of feet away, and I pull Henry to one side.

"What happened—the carriage accident?"

Henry's mouth tightens. "You fainted. I didn't know you had it in you."

I swallow what I want to say: a reminder of how my parents died. "It was quite shocking," I say instead. "But what about the woman? Is she alive?"

"Yes, she is quite alive and occupying one of the few bedrooms the tradesmen have finished with. It must have shaken her wits from her," says Henry, with less patience. "Seems to come from fine breeding, but she will not divulge anything but her name. The doctor is with her now."

"Have you sent for the police? Should we notify someone?"

Henry scoffs. "Tell the police what? A silly woman was out alone in terrible weather and had an accident? There's no need to waste their time."

"But—"

Henry puts a firm hand on my shoulder. "No police. All right?"

I nod. "Very well. Perhaps I should—"

"You should put some clothes on before you scandalize the staff," Henry interrupts.

As if prompted, two workmen come in with wooden poles suspended between their shoulders. I remember now: a letter sent to commission work to clean and repaint all the ceilings and moldings. They are yellow with pipe smoke and candle-flame. If I were more myself, I would have noticed such a defect already.

"Yes. Of course."

"I'm going to the Ajax Works. I've already told Cook not to bother with lunch."

No matter that I am still here, as is our guest. I clasp my hands before me. "Will you return for dinner?"

"I doubt it. I'll be expected to dine with a few people at the chophouse. Tomorrow."

Henry pulls his hat from the stand by the door and selects a walking stick, then returns to kiss my cheek. It seems suddenly preposterous—all this London fashion transplanted to the wilderness of the moors I can see even now through the open door. What use a top hat and patent leather?

The traveling chariot pulls round, hastily washed down to clear the mud.

"Wait—one last thing. What is our guest's name?"

He seems surprised, as though such things as names are beneath him. "Carmilla Kernstein."

"Carmilla," I say, tasting the syllables in my mouth. A little harsh, but with long, languorous vowels lingering between the lips.

"We could get no more from her." Henry leaves, striding purposefully across his threshold. He is finally what he has always longed to be: a landed gentleman, with a fine house.

I look around me at the worm-eaten paneling and the crumbling mortar. It will be a fine house once I am finished with it at least.

Henry is right: I have much to manage now we are arrived. The workmen are the first of many, and my fainting fit is more than simply an embarrassment: it is a threat to the careful operation I have planned to ensure we are ready for the shooting party. There is a little over two weeks until the Glorious Twelfth is upon us, and there is an unspeakable amount yet to do.

Returning to my room, I pick through my bags, trying to draw my thoughts together, but I stop, hand clasped around the bedpost, and close my eyes as a wave passes over me, a strange sense of vertigo. It is as though the two memories, my childhood and yesterday's accident, have become one, all the attendant fear and sorrow and horror twining through both. I can never escape the past. Its mark on me has been made too deep.

I feel a sense of relief when Molly arrives and takes charge of my own clumsy attempts to arrange my hair. The servants who traveled with us from London were forced to stay overnight in town, because the open-air dog cart sent for them could not travel in the rain. I wish for a moment to have had the same fate—but then I think of the woman we rescued: if we had not taken the foolish decision to chance the hill road in a storm, the poor thing could have been left for days.

I select a plain but elegant day dress in moss-green cambric and lace myself into my walking boots: we are far from the soft, sterile homelife of the city. Here, I must condition myself to be more robust.

There is much that lies before me—Henry's orders are heavy across my shoulders—but I cannot keep thoughts of our unexpected guest from my mind.

I pull the plan of the renovation work from the leather portfolio of documents I have brought from London. There are few bedrooms in use, and it takes little time to deduct where she has been placed. It is past time I greeted her.

With the memory of blood on my tongue, I venture to the end of the corridor that runs the length of this side of the upper courtyard. Nethershaw is formed of two square buildings set around two courtyards, with the central spur given over to the dining hall. Beside my bedroom and the room opposite, which I assume will be Henry's, there is one other room in a good enough state to be used immediately, close to the chapel.

I knock softly and enter—but to my surprise the room is empty, and scattered around it are Henry's things. His trunk is open, and a mess of collars and suspenders hangs off every chair arm, open pots of pomade littering the dressing table.

It is like a blow to the sternum.

I close the door quietly and stand outside, holding this new piece of information in my mind.

Henry does not sleep beside me.

He rests as far away from me as he can.

And then the next thought follows: the woman from the crash had been a few feet from me all along.

Swiftly I return to the corridor that holds my room—and my guest. I am met by an unknown man emerging from the bedroom opposite.

I fold my hands together stiffly.

"You must be the doctor," I say to the new figure. "Thank you for attending us so promptly."

He bows his head gravely. "I am Dr. Bartolomé. I only wish to have made your acquaintance under more promising circumstances."

"Of course we would be delighted to welcome you to dinner on a night that suits you," I add. "How is our patient?"

"Tolerably well, considering the terrible events she has endured. Bumps and bruises, of course, and naturally the shock to her nerves, and I'm afraid I have some concerns about the condition of her heart. She must build up strength. Plenty of rest, and gentle exercise by way of walks about the estate once she is ready. I am sure you will take a personal interest in the care of a guest under your roof."

My eyes wander from him to the door that conceals the mysterious Carmilla Kernstein.

33

A personal interest.

I thank Dr. Bartolomé, instructing him to give his bill to the housekeeper, then finally let myself into Miss Kernstein's room as though a trespasser in my own house. It is gloomy, the shutters closed, and no fire banked in the hearth. Only a single candle is lit on the bedside table.

As I enter, I have a sense of something slithering, a cool, dry susurration from the sheets.

"Good morning," I speak to the darkness. "I am Lady Lenore Crowther. You are at my and my husband's estate, Nethershaw. I hope the doctor explained how you have come to be in our care."

Another shifting, a body coiling, and a voice is nearer to hand than I expect when it comes. "Yes. The doctor. You and your husband."

Her accent is a little strange. Not foreign, exactly, but I cannot place it: something curious, and almost old-fashioned.

"He says you will recover with rest."

"Yes. I must rest." Her voice is soft and melodious, lingering on the hissing sound that moves between her lips like a breeze.

The darkness is oppressive, so I move towards the shutters and throw them open. Light floods the room through the twisted glass, and I turn to greet my guest—but the words die on my tongue. I am struck dumb in horror.

It is the woman from my dream.

Surely it is her—but diminished. Her skin is not milk-pale but ashen, her chestnut hair dull and brassy. But it *is* her, I am sure of it, reclining against the pillows in this remote, moorland house of which I am now mistress.

I twist my wedding ring to displace my agitation.

Impossible. It cannot be.

"If you will tell me where you were traveling to, I can send word of your accident." I school the trembling from my voice.

"There is no need." She speaks coolly, strangely composed for someone fresh from a terrible accident.

"Surely there is someone worrying at your late arrival." I am searching for some landmark of normality, a human edge that I can grasp. "Or we can write to your people to arrange your transport home. Where would they be found?"

"My people are everywhere." She leans back amongst the pillows like a queen upon a throne, heavy-lidded eyes watching me thoughtfully. I cannot understand the feeling it stirs in my core. "Do not fret, Lenore. Everything is as it should be." She smiles, mouth stretched wide, sharp incisors catching her bottom lip.

The sound of my name in her mouth unsettles me. It is too intimate, too close. For so many years there has been only Henry to call me by my Christian name alone, so plain and unadorned with title or status. She assumes command in this house that I have yet to bring to heel.

"You are of course quite welcome here, but I am sure you would prefer to recuperate in familiar surroundings."

"Thank you." She extends a hand towards me, and after a moment's hesitation, I take it, heart trembling. Her skin is so very soft, her fingers slim and cold. "I am terribly in debt to you for your kindness. I hope I may stay long enough to repay it."

"There is no need." I move brusquely to the door, fetching up a discarded glass of water, a dropped cloth. I cannot bear a moment more in this room. "Molly will bring you anything you need. There will be dinner downstairs each night, if you feel well enough."

Unable to look at her again, I flee.

*

The building work provides an immediate and demanding distraction, and I fall into it gratefully. Here, I know exactly who I must be and what I must do. There is no need for memory, no need for emotion. From the pastille tin in my pocket, I take a handful and shove them into my mouth, lips and fingers dusty with sugar. The sweetness is a succor.

First, I arrange my room to my satisfaction, moving the dressing table to the window, which shows a view of the moor so distorted by the ancient glass it is merely a smear of purple and green. I pause before the mirror and examine my neck. It is unmarked, of course. The two pinpricks I felt in the dream were nothing more than that: a dream, surely.

I move on to set up my bureau in a room adjoining the entrance hall. The dark wood paneling extends to every room, and I find it oppressive. Perhaps next year I can have the rooms modernized; this year, I must satisfy myself with ensuring the building is watertight, clean, and fit for guests.

I begin by working through the correspondence that has already arrived for me at Nethershaw: a mixture of responses to my inquiries for suppliers of meat and beer and flour, for men who will clear the gutters and shoe the horses and sweep the chimneys. The house has been all but shut up for years and comes only with a small and relatively inexperienced staff: a housekeeper and her husband, who I hope to keep on as head butler, a range of maids drawn from the local villages, who have held back the worst of the decay, and a few stray outdoor staff under the groundskeeper, who seems, at least, glad that someone will put the grouse moor to use. A decent cook has been a trial to find, and while we wait for the rest of the staff I have hired, poor Molly and Roberts, Henry's valet, have far too much to do.

I will have to establish all the running of a great estate from scratch. I think of Aunt Daphne pushing my spine straight with the toe of her cane; this was one lesson she could not teach me.

There is one letter among the pile that I was not expecting so soon.

I ease open the seal with a finger and unfold the square of daintily written paper, the hand slopes and curls in a way Aunt Daphne would have gifted a small nod of approval.

It is from Cora.

I read one or two lines of pleasantries remarking on the stifling weather in London, the people she has seen riding in Hyde Park, before pushing it to the bottom of my correspondence. Etiquette demands that I write a response—and promptly—but I think my new position allows me a little grace to delay my reply. I do not have any spare thought to construct a pretty lie, and I am embarrassed to tell her the truth: I fear that I may be beyond my depth. Cora must have sent the letter before we departed London—before she even came to call—and her presumption arouses unseemly irritation in me.

Cora is never out of her depth.

Instead, I take a fresh sheet of paper and write a few inquiries to local hotels to see if Carmilla had stayed with them before her accident. Kernstein seems an unusual name, so I turn to my small traveling library to locate *Who's Who*, and then, thinking of Henry's comment about fine breeding, *Debrett's Peerage*. I find her in neither. She must, then, have come recently from the continent. I do not have the *Almanach de Gotha* on hand—how Aunt Daphne would disapprove—so I write a further letter to Debrett's editor, asking his assistance in locating the Kernstein family.

I am grateful, then, for the unending list of demands that Nethershaw places upon me. I spend the next few hours walking the extent of the house, making small amendments to my plans of repair and renovation, noting the paintings requiring to be cleaned, the cracked windows to be fixed with new lead.

In the dining hall, the grandest room by some distance, the ceiling sags in one corner, and I send an attending maid to instruct the workmen to check the roof for broken tiles or any manner of ingress for rainwater. The hall is twice the height of the other rooms, and set at one end with a minstrel's gallery that I have read is an original from the medieval hall first founded on this site. Perhaps Henry's guests might enjoy a historical dinner; it is the kind of novel amusement I have attended before in far less appropriate surroundings. But the white stucco ceiling is filthy, smoke and grime encrusted into the swirl of plaster, and I feel doubtful it can be renewed before our guests arrive. Perhaps it is better not to do a thing and let the dim candlelight hide our many sins.

Nethershaw is, of course, not on the gas, with no prospect of a line being run so far out. Candelabras stand in every room, stubs of candles melted into the sockets, and in a few places heavy chandeliers hang from rusting chains anchored to the floor.

I am overwhelmed. This is more than the running of an estate. This is the salvage of a shipwreck, timbers snapping all around me as the waves surge higher. This house, Henry's reputation, our marriage: I am responsible for it all.

When the groundskeeper asks me what I want doing with an acre of grouse moor that has become too overgrown for the birds to find enough green shoots to sustain themselves, I think, for one hysterical moment, that I might cry.

"It must be burnt, my lady," he says when I give no answer. "That is the only way. Scour the old growth to make way for new."

I nod my assent, presenting myself as though I understand what he means. I must find a book on grouse and game. I cannot be caught out.

My watch marks time for my appointment with the cook, and I decide to meet her in the kitchens, rather than summoning her to my bureau, so that I can assess my staff.

In the moment of moving through one courtyard, I catch another glimpse of the moors beyond, and I am struck by how perfectly and totally alone we are. No gently rolling hills enfold this place, no landscaped lake or lawns. There are no roads across them, only the narrow pony tracks paved by some ancient people— no shelter, no way markers. Defoe's howling wilderness. Only the moors, unending planes of gorse and purple heather, bruised under the sunlight.

The kitchens are a cavernous space, dominated by an old range that takes up one wall. Modern when it was installed fifty years ago, it now seems like something from an illustration, coal-black metal hulking against the stones, radiating a monstrous heat. I have about enough time to take in the large central table around which a small team of maids are at work on pastry or mixing bowls, and the array of copper pots hung against another wall, before the cook ushers me outside, clearly displeased at my intrusion.

I give her my instructions: a modern menu that will be demanding this far from the city, with jellies and continental dishes I doubt the staff have encountered before; but it is what Henry's guests will expect, and I hope the remaining two weeks will be enough time for the kitchens to practice on us for our private repast. I assign a list of purchases to the cook, a plain, broad woman who I have read comes to us from a steel family that made our journey in reverse, leaving their pleasant house in the smogless western suburbs of Sheffield to establish themselves in London.

A sudden clamor of voices and canine yelps interrupt us, and through a door rush a pack of dogs, running low, with their teeth bared. It all happens so quickly I have barely time to snatch up my skirts and dart into the kitchens, as the cook slams the door closed.

It is done in the stable style, the bottom and top moving separately, so that we can all too readily see the hounds snapping and snarling as they jump against the wood.

I am too cold and hot at once, my hand closed tight around the cook's wrist as though she can save me from this threat. A man follows the beasts, holding a whip with which he urges the pack back towards the kennels.

When the dogs have been removed, a gardener is carried towards the scullery, leg elevated, though this does nothing to conceal the mangled flesh and bone where once his calf had been. I feel quite faint, and it is all I can do to remain quiet, upright, and swallow down my emotions.

I hear the kennel man speak as he shuts the last of the dogs away. "Money can buy a pack, but it can't buy training."

Of course. The estate has had no hunting dogs for years; these must be the hounds Henry has purchased for his grouse shoot.

There is bloodshed already.

For a decade, I have carried the burden of his secret, and now he brings another hunting party to our door.

How simple it is for him to bury the past.

I only pray we do not resurrect it.

4

SOMETHING IMPATIENT AND SNAPPISH has swollen inside me. I feel as though I carry some fragile, painful growth in my throat, and every small challenge or inconvenience threatens to burst open the pustule and fill my mouth with poison. I pass the next few days brittle as the plaster that flakes from the walls around me, and more than one unfortunate maid feels the sharp edge of my aching tongue. The tin of pastilles rests in my pocket as my constant companion: a pathetic crutch.

I do not know what has taken hold of me. Perhaps it is the cramps; they come as hard as ever. Though I have stopped bleeding, I find the laudanum bottle in my hand most mornings, tucked between my breasts so that I can slip a drop into my tea or wine. It is an incessant pain as raw as my anger, and it makes my body ever more a traitorous, alien environment in which I am forced to live.

My sleep is poor, bothered by the wind against the windowpane and the heavy creak and roll of the house, like some ocean-borne ship tossed by waves. The pain in my stomach has not abated, and I wake one night soon after our arrival twisted and stiff with it. The laudanum bottle at my bedside is empty already, so I take a pastille from the tin in compensation, and slip on my dressing gown to venture downstairs to look for something more to ease my pain.

I do not know what it is that stops me, a pace before the bedroom door, hand outreached to the knob. Perhaps I caught the faint sound of footsteps before they become clear, advancing down the hall towards me.

The housekeeper, maybe, checking that all is well, or Henry returning late?

The footsteps stop at my door.

I hold my breath, lift my hand lightly from the knob. My foolish heart is racing, and my palms grow clammy. This is my house; I should simply open the door and demand to know what this person is doing—but I am too much a coward.

Instead, I lower slowly to the floor, moving as soundlessly as I can, and peer through the gap at the bottom of the door.

There are feet.

Two: pale, mottled, and bare, long toes and anklebones standing taut against the skin. The whisper of white lace.

There is too much dust down here, and to my horror, I sneeze.

The feet move at once, steps swift on the creaking boards.

Screwing up my pitiful courage, finally I open the door—but too late. A flash of white nightgown disappearing around a corner, then I am alone.

*

I am avoiding our guest—I cannot deny it—and yet, she plagues my thoughts. I plan menus and order paint and plaster, mend linen and pay bills, attend the church, sitting beside Henry in the ancient Nethershaw box, and all the while my mind is on *her*. My dream come to meet me, languid and arresting and uncanny. Should I tell her I dreamt of her? No, that would make me seem utterly mad.

But what does it mean? Does it mean anything at all?

Molly delivers our guest her meals, a tisane or beef tea. Carmilla lingers among the pillows, Molly informs me, as she curls my fringe with a hot poker, chestnut hair fanned out around her ashen face, demanding softer coverings, a warmer fire, a more beautiful view. She is so hungry for so much.

"And, my lady, please, I must tell you. We have all seen her walking the corridors at night," Molly adds. "We hear someone trying doors, and when we look through the keyhole, we see her walking down the corridor, all that hair hanging down her back like a shroud."

I can see it so clearly, bare feet on floorboards, the hem of her nightgown dragging in the dust.

"That cannot be true," I snap. "She is an invalid. She has not been out of bed once."

I am speaking to myself as much as to Molly.

"Strange she won't say where she's from or where she's going. It's like she appeared out of nothing."

"Enough. You've been reading too much common literature."

"Yes, my lady."

We are all preoccupied by Carmilla Kernstein, and I am wary of it. I cannot let the staff see my own misgivings; I must captain this ship through whatever storms befall us. It makes no sense that I dreamt of her before I met her, so I cannot believe it to be true. I will not allow impossible things any quarter.

To hide my own skittishness around our guest, I insist on delivering her next meal. It is a sullen, sultry day. A thick pall of cloud lies low over the moors, the air heavy with unspent rain. The ceiling of the dining hall has buckled with damp after the storm, a leak in the roof spreading moisture across the beams and plaster; in this humidity, none of it will dry out.

I maneuver past a phalanx of workmen wrapping the damaged paintings in hessian and lifting them away, and continue down the twisted corridor to my room and Carmilla's. A soft knock at the door, and I let myself in before I hear a reply.

This is my house. I am master here.

The fire has been banked high, despite the weather, and the curtains drawn across the window. A scant scatter of candles light the room, one on the mantel, one on the washstand, one on the bedside table. It is cave-like and suffocating.

"I have brought lunch. Cook has made a little toast water and calf's foot jelly." I speak with false cheer, crossing the room with confidence, despite the dark, and settle the tray to one side of the bed. I stop. Breakfast lies untouched at the foot.

"Is our food not to your taste?"

A shifting, limbs and body and face emerging from the gloom. "Lenore. You do not visit."

Carmilla is half-shrouded in her loose, glorious hair. I see half a face: a full lip, the soft curve of jaw and cheek, one dark, thick-lashed eye regarding me intently. Her nightdress has slipped off one shoulder, exposing the smooth line of her collarbone and the swell of her breasts. I look away quickly.

"I am afraid I am quite busy with renovations to the house. I hope the workmen have not disturbed you."

"Why do you spend your energy on this wreck?"

I am shocked at her incivility, her lack of propriety. "Nethershaw is a fine old estate. It simply needs a little attention."

Carmilla sneers prettily. "A waste. Some things have no end. You pour and pour and pour your soul away, and they are always hungry."

"It is a house," I say weakly. "I am sure all will be well."

I want her out. I will not entertain Molly's superstitions, but I do not have time for a stranger to make demands of me. We know nothing about her. This could all be a trick; perhaps she has a gang of thieves lined up to rob us.

What a stupid thought.

I collect the breakfast tray and place it on the dresser, taking a moment to feed myself a pastille. I am being as foolish as the staff. I cannot throw her out when she is so unwell. What if she has connections? What if reports of our cruel treatment reach the ears of people who matter? My status is the driftwood I cling to so I may stay afloat above a deep, yawning ocean.

"I hope lunch is more to your liking," I say. "I will call for the doctor again tomorrow if you are still unable to rise from bed."

"Lenore. Wait. Come here."

The hair prickles on the back of my neck. She watches me so intently I cannot hide. It is only her eyes that remain unchanged, a dark sapphire blue that glitters in the sunlight.

Hesitantly, I rejoin her bedside, and she grasps my hand. Hers is cold and smooth.

"I have not thanked you for your kindness." She strokes my palm in some approximation of affection. "You take in a stranger. It speaks of the goodness of your heart."

My cheeks heat with guilt, as though she can tell the ungenerous thoughts I have entertained.

"It is only what any good Christian would do."

She hisses, eyes flashing, "Wash your mouth out."

"Excuse me?"

"You dismiss yourself. Do not."

Again, I find myself lost for words around her. Instead, I pat her hand awkwardly. "That is very kind of you to say."

"Will you stay with me a little while?"

I hesitate. There is much still to do, so much in fact I dread to face it, though I have no choice.

Carmilla looks at me with such strength of feeling, my resolve falters. Is caring for my guest not one of my tasks? I would be a poor host to neglect her. I do not stay with her because I want respite from my work but because this *is* work.

"Very well." I straighten the counterpane that is rumpled around her, then move the lunch tray to one side, tidying up one or two used glasses.

She extends a hand to me, the blue lines of her veins standing out stark against her ashen skin. "Come. Sit with me."

I let her draw me down.

"Tell me about yourself. How did you come to be mistress of this place?"

Haltingly, I give her a few particulars of my life and situation, my marriage, my orphaning, Henry's position and our coming to Nethershaw.

She seems dissatisfied, full lips curling over her teeth. "I am saddened, Lenore—you feed me only scraps."

"It is the truth."

"Part of it, perhaps, but is there not so much more to tell? Who we are is more than a series of dates and legalities. You are kind yet cautious. Mastered yet insecure. Will you not tell me *why*?"

I am quite taken aback, and for some confusing reason, there are tears prickling my eyes. How neatly and quickly she dissects me to my core. "I do not know what to say."

She takes my hand and strokes it, bringing me closer. "You are very pretty when you are honest."

"Am I?"

"Terribly. Will you tell me your story?"

Slowly at first, then tumbling like water over rocks, I begin to speak. It has been so long since I have told anyone of Aunt Daphne, of losing my parents, of the disappointment of my marriage. I feel quite mad to be speaking of it now, even though I offer only the smallest fragment of the whole, but perhaps a stranger is the one person with whom I can speak without fear of consequence. It is a heady mix of fear and relief to give in to this brief vulnerability.

When I am done, I look away, hastily blinking back tears.

"Ah," says Carmilla softly. "I see."

"It is only the past. No more than many have endured."

"And yet so much more than you deserved."

I pull my hand back and stand up abruptly, going to the window to hide my face; a wave of shame slinks through me. This is foolish—*I* am foolish, spilling my heart as though I am still a girl in short skirts, as though anyone cares about my history. If I give in to that impulse, the need to be seen, understood by another, then I do not know what howling wave of past pain may capsize me.

"It is nothing. Henry always says I am wedded to my own misery. I simply need to make a little more effort to be happy."

It is the wrong thing.

"How dull," says Carmilla. "I am tired. Leave me."

When I turn back, she has rolled over and closed her eyes.

I do not know why, but her sudden rejection feels as though a cloud has covered the sun. Something in me wants her light back.

She does not speak to me again as I take the discarded breakfast tray and let myself out. The world outside that stifling room feels mundane and dull. I went too far. I spoke too openly. It is only that it has been so long since it felt as though someone was truly listening.

I walk the halls of Nethershaw carrying a sense that things have shifted in a way more significant that I can name. It is as though a crack opened up beneath my feet the night I dreamt of Carmilla, and the dust has shaken loose around me.

There is the sense of vertigo.

And the drop below.

*

In the kitchens I return the breakfast tray, and meet a commotion. A maid is in tears, holding a bag clutched to her chest as Cook edges her out of the kitchens. I catch Molly as she leaves the laundry with an armful of darning to ask what is happening. She tells me: the girl was discovered that morning on her knees in the pantry, pushing into her mouth the last crust of four game pies that had been cooked the night before, devoured in some mad hunger. She has been dismissed. From the courtyard, we watch as she is loaded into the dog cart, dazed and groaning, to be driven back to town with no reference.

I feel a sudden rush of hatred for this place, for the unending burden of wifehood, of fighting entropy. All things fall apart, and I must expend so much energy each day to hold them in place. I thought marriage freedom when I sought it; I thought it safety. But sometimes, when my control slips, I think there is only safety and certainty in death.

Work. I must still my mind with work.

Henry spends much time at the steel works, and despite the best effort of his valet, Roberts, his room is ever in such a disarray. I come to his wardrobe to compile a list of mending for Molly and new pieces to be ordered, but I am confounded in my task. Henry's room is grander than my own, with a line of windows that look over the sloping moorland and the conifer plantation that falls within our land. I found an Ordnance Survey map of the moor and traced my finger over the names of this landscape: Higger Tor and Mam Tor, Kinder Downfall and Jacob's Ladder. They are names for conjuring, and I sense the edges of my London world fraying against the limestone and peat.

I tidy Henry's room. It is what a wife is for.

There is an old bed that is grand enough I wonder if it has been used for state visits. I pluck up the nightshirt and dressing gown from the quilt and hang them over the back of a chair. The washstand is a mess of shaving cream and brushes, the cutthroat razor half out of its case. The clothes press teems with dress shirts and sporting coats, ties and fashionable waistcoats lined in silk. All a little ostentatious for the crowd he wishes to impress, but he will not hear my gentle suggestions. I must give these through Roberts.

There, at the bottom of the press, is a long, leather box that I do not recognize. I withdraw it, expecting a watch chain or tiepin, but instead there is a fine chain of gold set with diamonds. A rush of warmth floods through me like kindling taking a flame. A necklace. I lift it from the silk lining and hold it up to the light to see the gemstones glitter.

It has been a long time since Henry last gave me something so precious.

There are noises outside the window—the carriage returning. Hastily, I restore to the necklace to its hiding place and finish tidying the last few pieces of clothing in the room, taking the old collars down to the laundry to be freshly washed and starched.

*

I married Henry a day before my twenty-first birthday, and three before Aunt Daphne died of heart failure. I was not surprised to receive the telegram upon our arrival in Paris. Aunt Daphne was a woman for whom life or death amounted to much the same thing— only now, she would reside in a coffin in Highgate Cemetery rather than the chair that was always drawn up to the window for her to monitor each passerby and assess their status.

Henry was for ending our tour at once. It was to be only a short one: a week in Paris and Rome before taking a steamer back to London. He had undertaken his grand tour after university and felt a sense of ownership over the continental cities that meant he had no need to witness their streets and breathe their air again to know them. There was no way for me to disagree, though I was struck acutely by the sentiment that Aunt Daphne had arranged to die as soon as the ink was dry on the wedding certificate. I was free of her, and I was not. The final net cast to draw me back to her and close the world off again.

I have not seen Europe since. I hold on to the scattered memories of France like gold coins that I can spend in moments of despair or desperation: the scent of coffee freshly roasting in the café below our hotel; the warm summer light across the honey and white stone of the Third Republic and its monumental architecture; the sluggish Seine beneath Pont Neuf, iridescent with oil like the scales of a snake.

The funeral was my first trial as a married woman. I thought I might stumble, that I would look for some more grown person to take charge, but I did not. Aunt Daphne would have been proud. I purchased Henry and myself black crêpe armbands as we waited for our boat train in Paris, in order that we should arrive back in England in mourning. I sent a telegram ahead to the staff at the Holland Park house that Henry had recently purchased to order my plain day dresses dyed black, and a new riding habit and day dress to be made up in bombazine and silk.

There was a coffin of plain elm lined with white jean, with handles of galvanized brass. Henry wanted steel, but I was young then and spoke in grief when I told him his merchandising was not welcome. He took offense and left me to make the arrangements so that he could take a meeting with a supplier of hunting knives to America.

The honeymoon was over.

I wished for some dear relative or acquaintance to take these grim tasks from my shoulders, but there was no one.

I was alone, as in all things.

I learned: learned, then, that mastery is the gift that befalls the isolated and unhappy. There was no help forthcoming, so I learned to take complete and total control myself.

It has served me well.

I knew what to do, and the certainty felt intoxicating. I was powerful. I was invulnerable.

I wrote to several newspapers of good report to insert a death notice. I appointed an undertaker who arranged for a hearse and white horses in black feather headdresses. I declined the mummers; I thought the pageantry unseemly.

I wrote to the director of Highgate Cemetery to inquire after the plot of land Aunt Daphne had purchased several years before. My mother and father are buried in Brompton; Aunt Daphne wished to avoid them even in death.

I sat at my bureau to write the order of service, and Aunt Daphne's voice came to me from twelve years prior, the words she had spoken at my parents' funeral. She had lifted my chin with the head of her cane and looked me clear in the eye. *Death is the end of all things. He lays low young and old.* Her voice rang so clear in my mind it was as though she sat a little behind me, and if only I could turn my head, we would be reunited.

I did not turn.

My complicated life with Aunt Daphne, my only family, my half-snatched childhood itself, was all over, and I did not yet understand what it had meant.

Naturally, I was not expected to attend my aunt's funeral. Women rarely did. But I was gripped by an anxiety that Henry might not attend either, and the thought of a funeral service delivered to an empty church struck a fear through me that I could not contain. It was a horror, an undoing too large. So I arranged a dress of stuff and crêpe, and left the house at the appointed hour to follow the hearse.

Henry surprised me by not only attending but by having arranged the most delicate and tasteful mourning for himself. The black crêpe scarf hung over his shoulder and the hatband fitted neatly around his top hat. He offered me his arm with a most sensitive look, and I was overcome.

He was good to me, once.

I hold on to that, like a prayer, like a plea.

Let this life of mine be about more than pain.

5

HENRY KISSES ME WARMLY when we meet in the drawing room before dinner, his fingertips lingering on the side of my throat, and I cannot help but think of the diamonds he means to place around my neck.

"How goes progress at the works?"

I sit beside him on a settle. Half the room is under dust sheets, and the smell of damp lingers in the upholstery. The house has come with more furniture than I know what to do with, the wrack washed ashore from so many centuries of life.

"No talk of work at home." He waves my question away and leans back, crossing his legs. "Tell me about *your* progress—the place seems half-destroyed?"

"Only half?" My lip quirks into a small smile. I give him a simple narrative of what has been done so far, leaving out the leaking roof and mounting bills. It will all be managed before he has to know of any of it.

"I knew I could trust you." Henry fixes the rumpled sleeve of my glove before kissing the back of my hand as he used to early in our marriage. "There. Do you not look fine in a grand house of your own?"

"As do you," I reply.

For a moment, I let myself lean into his warmth, the strong, solid bulk of him. He smells of smoke and the same dusky cologne he has favored for years. Oh, but I have missed this.

Henry's expression sours, and I am shot through with worry at what I have done wrong.

But no—he is looking over my shoulder, and I turn to follow his gaze.

Carmilla stands at the door, dressed in one of my more elegant gowns; a rich gold that complements her lustrous hair, which has been carefully arranged with a handful of diamond star pins.

It is a shock to see her in so mundane a setting. Out of the darkness, she is something more of a woman like me or Molly, but there is still something unreal about the easy grace with which she holds herself, a clean precision to her features that shows no blemish or flaw. She appears much recovered since this morning, watching us with bright intellect. It seems the night becomes her.

"I did not know you were to join us for dinner," says Henry.

Carmilla's figure is shown well in the slender, tightly laced bodice and low-cut neckline. I would half expect Henry to look at her with interest, but he only stands, inclining his head stiffly.

"Nor did I." I rise, quickly smiling, and place myself between them and this curious tension. "It is good to see you looking so well."

"I missed you, Lenore." Her voice is a low hum, rich and textured like velvet. "I prefer to be in your company."

"Oh." Color rises to my cheeks. I do not know what to say to that. I am strangely tense that she has spoken so before Henry, but that is silly of me; we have made no transgression.

Thankfully, we are interrupted by the dinner gong, and our small party of three cross to the dining hall.

In the hallway, Henry catches my elbow. "She's still here?"

"Of course. This is the first time I've seen her out of bed." I am brought suddenly to the memory of her feet outside my door the other night, but I dismiss it. Henry does not need to know of that either; real or dream, he will not appreciate to hear my flights of fancy. "I'll have the doctor come to assess her again soon, and I have made inquiries to locate her people."

Henry seems satisfied, giving a small grunt of acknowledgment before we enter and take our places at the table.

The meal is a simple one. I have set Cook the task of practicing many fine dishes and elaborate services before the shooting party arrives, and the kitchens need a little time before they are ready with the first. Tonight, there is a simple spread of cold lamb from the day before, and a salad, a small meat pie, vegetable marrow, and white sauce. If I had known it would be Carmilla's first meal with us, I would have ensured it was something a little more special.

As it is, she pushes the food around her plate, tearing off delicate strips of lamb and eating with flashing teeth, leaving the rest. Henry watches her with mounting irritation, eyes tracking her unusual manners, the watery blood from the meat pooling on her plate.

"Is our hospitality not to your taste?" he asks lightly, but I too well know the tightness in his jaw.

"It is very fine," she replies, licking her lips. "Lenore has done magnificently."

"Perhaps you are accustomed to foreign food, where you are from? I ate paprika on my tour, and I didn't care for it."

Carmilla only laughs—an intrusive noise—and I see a flush creep up Henry's neck.

"It is still rich fare for someone recovering from such a shock," I offer. "I'm sure your appetite will recover with time."

Carmilla's eyes flash, and another strip of meat disappears between her teeth. "Oh, my appetite is quite satiated. Is yours?"

"What exactly is wrong with you?" asks Henry, ignoring her question.

"Henry!"

"It is a reasonable question."

Carmilla watches us, her lips quirked in amusement.

"The doctor spoke about her heart," I say. "One must take the matters of circulation and the heart quite seriously."

Henry frowns. He can make no objection to that.

We eat in silence a little longer, Henry knocking back several glasses of hock, while I chew mechanically through everything on my plate, hardly tasting it, until my stomach begins to feel painfully full.

"And where is it you will be going once you are deemed well enough?" asks Henry.

"Oh. Quite far."

Carmilla loosely curls her fingers around her wine glass, still watching Henry, and he shifts beneath her gaze like a butterfly evading the pin. Perhaps it is the wine, or perhaps it is the light, but her lips seem startlingly red against her skin, as though slick with blood.

I know I should intervene and lead the conversation to a lighter, easier place, but I find myself empty of any inspiration to do so. Usually this is my most prized skill, but Nethershaw has drained too much of me already. I have little left to give.

The moor winds slap and rattle at the windowpanes, candles guttering in the breeze that finds its way inside. Above us, something drips from the sodden ceiling.

Henry sets down his knife and fork. "Look, I will speak plainly. Perhaps you would be more comfortable at a hotel in town? Warmer, I'm sure, closer to the doctor. We have plans to entertain soon, and it will be quite disruptive to you."

Carmilla leans her chin on her hand, eyes fixed upon my husband, unblinking. "You would prefer me to leave?"

I am losing my patience. There is no need for Henry to behave like this. It is childish and unbecoming, and I thought I had better impressed upon him the importance of manners—of control. It is all we have to stand between us and the void.

"Let us discuss this tomorrow. It is not dinner-table conversation."

This was a mistake. Henry's face darkens.

"This is my house and my table, so I'll talk about whatever I like. Frankly, Miss Kernstein, yes, it would be preferable for you to recuperate elsewhere."

Carmilla weathers his mood like the moor weathers the storms that blow across it: simple, certain, unmoved. She turns, those hypnotic eyes now trained on me.

"Lenore, would *you* prefer I leave?"

Would I? Instinct says yes, at once. Though I may not speak it as plainly as Henry, I, too, am troubled by her presence and the mystery that surrounds her, and with all that is expected of me, it would be far easier without her.

But there is instinct, and there is attraction.

Carmilla holds an allure, like ghosting a finger around the edge of a flame: the temptation, the beauty, and the anticipation of pain.

I should want her gone.

And yet.

"I won't hear of it," I say lightly, giving no fuel to the tension running tight between Henry and Carmilla. "Miss Kernstein is in my care, Henry, dear, and until the doctor gives her a clean bill of health to travel, I cannot countenance it. I could not bear it if she fell to some harm on my account."

Carmilla's smile widens, her incisors slipping over her bottom lip, and she looks upon me so warmly it is as though I am now the fire, for so greatly do I burn with something I cannot name. My stomach rolls, and I hide my face in another glass of wine.

No. Henry will not send away my guest.

He is wrong. This is *my* house.

*

"I do not like that you contradicted me in front of a stranger."

Henry summons me to his study after dinner with the crook of a finger.

"She is not a stranger."

"Oh, enough, Lenore—the woman is a chancer. Can you not see it?"

"She's harmless. She's hardly left her bed."

"Yes, exactly, and soon she'll have been here a month, and you'll find her so essential, we will have to drag her around with us everywhere I go. Stop being so naive."

"I am not being naive; *you* are being unkind." The words move from thought to lips with no intercession, in a way I have rarely experienced. I grip the back of a chair for support, so in shock am I at myself. "What I mean is, perhaps in the world of business you must be so cautious, but I do not believe that to be the case here."

Henry's jaw is tight, muscle flickering beneath his skin. "She was watching me the entire meal. It was disturbing behavior."

"She is eccentric." I take his arm, lead him to a seat, and pour him a glass of brandy. His body is stiff and unyielding, but after a moment, he allows me to serve him. "I like her. You must be able to see that it is a little lonely here. Allow me a friend."

Henry drinks the brandy mechanically, then sets down the glass, a decision made. "Very well, but this is on your head. Things *must* be ready for the shooting party. I would not choose to indulge such distractions, but if you think you can still achieve the high standards I expect . . ."

"You said before you trusted me. Don't you?"

A decade ago, Henry placed his trust in me, and that pact has grown thin and stretched over the years. I am unsure where this boldness has come from, and I fear I may pay for it, but there is something a little petulant and stubborn in me tonight. I have chosen Carmilla, and I will have her.

Henry takes my wrist firmly enough it hurts. His fingers are cold from the glass and the green of his eyes is piercing.

"Do not make me regret this, Lenore."

*

I touch myself that night.

I am efficient, and quiet, knowing well how to achieve the release I hope will settle my tense body. It was a discovery made through accident and curiosity as I grew, something about which no one had ever spoken to me—certainly not Aunt Daphne— nor had I heard any whisper or sly comment from the servants or any others. I was entirely ignorant. It seemed simply a mechanical release that offered small comfort in the bleakest, coldest hours of my lonely existence, a way to sleep when my mind tangled and tortured me. With Henry long neglectful of our marriage bed, it remains thus for me still. Perhaps I am a little ashamed of myself, if I think about it, so I simply do not think about it at all.

Tonight, though, my ministrations are not effective. My body will not respond.

Damn Henry dragging me here. Damn Nethershaw for its ruin and rot. Damn Carmilla for the sudden burden she places on me.

An image, then, flashes through my mind: the nightdress slipping off her shoulder, low enough that the soft swell of her breast is revealed, and the delicate flush of areola, the small peak of her nipple against the fabric.

Heat builds beneath my moving fingers, and I chase the sensation for the smallest moment before it comes to me what I am doing, and I yank my hands away at once.

My cheeks are flushed with shame, as though Carmilla would know at once what I have done, thinking of her.

I roll onto my front, bury my face in the pillow. I take those thoughts and parcel them off into one corner of my mine, slice them away cleanly so it is as though they do not exist.

I should have the dining room chairs reupholstered. There is still time, if I act swiftly tomorrow and pay handsomely. Perhaps a few more indoor plants can be obtained from a nursery, they would look well in the drawing room.

Sleep does not come.

I am troubled by pain in my stomach again. It can no longer be my courses, so perhaps it is indigestion, and I would well believe it after all I ate, but when I bring up my dinner into the chamber pot, it is tinged with red, and I feel the first notes of fear.

I have been in pain for several weeks now; I had thought it only the slow mount to my monthly bleed, but there seems no end in sight. I cannot control this, my body and I are unwilling prisoners together, and it makes its protest louder than my thoughts can contain.

Something is wrong with me.

In the morning, Molly does not wake me, and my washbasin stands empty. It is unlike her, so I put a wrapper over my nightgown and go below stairs to seek her out.

I encounter the housekeeper, Mrs. Smith, coming towards me.

"If you're looking for Mr. Crowther, he left at first light—rode into town to collect the new carriage, I believe."

I flush, embarrassed to be caught off guard. I was not thinking of Henry at all. "Oh. Yes. I knew that." I did not. It is frustrating for Henry to be so changeable; I am made a fool when my authority is all I have to wield in this house. "I am looking for Molly."

Smith frowns. "She went up half an hour since—I thought she would be with you."

"She is not. I would not expect to need to hunt for my own servants."

"Yes, my lady. We will find her straightaway. I can send another girl up to do for you." The housekeeper bows her head, and I know I have shamed her. It shames me, too, the small pleasure I feel in displacing my own embarrassment and frustration onto someone else.

"No. I don't want anyone else." My fingers twitch for a pastille. How I dislike myself sometimes, and my own feeble will that indulges such cruel impulses. "Well. Never mind. I'm sure she's somewhere."

"Yes, my lady."

The workmen have already arrived, so I take the servants' stairs to avoid their stomping boots and the racket of hammer and saw. After losing my dinner to the chamber pot, I am hungry again, so I take a few pastilles from my room.

It is there I hear something. Beyond Carmilla's door, I hear her voice.

And another.

I find Molly knelt beside Carmilla's bed like a supplicant, her hands tenderly holding a brush of mahogany and boar bristle, from which she is unwinding chestnut strands of hair and putting them greedily in her mouth. Carmilla smiles down at her, lips stretched wide and cheeks flushed with excitement.

For a moment, I am frozen. I cannot understand what I am seeing. It is as though my mind attempts to decipher a foreign script: the lines and movements of what is before me are so unfamiliar that they impart no meaning.

"What are you doing?" I ask, when I find my voice.

It is as though Molly comes back to herself with a jerk, and she looks anew at the brush in her hand, pulls the hair from her mouth with horror.

Quickly, I shut the door behind me.

No one else need see this.

"Give me that." I snatch the brush from Molly's shaking hand and push it into a drawer. The hair lies limply across the bedspread and the carpet. I scrape it up—there is so much of it, thick and shining in the sunlight—and toss it out the window.

Molly has retreated to a corner, looking at her own hands as though they have betrayed her. "I'm sorry, my lady—I'm so sorry. I don't understand what came over me."

"It is all right, Molly. Do not think on it again."

"But—"

"It did not happen. Do you hear me? Go to my room until you can collect yourself. Mrs. Smith is looking for you."

With a bob and a thanks, Molly flees, and I am left alone with Carmilla.

This is her doing. I am sure of it. I do not understand how, but I know it somewhere in my gut.

I round on her, hands twitching. Molly is under my care. She has been with me since she first entered service. I brought her to this house. And Carmilla has—she has . . . I do not understand what it is she has done, but I must not allow Molly to take any blame for it.

Before I can speak, Carmilla looks at me sincerely, mouth in a delicate pout, and says, "She must be so hungry, the poor thing."

I blink in confusion. "What on earth are you talking about? She was eating your *hair*. How did this come to happen?"

"I suppose she wanted to know what I tasted like." She says it so simply, as though I am quite naive to not understand.

"It is perverse!"

"Have you never done anything a little perverse, my dear Lenore? Just to know how it feels?"

Carmilla cannot know that my cheeks burn with shame for what I have done only the night before, thinking of her. Without meaning to, my eye drops to the swell of her chest below the delicate cotton nightgown, then quickly away to the floor.

"You say that as if it is any answer at all," I snap. My carefully nurtured patience is wearing thin.

I think of sitting on the bed with Carmilla's hands on mine, mouth open, all my history spilling forth. She is not Henry. She is not Cora. Somehow, all my steel edges bend and flex with her, and it unnerves me.

"What is your answer, then?" Carmilla cocks her head to the side, like an animal considering its prey.

"I . . . I don't have one. But Molly would not have done that of her own volition."

"Wouldn't she?"

"Of course not."

Carmilla sits forward, chestnut hair pooling around her shoulders, lustrous in the candlelight. "You know her mind so perfectly? Every want? Every dark impulse? Do you know everything in her that longs to be free and be felt?"

It is as though she is asking me to cross some invisible line with her, to step over into a world I little understand and much fear.

My hands tremble where I knot them into my skirts. "It is too strange. You must not let something like that happen again."

It all changes in an instant. Carmilla's expression lightens and she laughs at me; the tension snaps, she beckons me to her, as sweet as honey and as comforting.

"Oh, Lenore. How easily you are all shocked. Never mind a little strangeness—what does it matter to you? Come and sit with me a while. I would be grateful for the company."

My hand finds hers of its own volition, and I am drawn down into her embrace. She strokes my hair, arranges us side by side on the bed and presses a book into my hands, demanding I read a chapter to her while she closes her eyes.

It is easier to comply.

I cannot begin to understand what I have witnessed; it threatens to overwhelm my faculties if I give it any closer attention, and I am nothing if not a coward. Better, then, to close up the memory of Molly knelt with her hand to her mouth, place it deep and dark among all the others I would rather forget, my own moments of madness.

This, at least, I know how to do.

"You have the most beautiful voice," says Carmilla when I finish the chapter. "It is most soothing."

"Oh, I am sure it is quite plain."

"It is a melody to me. You are a song, Lenore, harmony and discord. I am learning to sing it."

"How curious are some of the things you say. I'm no more a song than a painting or a dance."

"You think yourself a tool, needed only when useful. You are wrong."

I take a sharp breath in, cut so suddenly. I feel utterly naked and exposed, as though Carmilla has sliced me neck to navel in one line.

"I should go." I move to rise, but her hand holds me firm.

"Don't you love this house?" she says.

"What?" I laugh. "Love rot and decay?"

"All the crumbling mess of it. I thought it a wreck that consumed you, but now I see its magnificence. This place is wild. It is defiant and difficult and free. Do you not love it for that?"

I look again around her room, at the vast fireplace with its delicately carved mantel, the uneven boards that have survived centuries, the warped beams and persistent stone walls.

Yes, I suppoze it is wondrous, in its way.

"I apologize for my husband's behavior last night," I say. "He has his reasons, but I would have hoped he could express himself a little more tactfully."

"It was quite tiresome," she agrees. Her candor shocks me, but it comes with a flare of pleasure at having my annoyance indulged and affirmed.

"I have tried for many years of our marriage to instill a sense of propriety," I add, "but he will let his temper get the better of him."

"He is his own person. You should not be responsible for his behavior."

"Well. No. I suppose not."

Carmilla has nestled so close that she rests her head against my shoulder, breath ghosting against my neck, a closeness I am quite unaccustomed to. I hold myself so still; I would not disturb her and lose this intimacy.

"Do you prefer I go, Lenore?" She strokes my hand again, and I feel a strange shiver of something between my legs.

"No," I say, a little too quickly. "I do not."

Her smile is delicious and wicked and just for me. "Good. I think we have so much more to do together."

*

Henry arrives back at Nethershaw in a new carriage drawn by two fine bay stallions. They clatter up to the entrance like a clap of thunder in the mealy sky, nostrils flaring and eyes rolling as Henry drives them at top speed, before hauling on the reins and overshooting the front door by several feet. The groom who drove us from the station sits beside him, holding his hat on with one hand but otherwise entirely enamored by my husband's reckless style. Henry hops down and slaps the flank of one horse.

"Are they not fine?" he asks, circling his new acquisitions, for I assume he purchased them along with the coach.

"I did not realize you had made arrangements for a new carriage," I say, displeased by how shrewish I sound. Henry has bought diamonds for me. A great surprise. Our anniversary. I should try harder to be happy.

He laughs. "A gentleman could not be seen dead in that ancient thing. I instructed a maker on my last visit and found it was ready to take into my possession. Naturally, I needed a pair of horses that would match its finery."

I do not say that the horses look wild, stamping on the cobbles and straining at the traces, nor that they will upset the balance of the stables. The groom has taken over, trying to gather the reins in one hand.

"You may take it into town if you like," Henry offers, pleased to be generous.

A note of the north enters his speech; it has been so long since I last saw him in his place of origin that I had all but forgotten the accent that flattens his vowels, no matter how many years he spent at Harrow and Cambridge to smooth them out.

I smile. "You sound like you belong here."

His expression grows fixed. "I built the prosperity of this city. It is mine."

"I could hear it in your voice when we first met—so different from all the typical men at every party."

"No, I wasn't." He is abrupt. "I went to school with half of them. We are the same."

I realize I have stepped on unsteady ground and steer quickly away. "Is all well at the works?"

Henry ignores me and goes to the carriage door, brushing off our exchange as though it never happened.

He opens the door, and I think he means to leave again, but then he extends his hand and helps someone descend. A woman.

Cora.

6

My smile becomes stiff.

"Look who I found," announces Henry.

Cora is dressed prettily in a dusky-pink day dress with a smart bustle that bobs behind her, a straw hat tied under her chin with a matching ribbon. The brim is decorated with a diffusion of cloth roses that would look foolish on me, but on Cora they only accent the delicate flush of her cheeks. Her youth clings to her like dew, brightening her eyes and softening the lovely curves of her face. She is younger than I ever was at her age, cushioned by her good birth and money, so that the world is still a plaything to her.

She comes to me at once and gathers my hands in hers. "Lenore, how I have missed you."

"And I you." I do not miss a beat, despite the sour feeling spreading through me.

"Did you receive my letters? I knew you would want me with you—an estate! How marvelous it is."

I think of the stack of correspondence mounting on my desk and feel both guilty and frustrated. I should have read them sooner, and then I could have instructed her not to come.

No, that is an ungenerous thought.

I am gripped by something like dread, and I do not understand it. Cora is my friend. I have spent more than a year in her company at balls, luncheons, excursions, and assemblies, intoxicated and infuriated at once to be drawn into the fantasy world she offers; one where things come easy, where all is beautiful and good and hopeful, and storm clouds are but passing. I dread her, and I crave the fantasy.

"Of course," I say. "How delightful to have you here." I look to Henry, who is standing behind her. "How did my husband know you were in town?"

Cora laughs delicately but does not answer my question. "I have been staying a night or two at the Victoria with the Carstairs. They have invited me to dine with them tonight—they wish to introduce me to their nephew. Not that I shall entertain him! But of course I wanted to be here with you."

The Victoria—when Henry insisted there were no hotels in town suitable for us to stay at.

Cora hooks her arm in mine and draws me inside, keeping up an incessant chatter.

"You must tell me everything. Molly, have some tea sent to whichever room it is Lenore likes best. Look at those hills, what a sinister view! How like a novel. Don't you think I am clever to have worn these shoes? I am a very good outdoors woman—everyone says so. I could walk all day to a romantic ruin and still look smart in these."

I allow myself to be led, my thoughts filled with Cora's noise. We must give her the best room, of course, if there are any that are not an embarrassment to me. Carmilla occupies the only decent one, but perhaps there will be one that is at least clean and free of workmen.

Why did Henry do this? Why must he demand so much from me then disrupt my path at every turn? I have been loyal to him for a decade, held my tongue when one word from me could have capsized him in those early years. Can he not give me some peace?

Tea is delivered to the smart drawing room that faces the dark thatch of conifer plantation at the edge of the moorland. It is the quieter side of the house, sheltered from the excesses of weather that strike the windows facing the limestone of Hungerstone Edge. Wind gusts over the stubble of heather, sun beats relentlessly against the glass, and rain drives its way into the mortar. Those rooms are the more damaged, taking greater effort to buttress against decline. Here, the drawing room is a little dark, papered in an unpleasant shade of yellow I thought looked less sour in the book of samples, but it is the most presentable.

Cora examines the objects on the mantelpiece: an old carriage clock that tells no time, an empty snuff box, a basket of tapers to light candles from the fire. I find myself watching her too closely, looking for some sign of judgment. I will have done something wrong, shamed myself in some capacity—I am sure of it. Cora will see the rime of dirt, my unkempt hair, or disorderly servants, and know me squalid, lacking, out of my depth.

I shut the roll top of my bureau, before Cora can see her unread letters, and smile mechanically.

Molly pours two cups before retreating to the kitchens. The two of us sit for a stilted moment, Cora and I sipping at our tea, making idle conversation about the trains from London, the weather, my decoration scheme.

"Ah!" Cora claps her hands together. "I have something for you."

"Oh?"

"Hold out your hands and close your eyes."

"Cora, really—"

"Humor me, please."

A little wary, I do as I am bid and hold my palms upturned to the air.

There is the sound of Cora's skirts rustling, the creak of boards, and then something light and thin is placed into my hands.

"You can look now!"

I open my eyes to see a slim fan in its embroidered sleeve. It is a delicate pink, embroidered with flowers and trimmed with lace. When I remove the fan itself, it is fine, detailed carving work in ivory and silk, painted with roses and trimmed with more lace. Quite expensive, and quite, quite wrong for a woman of my age. It is girlish—coquettish even—and perfectly suited to Cora. On me, it would be an embarrassment.

I smile, tight-lipped. "It is lovely. Thank you for thinking of me."

"Isn't it sweet? I saw it and thought at once of you."

I make some pretty comments about the fan, speaking from habit more than sincerity. I am not rich in friends. I have spent my adult life at the work of establishing Henry's position and my own role within society, to build each new step before me, each one an assurance I will not end up like Aunt Daphne, or my parents, bankrupt and dead. There are many acquaintances upon whom I may call, but none familiar enough that I would stay for long. All have their own families, their own childhood friends, parents, aunts, uncles, cousins—a world of people who take priority.

I have Henry, Cora. I must take what I can get.

I run my fingers over the carved bone, thinking of the flash of teeth every time Carmilla smiles.

For now, at least, I have her, too.

"Tell me, what do you think of my plans?" says Cora, and I wonder if I have drifted so far from the conversation that I have missed something vital.

"Plans?"

"That I wrote to you about. I think I shall study art. Isn't it a delightful idea? I showed my work to a gentleman at the Slade School, and he says he has never seen a woman show so much promise. He invited me to submit my application immediately."

"I did not know you were so interested in the arts," I say.

"Perhaps if I am bored, I will do it. I think I shall travel to Rome before I marry and spend a summer painting. Or perhaps I shall marry first, and my husband can take me for our honeymoon."

Cora has taken up a position before the fireplace as though on a stage, and arranges herself so that the light falls well on her petite frame.

"Lord Walham called on me three times last week. I shall show him my art—he will be very interested."

At this, I hear a snort of derision from behind me. Cora and I turn as one to see Carmilla in the shadow of the doorway, leaning on the frame for support. Her hair tumbles loose around her shoulders, and she wears only a light robe over her nightdress, the white lace peeping through the blue silk.

Again, Carmilla has appeared noiselessly, just as she did before dinner last night. I am uneasy at the thought of how effortlessly she can slip through space, where she might go, what she might see or hear unnoticed.

I think of bare feet on floorboards, the nightdress disappearing around a corner. Night walking.

"Who is this?" Cora asks. "You did not tell me you had invited another guest."

I am surprised Henry did not inform Cora of the accident as they rode in from town together; I would have thought half of Sheffield would know of his heroics by now.

I give Cora a small shake of the head before going to Carmilla's side.

"Are you sure you are well enough to be up?" I ask her softly, searching her face for signs of weakness, but she seems strangely restored.

Carmilla touches the tightly pinned set of my hair. "Yes, dear Lenore. How pretty you look in red. Like blood and roses."

I remember Molly and the hairbrush, and my unease grows. Carmilla is strange—I cannot deny it is a strangeness I have found alluring, but now, with Cora's fresh gaze, her talent for normality, I fear that she will see something more in Carmilla than she will like.

It is a risk, to keep Carmilla here.

How frustrating it is that Henry might be right.

I flush and remove her hand. "Will you join us?"

Carmilla ignores me, drifting into the room to extend a hand to Cora, palm down as though she expects Cora to kiss it.

"Carmilla Kernstein," she says, voice like honey. "I found myself in grave need of assistance, and dear Lenore was good enough to let a stranger intrude on her hospitality."

I recount the story of Carmilla's rescue and her recovery with us.

Cora ignores the hand and delivers a kiss to both cheeks. "Oh, you poor thing, how terrible. How glad I am that you have found respite."

Carmilla is too cool, receiving Cora's embrace disinterestedly.

"Won't you take tea?" says Cora, indicating a seat on the ornate Louis XIV sofa that is at odds with the heavy stone of Nethershaw.

Carmilla ignores her, instead drawing my tin of pastilles from her pocket. "You left these."

"Oh." I reach for them, embarrassed, but she doesn't hand them over.

"Where did you get them?" she asks, eyes sharp.

"You can have them if you like," I offer, but she bares her teeth.

"Throw them away. They're disgusting." Her words are as sharp as a slap.

I snatch them off her and push them into a drawer, stomach rolling. Did Cora hear?

"We will dine later." She glances at Cora and says so only I can hear, "I would have you to myself."

My breath comes short, and I do not know why. Before I can respond, Carmilla is gone, a flash of nightdress trailing on the stairs.

Cora's trunks are taken inside, and while she oversees their installation into a guest room, I find Henry as he comes in from stowing his new mounts.

"How strange you should find Cora in a busy place like Sheffield."

Henry tosses his hat to Roberts and takes the mud from his shoes on the boot scraper.

"I met the Carstairs on business, and they told me Cora was expecting to join us today. Not that I knew anything about that. I suppose you've been ignoring the one person who's *actually* bothered to try and be your friend."

He is cold and short, and I fear that I pushed him too far in my defense of Carmilla last night.

"I confess I have been too busy to attend to all my correspondence. The shooting party has been my priority."

"Don't blame this on me—I dare say you've been occupied with your new hanger-on." He glances upwards to where Carmilla has returned to her lair. "You seem so keen to host guests. I thought you'd be happy to add to your menagerie."

Sometimes, I think Henry is more beautiful in his cruel moments. His mouth takes a sneer handsomely, the low set of his brow something Byronic. I want to tell him it is not I who brought

Carmilla into our home, but I do not know what use that will be. Instead, I return his smile, because what else is there for me to do?

"Of course I am pleased to see Cora, but it is so sudden . . ."

"You're very lucky to have such a thoughtful friend who cares about you."

"I am."

"I want you to come to the works with me in a few days."

The change of topic is so abrupt that I only stare at my husband as he peels off his jacket and rolls up his sleeves. The heat is beginning to build, and sweat sticks curls of his hair to his temples from the vigor of the drive up.

"Me?"

"Yes, you. You are my wife, aren't you?"

Then the memory comes to me: the overheard telephone call. The surprise. I think of the diamonds nestled in their silk. A warmth rushes to my cheeks.

I have upset Henry, and perhaps this is an important moment to repair his regard for me.

"If you think you have need of me . . ."

He softens, pulls me close with a hand at my waist. "I need you. A few gentlemen are visiting whom I wish you to meet. This is a critical time for Ajax, and you always help me show my best face." He tucks a strand of hair behind my ear, lets his fingers trace the shape of my jaw, and I am transported back to the rushed, hopeful days of our courtship, when he would touch me like I was a treasure he had discovered hidden among junk, an unexpected windfall. "I've put my future in your hands from the start, Lenore. I still do."

I wrap my fingers around his and place a kiss to his palm. "You know you can trust in me."

He hangs his head, takes a slow breath at the feel of my lips on his skin. "You know there is much that lies heavy on my conscience. But I have always thought we could really *make* something together." There is a light dancing in his eyes when he looks at me that I have not seen for many years: the excitement of the young man I married, burning with a hunger to succeed, to crack the world open and claim it all for his own. He takes my hands and squeezes them. "There is something very special I would have you see."

My smile now is genuine, and I am buoyant with hope. "Then I will be ready at the hour you set."

He kisses my temple. "That's my girl."

*

Carmilla and I dine alone.

Cora is at dinner with the Carstairs, and Henry drove her back to town, citing chophouse socializing for some business matter. I know he does not like our guest, and after her behavior last night, I have begun to suspect she does not like him either. I am grateful, then, that he has so much to attend to in the city, and so I am spared their crisp, uneasy dialogue.

I can enjoy Carmilla to myself.

What a thought. Do I enjoy her?

Cook is practicing a menu I have designed for the shooting party. We start with mock turtle soup and red mullet, which is replaced with Fricandeau de Veau à la Jardinière. Carmilla eats sparingly, spearing a sliver of fish on her fork and placing it delicately between her lips.

"You seem much recovered," I say, and it is true. Her lips are full and red, and her skin is luminous. She never pins up her hair, letting it fall around her shoulders like spun gold.

"Thanks to your ministrations," she says. Sometimes, her voice is low and soft, like the movement of wind over the heather; sometimes, it is faint and wasting. It is as though she is one woman in the day and another at night.

"It is nothing. I am only glad to see you well."

Carmilla drinks from her wineglass, staining her lips dark. "Your husband must have much pressing business to keep him from so pretty a wife."

I smile, despite myself. "Indeed. Henry's steelworks are flourishing."

"What is it he makes?"

I falter. "Cutlery, I believe, for the most part, with a special attention to knives." I lift the carving knife from beside the haunch of venison that has arrived for our next course. It is perfectly balanced and wickedly sharp, the blade curving slightly at the tip. "This is one of his. Is it not fine?"

She considers it, expression unchanged. "He is ambitious," she offers.

"As most young men are."

Carmilla makes a noise that could be assent or disapproval, and sips a little more wine. "And young women? What of their ambitions?"

I laugh. "I am hardly young."

Carmilla's age is hard to determine, though now I try—there are no lines on her face, nor gray in her hair, but she holds herself with such ease and certainty, I think her closer to my age than Cora's.

"Are you not the same age as your husband?"

The footmen arrive to change the savory for the sweet, a dish of strawberry cream and a raspberry tart with custard.

"It is different for women," I say when we are alone again.

"How so? Do the natural processes of aging not affect men? Do they not grow slow and gray-haired?"

I am beginning to feel irritated. The frustration I have nursed for too long subsided with the discovery of the hidden diamonds, but Carmilla has needled it to the fore. Perhaps the customs of guests are different wherever it is she is from, but I do not know how to respond to such provocation.

"I am sure you well understand what I mean," I say.

"I do, but that does not mean I comprehend it. I think what you truly mean is that it is different for a woman's appetite."

I pause at her choice of words and put down my spoon of strawberry cream. "What is it you intend to say?"

Carmilla makes a noise of distaste and impatience. "It is what *you* say, Lenore. You think Henry has license to entertain every appetite that wakes in him, and that you do not."

"But of course. We occupy different spheres of life. He is responsible for the Ajax Works, as I am for Nethershaw, and each makes different demands and offers different rewards."

"And this is enough for you?"

My temper frays again, her presence like sand wearing me thin. "It is naive to think one is owed anything from life. We endure it; we survive it. That is enough."

Carmilla sneers, her pretty face curling into something sharper. "What a small, pathetic future you build." She leans forward. "I wonder for what you hunger, and whether you allow yourself to feel it."

I stare at her. I do not like her words. The rich venison and fish sit heavy in my stomach, and I hate myself for having eaten so much.

"It is a future envied by many," I say instead. For it is. I have *fought* for this life, when I could have so easily drowned beneath the waters of my misfortune. No one has loved me for so many a long year, I have done it all from spite. If the world offers me no kindness, then I will take from it armor and sword, create an unassailable fortress for myself, and lock the door.

"You are not listening to me." She sits back in her chair, taken with a strop. Her beautiful face becomes dark with shadows, and her eyes glitter.

Somewhere near the kennels, the dogs begin their howling; the sun is setting, and soon we will have only the stars for company.

She tilts her head. "Do you think they're fucking?"

I fumble my wineglass, spilling claret across the white tablecloth. "I beg your pardon?"

"Your husband and that smug little girl."

"I do not know the customs where you are from, but in England it is not appropriate to discuss such a matter." I sound as unreal as a marionette, the words falling from my mouth without any genuine emotion or thought.

Carmilla's face lights up, and she leans forward again, drinking in my discomfort. "You do think it. I wondered if you were alive enough to care."

"Not that it is any of your concern, but I know that my husband is loyal to me."

Do I?

I hold a kind of power over him that he cannot easily negate. That is not the same as loyalty in every aspect.

"If you were so sure, it would be a simple thing to ask him."

"I do not need your marital advice."

"No. I think you are too much a coward to ever risk learning the truth. Easier to die for a delusion."

My face feels hot, and I push back from the table too sharply.

She knows nothing of what I truly am. What I have done to survive.

For what do you hunger?

79

I cannot bear her company for a minute longer. I cannot bear this.

The sooner Carmilla Kernstein is gone from my life, the sooner I will feel in control again.

*

I take a fistful of pastilles from a new tin on my dresser, and eat them one by one as Molly takes my hair down from its pins. They are so sweet I feel sick after the second or third, but I continue until my tongue is thick with fur and my teeth ache to their roots. Carmilla called them disgusting. She judges me.

I push another between my lips, cracking it with the clench of my jaw. Why do I care if she judges me? This is my house, and I am its mistress; it is not for her, a stranger imposing upon my hospitality, to make judgments over the way I choose to live.

Molly helps me into my nightgown, and when she is gone, I eat another four pastilles, until the tin is empty. I hate myself for it.

I fix the shutters closed, pausing to look through the glass, but there is nothing to see. The moon and stars are concealed by cloud, so it is as though we have been plucked from the face of the earth and set amongst some inhuman landscape of nothingness. When Lucifer fell from Heaven, was this how he found Hell? A cold, blank world into which no good thing could be born?

Molly brings me a posset, and I drink it. The night is cold, and the fires have not been lit for so long, damp has seeped into the fabric of the building, so I lie between the sheets, shivering as I have not done since leaving Aunt Daphne and the frigid house on Mount Street.

I pass a few hours in a fitful doze, rousing to the sound of distant church bells tolling the hours.

Three bells chime.

I wake to a weight settling on my chest.

My eyes fly open, but I cannot move. I am fixed in place by the great pressure above my heart that all but squeezes the breath from me.

A shadow obscures my vision.

The shadow from London has followed me.

I try to scream, but nothing emerges from my lips save a whimper.

The room is so dark I can barely distinguish it from the night air, but its presence is incontrovertible. I feel it shift as though it has sensed that I wake, and I have the sudden impression that a great cat of some kind has prowled around my bedroom and made its home upon me.

In the absence of my ability to move, I concentrate on what I can feel. Is that the sensation of fur against my thighs? A claw at my breast?

Then a tongue at my neck, soft and hot. The shock of it sends a wave of confusion through me. Two sharp darts press into my skin a few inches apart, and I gasp, the barest of sounds.

The shadow shifts, and its smoky body pours off the bed, leaving me heady with confusion.

I wake to the dull, navy light of early morning. My door is ajar, and I hear the soft patter of feet in the corridor outside.

Returned to my strength, I stumble out of bed, angry. It is Carmilla, playing some trick on me—I am sure of it.

The crooked corridor is empty. When I try her door opposite mine, I find it locked. I press one ear to the wood, almost expecting to hear her cold, glassy laughter.

There is nothing; only the hectic beating of my heart.

7

I HAD MY FIRST audience with Aunt Daphne the day I arrived at her house. A frost of parental blood still marred the lace trim of my skirt as I was summoned into a parlor overlooking the square outside. The last of the daylight was all but gone, but no lamps had been lit inside. I can still remember how vast the room seemed to me at twelve, how strange and alien its landscape of console tables and antimacassars.

When I left to marry Henry, I could see it for what it was: a dull, faded space crammed with the detritus of a life frozen too long in the past: heaping piles of magazines so old their bindings had cracked, old tins of sweets, withered clementines in a basket, the desiccated bodies of mice in ancient traps, flowers dried and dead.

That night, it was like something from a dream that I moved through slowly, afraid to touch anything for fear of precipitating a collapse. At last, I discovered Aunt Daphne by the window, her chair pulled close to the glass so that she could watch the world below through a pair of small eyeglasses. She wore black—I remember thinking like the Queen—and it made her more inhuman in my eyes. She summoned me with a crook of her finger, said nothing as she cast her gaze over me. I felt on trial without being asked a single question, and I did not know how it was that I could account well of myself.

Dinner was brought to Aunt Daphne on a tray, a second smaller plate added for me as though an afterthought, which I supposed it was.

Still without speaking, she indicated that I sit on a footstool by her side. The plate was passed to me to balance on my lap, an oily mess of bony fish and toast burnt on the fire. Aunt Daphne ate loudly, lips smacking and whiskery chin working as she picked the spines from between her teeth.

I could not stomach a mouthful. The world had cracked open, and nothing held any meaning. To eat, to not eat, to speak or not speak—it was all the same.

"You know your letters and figures?" It was the first thing she said to me.

"Yes."

"Did they send you to a school?" The word like a piece of gristle on her tongue. *They*. My dead parents.

"No."

"Dance?"

"What?"

"Do you dance?"

"Oh. A little?"

She peered down at me again. "How old?"

"Twelve."

And that was it.

The next morning, I learned my first great mistake.

I came to breakfast in dread, still blank from the shock of the day before. I could only bear the memory of the crash if I simply turned away from it each time it rose in my mind, and I had lost much sleep in this endeavor.

Aunt Daphne summoned me to her side again, positioning me on a footstool at her feet.

"I don't appreciate your attitude."

I smiled in shock. "I'm sorry, Aunt Daphne."

"You sit at my table putting on such a performance I could think myself at Drury Lane."

The sense of unreality snapped in an instant; I was suddenly as immediately and completely in the moment as I had been when the crash occurred. I could feel the prickle of cold air on the skin of my neck, and the sharp line of light below the lowered window blind, each detail picked out so cleanly I could see it all at once.

"Not a word of thanks for eating my food or sleeping beneath my roof? It is astonishingly self-involved. Do you think I want a girl under my feet acting the little princess?"

I felt sick, the ground lurching beneath me. I had thought myself in one place, but indeed I was in quite another.

"No," I breathed.

She leaned down from her wingbacked chair, pinched my chin beneath her sharp fingers and twisted my face towards her.

"I am a charitable woman who has allowed you, some offshoot of a feckless cousin, to live here, but I will not tolerate rudeness. I will not tolerate entitled behaviour. Are you entitled?"

"No, Aunt Daphne."

She frowned. "Your parents are dead. It happens to everyone. Don't think yourself special."

"No, Aunt Daphne."

Her thick, yellowed nails dug into my skin like glass. "You have been educated, have you not?"

I nodded as best I could against her grip.

"And yet not in manners, it seems."

"I'm sorry, Aunt Daphne," I said again. "I am very grateful to you for letting me stay here."

"Hmm. Better."

It was the first of many transgressions.

I learned quickly that my wants and needs were unwelcome, too great for any reasonable person to fulfill, and in time I came to agree with her. I *was* too much, too loud, too emotional, too clumsy, too self-involved. My existence was a burden to all involved with it, and I resolved to never make any demand if I could help it. Then, perhaps, I could be tolerated. Then, perhaps, I could be loved.

I remember few clear details of my life that came after. There is something like a panorama attraction in its place: a long track of similar road with only the occasional deviation or delight. It is as though my young mind rapidly grasped that whatever manner of life to which I had been accustomed was superfluous to the future. The only way to survive the position I now found myself in was to sever my existence neatly at the point of the carriage accident and discard what had come before. Who I had been died alongside my parents, and I was born again in that funereal house with Aunt Daphne.

What I remember most is my aunt herself. The faint, birdlike body with sharp fingers, and eyes unclouded by cataracts, all the better to see my every deficiency. The trill of her voice and the tilt of her jaw.

She kept me by her feet that day and the next, a silent audience to her narration of what transpired outside her window, her critical comments and observations that I was only to acquiesce to. Sometimes I nodded incorrectly, or looked at her in a manner she decided was sanctimonious. I felt quite mad at these times. Anything I said or did, I discovered, meant something else entirely according to Aunt Daphne. Silence didn't serve me, nor did any pretty speech. All I could do was train myself in her whims and weathers and endeavor to match myself accordingly.

I had no other choice.

I had no expectations. I had no one who loved me—no one who dreamt sweet visions of my future and made careful plans to shepherd me through childhood and into a kind, compassionate world.

All I had was myself, and the weight of that burden was almost more than I could bear.

*

I think Carmilla needs to leave.

Oh, I do not feel easy about this thought. I do not have any conviction that I am thinking clearly on this matter.

I lie awake through most the night, guts cramping and nausea rising in my throat. This illness that grips me feels like a premonition: there is something not right at Nethershaw, and my body senses it even if my mind cannot truly grasp it.

If I see Carmilla this morning, I will lose myself to the soft caress of her hand, her honeyed words and knowing gaze. I must rise early, with the birds, and be about my business before my hand falters and I lose my way.

With stout walking boots and a broad-brimmed sun hat tied beneath my chin, I follow directions in the guidebook I bought for Sheffield and its surrounding country, and make brisk work of an hour's walk into the valley to Hathersage train station. It is a small engine that pulls us through the moors, past Grindleford, Dore, and Totley, and into the city.

It is a bright, broad blue day, and the city is quite changed from the rain-slick warren of streets we passed through on our arrival. Smoke plumes lift into the clear air in all directions, and the streets rise and bend with the hills around the rivers. Newspaper boys crowd the station, hawking papers to passengers, crying headlines of murder, industrial accidents, scandal, and fraud in the steel mills of Sheffield. It is good to be in a different place, to break the spell of Nethershaw and be reminded of the noisy, dirty, mundane world that carries on with little heed for my own anxieties. My stomach is still in knots, and I hope the exercise of walking between my errands will help my acute indigestion pass quickly.

Dr. Bartolomé's house is a smart building on Eyre Street, where it crosses Surrey Street, not so far from the station. He is, of course, out with patients, but I expected this and have written a short but persuasive note requesting that he attend us at Nethershaw with utmost haste, and I have folded a banknote in with it as payment in advance. If Carmilla is well enough to torment me, the doctor will surely see that she is well enough to leave.

Turning up Surrey Street towards the town hall, I feel faint with nausea.

I am a traitor, am I not? I have sided with Henry over Carmilla, for no other reason than it suits me better. I wanted Carmilla to remain when she spoke sweet words to me, when the draw I felt towards her was too strong to deny, but now she has vexed me, I have turned on her so easily. I feel something unspoken slipping between my fingers, like I am sliding over a precipice and scrabbling to find some desperate handhold. I cannot lose my grip.

My next point of call is the police station. It is something I should have done as soon as we discovered Carmilla and the crashed carriage, but it did not seem so serious a matter then, and my mind was firmly turned towards the preparation of Nethershaw for the shooting-party guests.

Set down the narrow Castle Green near where Lady's Bridge crosses the Don, the police station itself is a tall, anonymous building in dirty, Italianate sandstone, four stories high. Sandwiched between the market halls of Exchange Street, the scent of piss and crushed vegetation is high in the air. Few ladies venture between the men unloading crates into the vegetable markets and bustling into the Corn Exchange. Perhaps I should not have come. This is Henry's world, not mine.

I stand before the police station, mute, watching the officers come and go in their distinctive blue coats and egg-shaped hats, listening to the clatter of the doors and boots on steps. I half hope someone will ask me if I need help, usher me inside and take the decision from me—but no one does. The memory comes to me of that first morning after Carmilla's arrival, of Henry hushed and firm, *no police*. There is something brittle in Henry lately that I have not noticed before, something I must work on repairing.

Very well. No police.

I continue on towards the river, a headache keeping pace. I must assign the cause of my distraction to this pain, for I step out unthinking into the street into the path of a rushing mail coach. The horses rear, the driver yells, a woman somewhere screams, and it is only a sudden, yanking hand on my arm that pulls me back, seconds from death.

I stand shaking as the market seller who was my savior yells at me for my lax attention. I do not hear him. In my mind, the crash that took my parents replays: the splintering of wood, the hot slick of blood, the violent forces brought to work upon my body.

Cold with shock, I push past the man and flee. I am urgently in need of a moment to sit down and rest. I cannot enter a public house, nor do I have any acquaintances here to call upon—a hotel tearoom is the only respite on offer, so I turn to take the steep, sloping street towards Victoria station and its hotel. The red-brick building is solid and square and modern, towering above the low station building to one side, and I disappear into its bulk, sinking into a settee in one of the smart sitting rooms.

I am brought tea, and I let it sit before me, cooling, as I shut my eyes. This headache will not desist, and again nausea rises through me with the pain in my stomach.

I know I should be worried about the way my body bucks and breaks beneath my hand; it is its own animal, with its own limits, that I have not cared to mind. It betrays me with its wants and needs, its pains and limitations, and I am furious to be tethered in this way. I thought us prisoners together, but perhaps we are enemies, working tirelessly to move in opposite directions.

Gradually, my heart rate slows, and feeling returns to my limbs as I come back to myself. I thought escaping Nethershaw would be a relief, but it seems there is no corner in which I may seek rest. My duty calls me: there is only on and through.

I take a little tea, cupping my hands around the china and watching the come and go of guests and visitors, enjoying a moment of anonymity. Beside me, a family of five fuss over their train tickets, who will carry the traveling rugs, whether the children's shoes are laced tightly, whether anything is left behind. They move so easily together, casually stepping in and out of each other's space, touching and gathering, so sure in their belonging.

When they go, a mess of cups and plates and crumbs remains in their wake, and a hastily tossed newspaper lies open across the seat of a chair.

A name catches my eye: *Ajax Works*.

I take up the paper in curiosity.

It is a short article touching upon industrial relations, a topic that goes far above my head, mentioning names and dates and something called the Sheffield Outrages, which I have faint recollection as an event of my childhood but did not realize involved murders and explosions in the very city in which I sit now. I am struck by a moment of fear for Henry. Is he quite safe, if such unrest occurs again?

I think, then, of the journalist who accosted me in London, of his probing questions.

I hope that this is only a journalist digging for a story, and nothing more.

My thoughts are interrupted by a familiar voice, and I put down the paper to see Cora and Henry walking from the hotel interior, deep in conversation.

"Cora?" I call. "Henry?"

They stop at once, and Henry takes an abrupt step sideways from Cora.

It is like a blow to my chest.

"What are you doing here?" I ask.

Carmilla's words ring loud and piercing: *Do you think they're fucking?*

"Lenore!" Cora is the first to my side, beaming and pretty in a delicate lavender day dress, and small bonnet with ribbons in matching silk. "Henry came to drive me back to Nethershaw. How clever of you to know we would be here."

"I didn't," I say. Can I see anything between them? Any shift in energy that will belie the truth of why they were here together?

"Well, what fortune. Are you finished with your business here? Do say you'll travel back with us?"

I nod my acquiescence.

Henry comes up behind her, stiff and humorless. "The carriage will be waiting," he says, uninterested in further conversation.

I rise from the settee, and at once my head spins, a sense of sickness rising in my gullet, and I think I may humiliate myself in front of all these strangers. I cover my mouth with my hand, sway on the spot, sweat prickling my forehead.

Cora takes my arm to hold me up, but it is not enough and I crumple back to my chair.

"Lenore, are you well?"

I wave her away, and she hovers anxiously. I wait for the nausea to fade, then this time rise more slowly.

"I am fine. Let us go."

Cora takes my arm again, and we go outside to where the carriage has drawn up to the front of the hotel. Henry, Cora, and I take our seats, lowering the windows against the already stuffy air of three bodies too close together at the height of summer.

I *am* fine. I have to be.

I have no time for weakness.

*

Nethershaw is in pieces when I return. There are open rents in the walls where rotten plaster has been dug out, gaps in the floor where wood-wormed boards have been pried up, the walls are bare of art or hangings, the furniture covered in dust sheets. It is enough to distract me from my poor health, and I go from room to room, receiving reports from the workmen, noting spilled paint, torn curtains, the wriggling larvae of moths exposed in the weave of a rug. It is barely more than a week and a half until our guests arrive, and I am a little hysterical at the sheer impossibility of the task Henry has set me. He swans around Sheffield with Cora while I take both our fates on our shoulders.

What *was* he doing with Cora?

The doctor arrives before I can reach my next thought, another task before me. The money left with my note has worked its purpose by bringing him without delay, and I deliver him to Carmilla. I leave Molly as a chaperone and hide in my busyness. I have brought this man to winkle Carmilla out of my home as though he is a knife and Nethershaw the shell, and I feel too guilty about my actions to stay to witness them.

Dr. Bartolomé finds me at my desk, working through a ream of invoices.

"Lady Lenore, I'm afraid I must request you extend your hospitality to your guest a little longer."

"What?" I rise, turning over the papers so that he cannot see the financial mess spread before me. "But, Doctor, she seems so recovered. She has been taking meals with us."

"Do not worry yourself overly, she does indeed improve, but with a condition of the heart, one must take the most delicate care. I am concerned that her pulse remains sluggish and erratic."

"I see. Of course."

He writes out another instruction for a tisane to be made up by the cook; then I pay him, and he is on his way.

This is not the outcome I expected. What am I to do? I cannot cruelly turn Carmilla out. Should she become severely ill from my ungenerosity, the news would ruin me. And for all she enervates me, I am not so heartless as to begrudge her her recovery. Perhaps I can simply avoid her.

God, it is all I can do not to succumb to despair.

I consult with the cook on menu cards and inspect silverware and balance the books to pay for all the extra staff the housekeeper has hired for the shooting party.

"Are you still working?" Cora idles by my desk, peering at the mess around me.

"There is much to do."

"But you were so unwell earlier."

"I do not have time for it."

"Did you see the doctor? What did he think?"

"I said I do not have time for distractions," I snap, slamming my pen down. "It is an upset stomach—it is not a matter for the doctor. Only children and the feebleminded call upon a doctor for every little discomfort. The rest of us simply get on with it."

Cora has flushed in shock and embarrassment, and at once I feel a sick wash of shame.

"I meant well," she says, and I think she might cry.

"Cora—I'm sorry—"

She flees, and I turn back to my papers, knotting my fingers together in my lap. I do not know what came over me, what cruel, capricious instinct led me to mistreat Cora so when I know she is harmless at heart. It is not a crime that she does not understand the pressures upon me—nor is it to walk with my husband in a public hotel.

I am struck by the sudden thought that this anger growing in me is directed at the wrong place. It is not Cora's naivety that riles me.

I cannot put the thought together; it slips from me, and I am left only with my shame and guilt. Aunt Daphne was right: my unpleasant ways place a burden on those around me.

Is this it? The moment I falter?

No. I cannot let in any weakness. I must not. It does not matter that I cannot sleep for nightmares, or that Henry has set me up for failure, or that I have tried and failed to remove Carmilla.

From a drawer in my desk, I pull a tin of pastilles, and one by one chew through so many that my mouth is thick with sugar and my head pounds and I feel wretched.

It is a better pain. A more familiar one. One I control.

In this place I know who I am, and all my suffering is mastered.

8

MY DEBUT INTO SOCIETY at nineteen was a shock as great as the day I lost my parents and found myself locked away with Aunt Daphne. After seven years of isolation, expulsion into the world was an overwhelming riot of noise and color and, everywhere, people: people who knew with ease how to speak, how to dress, people who knew they were welcome in every room, entitled to every invitation.

I remember very little: only a mass of white silk; nausea so great I did not eat or sleep for days before my presentation; the rush of blood to my heart that left my limbs unreal and floating; Aunt Daphne appearing in society for the first time in decades, in a dress so out of date some wit sold a sketch to *Punch* the following week.

And then Henry.

I had a task: to marry. I did not take pleasure in music or the taste of sweet sherbets or the smell of fresh flowers. I did not weep at the theater or thrill with excitement at the races. I was systematic and precise. Studied. Once I understood what it would mean to debut, what society would expect of me, there was finally some sense of purpose to my hollow life. Aunt Daphne could teach me nothing; so it was from books I learned to carry myself, to make pretty conversation. I studied fashions from magazines, the order of precedence from etiquette books, read advice on how to manage household staff.

If I were to survive my life, it fell to my own hands to find salvation.

I needed money, security, and speed. My high birth and my face would open doors, and my parents' bankruptcy would close them just as quickly. For that is what we learned of my mother and father after their death: our lifestyle was a façade propped up before the collapsed house of debt behind it. Whatever money had been amassed by the family who had borne my father's title for centuries had been annihilated by him in one lifetime of bad investments, gambling, and incompetence.

Henry was so rich, coins dropped from his hands as he moved: gold on his fingers and wrists, crisp, perfect tailoring new every day. He did not look at the shine on the palms of my gloves or notice that the jewels at my throat were all paste and paint. He attended the event as the guest of a school friend presenting his sister, and watched each girl like cattle at auction.

I knew him. I knew every man in the room; I had made sure of it. Money, a generation enough away from the factory floor that he was welcome at most events, but not so many that he was in high demand. Ambitious but sharp, handsome but pragmatic. The role of society wife lay open in his household, and I meant to make my application.

I had no mama to orchestrate introductions or paint the delights of my reputation. I would have to do this myself.

At the opening of a new exhibition at the Royal Academy, I endeavored to lose my footing ascending a flight of stairs ahead of Henry, tumbling artfully in his direction. He caught me with a delicate hand at my waist and shoulder.

"Thank you," I breathed, letting myself hang in his arms a moment too long.

"You ladies must take care with your trains," he said, righting me with a brief but uninterested smile. There was the hint of the north in his vowels, and I found that I liked it. Something that marked him out as different, just as I was marked.

A week later, at a dinner held by mutual acquaintances, I made sure I was introduced to a friend of his while he was in earshot, the words "Lady Lenore" ringing out clear over the chatter of those of lower rank. He looked over, his eye assessing the swell of my chest and the neat heart of my face, and at the last moment, I returned his gaze, gifting a smile, before disappearing to the other end of the dining table.

At a ball the night after, I danced with every man but him, laying foundations for alternative paths should my first plan fail. I felt him watch me with each turn about the dance floor, and I prayed he felt envy.

I underestimated him.

It took a few days, I learned later, for Henry to make his inquiries about me.

At a charity bazaar one stuffy afternoon, I slipped onto a secluded terrace to take the air, tired and faint with humidity and lack of food. Fanning myself with a program, I became aware of a presence behind me.

Henry had followed me, and now stood between me and the door.

"Good afternoon." He stood, hands in pockets, looking at me brazenly.

"Good afternoon," I replied with careful propriety. "I do not believe we have been introduced?" There was still an anxious thrill in using the careful manners I had practiced in my room, the sense of slipping into deep water where my toes could only graze the bottom.

"Oh, let's not pretend." He smiled, a dimple appearing in one cheek. "You know exactly who I am."

Over his shoulder, I could see the bazaar still in full swing: no one had noticed us.

"Yes, I do."

"And I know who you are." He looked me up and down, the pale-lilac dress and expensive shoes bought on credit, my hair done simply by my own hand, paste jewels at my ears and throat that had fooled most of society. "Lady Lenore Hansford, daughter of the Earl of Dorset, though you grew up in London. Your parents died in an unfortunate accident seven years ago. And then you become a mystery." He circled me as he spoke, brushing close enough that I felt the heat of his body.

"I was brought up by an elderly relative, sir. No mystery."

"Mmm, so I have heard. Then here you are, the beauty of the season, and yet no one has made a bid for you yet. What do they sense, I asked myself."

Leaning against a stone railing, he took a cigarette from his case and lit it with a match.

"If you know who I am, then you know I am a man of business, and business runs off information. The business of my future has its needs. In a marriage, I am looking to fulfill those needs. There are many pretty girls here but fewer who are capable of being wives. The information I needed was whether you were just a pretty girl— or a wife."

The riot of the bazaar felt so close, the tables of women hawking pen wipers and antimacassars, a penny for a lady of fashion to lick a stamp, the actresses serving at the bar, and the card and canvas painted to resemble a Venetian palace. The lights and perfume, the chink of coins.

I made a decision. "You need rank and status."

Henry's control was excellent; the only tell was a tightening around his lips that flattened his dimple. "Yes. And you need money."

Though I knew it was coming, the words still sent some unthinking, animal bolt of fear through me. I felt unreal, my solid body dissolved and gone.

"Yes." Threat and survival. That was all life was. "If you take a wife who needs nothing from you, then you will live forever in her debt." I did not know where the words came from, the false confidence that I wore like a mask. "You cannot marry one of those pretty girls. You need someone who understands that the world is not a neat, simple thing. It is harsh and unkind. I know that truth."

Henry smiled, a bright, handsome expression that spoke of calm, of security, of assurance, then held out his hand to shake on a business deal.

"I can work with that."

I left the bazaar engaged and trembling with relief and euphoria. I had done it. Henry had secured himself status and an aristocratic wife. I had secured myself a future.

I think of Cora now, happy to trade on her confidence in her own desirability, and refrain from taking the first proposal made to her—her assuredness that whatever she wants will be easily granted. If she wants to dally now, there will be no price to pay.

I consider her like a specimen in a display case, a strange creature of which I have no native understanding. I have never known what it is she wants from our connection, but nor have I been able to refuse it.

If Cora is an English rose, I am milk thistle: a weed, persistent and desperate.

This is the bargain I have struck: to lose my softness in exchange for survival.

*

Pain takes me into its arms and makes a home in my body.

At breakfast, I insist on eating downstairs, but I only make it as far as the sideboard before I collapse. The world spins around me unkindly, and I can grasp at no solid thing; even my body betrays me, twisting into knots and ripples as spasms pass through.

Molly and the housekeeper carry me to my room and lay me among the green vines of the wallpaper as though I am Titania in her faerie bower. I do not understand what is happening to me. The pain comes like it is retribution for the transgression of my existence, and my body is the rack upon which I will be punished.

Aunt Daphne used to pinch the fat of my arm and tell me I was too skinny, though my dresses had been let out that month, or when they were taken in, she would look sadly at me and talk of the soft figure of her youth that had looked so well in the fashions of her day. There was no state I could exist in that was not a burden in some manner.

I am a burden now as Molly holds me over the chamber pot for my guts to empty themselves, or when I double over to retch into a pretty dish painted with foxgloves.

When she brings a clean pot, she speaks softly. "Do you think you could be . . . *enceinte*," she says in the delicate French that is the fashion in town.

I am sour with shame, but I must not let her harbour false ideas. "No."

"I've heard it can come on very quickly for some women."

"It is not possible."

I let my meaning lie in the silence between us, and she is the one who colors. I have not been a wife to Henry in that way for so very long.

"Something you ate, my lady," says Molly, and I am grateful for a place to direct my humiliation, though I am too tired to do more than send a scathing note to the kitchens, suggesting that they do not deliver such a meal to the guests of the shooting party.

Molly asks if she should summon the doctor, but it feels excessive to bother him again so soon. I am sure I will recover in time, and I would rather rest in private than have some stranger trespassing on my body.

Carmilla does not suffer as I do, though she is wan again in the day, still weak as Dr. Bartolomé said, drifting to my bedside in the cloud of gauze and silk that my night things become on her. She lifts my hand to her mouth, whereupon she lays many kisses.

"It is too awful, my darling, what they do to you."

I think she means the cook, and I nod in agreement, pleased to be vindicated.

Despite her own listless movements, Carmilla seems delighted to take her turn to minister to me. It brings a pang of guilt: Yesterday, I was entirely set on removing her from Nethershaw. Now, she is the only one who can tolerate my distress.

Henry and Cora meet my sickness with irritation and horror. Henry takes no interest in my state, while Cora presents herself at my door only briefly, a cloth held over her nose and mouth as she offers great gouts of sympathy, while explaining she cannot possibly attend my bedside for risk that it may be catching; her delicate constitution would not withstand it.

Only Carmilla stays, strangely kind and patient.

As the pain recedes, I come back to myself enough that I do not quite know what I think of her solicitousness; one childish half of me longs to be tended to, but it is at war with the half that is tense with suspicion. What does this care mean? What sort of bargain do I enter into if I accept it?

I still do not understand my guest, and I do not know what it is she wants of me. I am gray and vague with fever, slipping between life and the underworld of sleep.

Carmilla curls at my side. "Lenore, there is something I must say: I am sorry for how I have behaved with you."

The words shock me. I did not think her a creature capable of contrition. "There is nothing to apologize for."

She tugs my hair painfully. "Stop that. Listen to me properly. I pushed you too quickly—I see that now. You need a persistent hand to come to heel."

I blink up at her in confusion. "What are you talking about? I don't understand."

She strokes the hair back from my face. "You will. There is so much for you to discover."

It is all I can do not to nuzzle into her hand like the touch-starved creature I am. "Please. I am unwell. Leave me out of your games."

"I am not here to hurt you, Lenore. I heard you calling me for so long."

My brow furrows in pain and confusion. "I do not recall . . ."

She fades in a haze of sweet night jasmine scent and soft laughter, and I sleep or wake—I do not know which—and find myself alone again.

*

When Carmilla returns, she locks the door behind her and throws open my windows to the lowering moor. It is bruise-dark under another veil of low cloud. In the distance, a shaft of sunlight pierces the earth like a finger of God, tracing over fell and tor to pick out the stunted canopy of a tree or the glittering line of a stream. Henry has bought all this land, and what is there to show for it?

A crumbling house fit for ghosts, and peatland too waterlogged and exposed for anything to take root. At night, the wind rattles the windows and sends gusts rushing down the chimney breasts to burst forth in clouds of ancient soot. In my sickbed, I can feel only bleak about it. There is no amount of effort I can spend that will change the bricks of this place.

Carmilla stands to one side of the shutters so that the light does not strike her.

"Do you know the moors?" I ask, thinking of her solitary carriage on the hill road.

She shrugs, then climbs onto the bed to stretch herself out alongside me. "Your English countryside is all much the same to me. So little grandeur. You are a small country and a small people."

She gives such insults generously, as though her opinion is a gift.

I can hear the workmen's carts rattling over the cobbles and their coarse voices from all directions. They need steering, monitoring. Henry has still not given me a list of names for the shooting party, and I do not know how many more rooms I must ready. Perhaps I can turn mine over to someone, but the thought of losing the one place I can close myself into safely makes the panic return. I can only stand the demand of everything beyond these walls if I have a door I can shut and lock. I will know peace no other way.

But that peace has been breached now by Carmilla, who has taken up a lock of my hair and is twisting it around her fingers. I was too ill last night to have my hair put in rags, and all its curl has dropped.

"Will you bring me my writing slope? There is work I must attend to."

"I will not. You must work at recovering your health."

"I am quite well enough to write. Henry has said—"

"Whatever it is, he can do it himself."

"He is my husband," I say, unsure what to do about her open dislike. "I must do as he asks."

She makes another noise I cannot interpret.

"My husband rescued you and brought you into his house as a guest. I would rather you not speak ill of him before me."

Carmilla laughs, and it is infuriating.

"What amuses you?"

She sits up cross-legged in her nightdress like a child, and I wonder how I have let this stranger become so intimate so quickly.

"You berate me for speaking ill of your husband, but you speak ill of him in every look and gesture. I only give voice to what it is you feel."

I blink in surprise. "I do not think ill of Henry."

She laughs again.

"I do not." I am indignant. "Do not laugh at me."

Though the cramping in my stomach has retreated, I feel as weak as a fledgling and entirely at her mercy.

Aunt Daphne did not like it when I was unwell. She would tolerate a day or two of my needing to be nursed; then her temper would change, and she would shift the attention to her own put-upon position, the burden she was under caring for this child she had not birthed. I knew by that point I would be alone with my weakness, and there was no point expecting different. It has been easy, then, to expect nothing of Henry.

Against this backdrop, Carmilla is too much. I do not know what she wants of me.

She studies me for a moment. "What else do you want?" she asks.

"In what sense?"

She makes an expansive gesture. "In all senses." When I cannot find a reply, she relents. "Very well. What shall we occupy ourselves with in this moment?"

I look at my hands on the counterpane. They are pale and narrow-fingered; the veins stand out as they did not when I was young. Aunt Daphne's hands were blotched with liver spots, the skin drawn tight and fragile like crêpe paper.

"I have already told you. I must make arrangements for the shooting party. Henry will be angry if I let him down."

Carmilla sighs. "Henry, Henry, Henry. You are not listening to me."

"I am. Tell me what it is you mean, because evidently you tax my intellectual capacities."

She regards me, mouth in a delicate moue. "Only if you no longer say such pathetic things about yourself."

I nod my assent. My guest is quite unpredictable.

"So what if Henry is angry?" she continues. "What is wrong with that?"

I do not know at first how to answer. I think through my words. "What is right about it? I should do my best not to anger anyone."

"Why?"

I am flummoxed. My face grows hot, and for some reason I cannot comprehend, I think I may cry. "Because it is bad. Are we not all taught that as children? If I have made someone angry, then I have done something wrong. We should endeavor to bring happiness into the lives of those around us."

Carmilla yawns. "That is quite boring. What of bringing happiness to yourself?"

"I . . . That is not—that is a selfish way of thinking, to only concern oneself with one's own happiness."

"The people you endeavor to make happy—they are selfish then, to care that you do not anger them but only please them?"

"No. That is not—you are twisting my words."

"My darling, your words *are* twisted. I am but smoothing them out."

I am not her darling. I want her off my bed and out of my room.

"I feel ill," I say, rolling away from her. "I will sleep now."

I close my eyes, willing her to go, but I do not hear the door close. When I look again, I find Carmilla at my dressing table, holding a tin of my pastilles, about to empty them out of the open window beside her.

Anger snaps through me like wind on a flag. "What are you doing? Those are mine."

Carmilla sniffs the powdered sugar on her fingers. "I do not understand it. Why do you eat these?"

I am hot with shame and struggle from the sheets, taking the tin from her hand to push it into a drawer, locking it. "Because I like them. Why else?"

She watches me with something like sadness, and it makes the shame burn hotter.

"Why does it matter to you what I do?"

"What are you doing to yourself?" she says, and I do not understand. She says too many things I cannot understand; I surprise myself with how much I hate it. Talking with Carmilla is like walking through sand dunes.

"Leave me in peace."

I return to bed and bury myself under the sheets.

I think she will refuse again, but instead I feel the brush of her skirts as she passes, and hear the soft hiss of fabric dragging on the floor as she leaves the room.

I am disappointed.

*

It is three of the clock when I rise, restless in the night with pain. The grandfather clock in the corridor beyond chimes its simple notes, and somewhere distant is the slow toll of church bells. The room is sultry and close; sweat slicks the backs of my knees, and my hair is lank.

The window does not open easily. I work at the catch that is stiff with age, until it gives all at once and the fresh, heather-scented air washes in. I hang my head outside for a moment or two like a swimmer breeching the surface. There is a coin-bright moon hung low over the hilltops and a thick belt of stars around it. By day, I am stranded in this remote place, but by night it feels like a freedom; the world recedes, and the darkness welcomes me just as I am.

On the moorland that spreads out from the borders of Nethershaw, there is a white speck, moving slowly towards Hungerstone Edge in the distance. I frown. It is a long, slim figure in a white nightgown, chestnut hair like a cape around her shoulders.

Carmilla.

Impossible. No one can be abroad at this hour. I am seeing things.

A cloud crosses the moon, and in shadow, the figure vanishes.

9

CARMILLA LEAVES ME ALONE the next morning, and I remain curled in my sweat-soaked sheets feeling deeply sorry for myself. I slept fitfully, but the shadow did not visit, and I see no figures in the grounds, so when I wake, I feel a little more distant from the strange mood that had struck me. I take a little bread soaked in warm milk, and when it stays down, I rise and dress. I cannot let myself sink. These waters are too deep, and I do not know if there is a bottom to them.

In truth, I do not know what it is I am so upset by, so the best thing I can think to do is to ignore it. I put on a sensible twill traveling suit that will be hard-wearing in these primitive conditions. Carmilla claimed my more delicate gowns days ago, exclaiming over the fine silks and velvets. I have not considered it before in my busyness, but it is strange that we found no trunk or personal effects in the wreck of the carriage. It suggests she was not intending to travel far, in which case, are her people nearby? Or perhaps it is a sign of how urgently she fled. I cannot glean an indication in either direction. She is resolute in her refusal to divulge her origin, and yet at times she carries herself so lightly I cannot imagine any trouble weighing her down.

Molly brings my letters to me at my desk, and among them is a short response from Debrett's, begging my pardon but explaining that they can find no record of the Kernstein family, nor could their continental counterparts. The trail has gone cold.

Carmilla rises indulgently late, and now that she sees me well again, my hours are again occupied by her entertainment and care. Her sheets are too coarse, her posset too sweet. There are not enough books to interest her; then her head aches too greatly to read. Henry is much occupied with his own business, and Cora has taken her writing slope to the conservatory to work through her own correspondence. Carmilla is mine alone.

Once she has dressed herself in one of my loaned tea gowns, she takes the largest chair closest to the fire in the drawing room, then pulls me to sit beside her as though it is a love seat, our bodies flush. She clasps my hand and lays upon me so many pretty compliments, I cannot but be moved to think well of her. The soft heat of her skin, the wave of her bronzed hair that tickles my throat, and the languorous way she reclines against the arm of the chair, twining our fingers together to keep me pinned, like a cat with one paw on the tail of a mouse. It is intoxicating, a flame I cannot but reach out to touch.

We play cards, hidden in a dark corner of the drawing room, heads close together as if in conspiracy.

"What would you have done, if you had not married Henry?" asks Carmilla.

"Please, let us not speak of Henry again."

Carmilla flicks my arm playfully, causing a flash of pain she then soothes with a stroke of her hand. "I do not speak of him, but you. Did you dream, as a girl?"

"What girl doesn't?"

"But did *you*?"

I take a card and add it to my hand, then discard one. "No," I say softly. "It did not seem possible."

Carmilla takes her turn, leaving the silence to expand. "Who taught you not to dream?"

I rest my head on my hand, suddenly too tired to hold myself up. I do not want to resurrect the past. Already, I feel the tightness in my chest, the low, heavy sense of doom in my heart.

"Everyone. No one. Life itself, I suppose. A dream is a dangerous thing." I throw down a card, unthinking.

Carmilla deliberates over her next move, finger pressing against her lip. "Disappointment can be too much to bear, yes."

"Better not to invite it in."

"I do not agree." She discards, then lays down her hand, cards neatly aligned in victory. "Disappointment tells us what we truly wanted. And to want is to be alive."

I've lost.

I sweep the cards back together, neatening them and returning them to their case.

"Will you eat those pastilles again today?" she asks, and it shocks me out of my trance.

I disentangle myself from her and clear my throat, pretending I did not hear her. "I must return to my duties. If you need anything else, ask Molly. I am occupied."

It is better to be too busy to know my own thoughts.

I assess the progress of the house: two more bedrooms have been cleaned and hung with fresh paper, but already it curls at the corner, peeling away like dead skin. The window frame in another room has come apart from the wall, letting in rain over an unknown stretch of time. The wood is so soft I can scoop it out with my fingers. Many of the outbuildings are beyond repair, although the stables and the icehouse are functional enough.

In the dining hall, I listen to a workman explain what is wrong with the ceiling as though I understand the technical terms he rattles off; there is a mass of scaffolding under the sagging plaster. It cannot be fixed. It is as though the house resists my work to tame it, as though it wants me out.

In my weaker moments, I think it was a mistake to come here.

All the while, Carmilla watches me from dark corners, idly turning the pages of the penny dreadfuls I assume she must have obtained from the servants, or else reclining with hooded eyes, watching the world move around her. Each time I catch her gaze, I feel tipped off-balance, like missing a step on a staircase and feeling the world tilt between safety and doom.

To escape, I walk the grounds of Nethershaw in stout shoes to clamber over stone and stile, noting the farm in the lee of the valley and the girl throwing grain to the hens, and in the distance, a speck of a village, little more than a church spire, a meager huddle of slate roofs around it like ivy wrapping an oak.

I have survived everything that has befallen me before now. I will survive this. By skill or force of will, I must endure.

I come back to the house, numb and exhausted. Cora is slipping out of Henry's study, glancing around cautiously. I pause, motion-less on the threshold.

Do you think they're fucking?

Carmilla's words appear bright and sharp in my mind.

I feel sick.

First, they are together at the Victoria Hotel—now this.

Cora sees me. "Lenore! There you are." She descends on me rap-idly and presses kisses to each cheek as if to smother my thoughts. "You seem so much improved today."

"What were you doing in Henry's study?" I ask, stiff within her embrace.

"Hmm? Oh, I saw Lady Bambury, and she's insisted we must join her for a picnic on Tuesday—I'm not sure what you'll think of her crowd, but it should be a pleasant afternoon. Bambury House has the most wonderful collection of Dutch landscapes."

"Of course we must go," I say automatically.

Henry comes out of his study and, seeing Cora and me, freezes.

I wonder how he will dissemble with me. Oh, I hate this, I hate this. I want to know what is between them, and at the same time I do not want to see it.

"You're well?" he says, choosing to join us.

Do I imagine that his mouth seems red? Do their eyes flicker towards one another? Does he think of her naked body when he sees her standing here?

I swallow back the bile. "I am well."

He steps closer and takes my hand, a look of concern on his face. "Perhaps you should rest a little longer. I am worried that you are pushing yourself too much." He strokes his thumb over the back of my hand. "I need you to take care of yourself," he says, so softly I half believe him.

Am I mad? These thoughts that plague me—I do not understand them.

Carmilla has joined us, draping herself across the newel post of the staircase as though standing for even a few minutes without aid is beyond her.

She has done this to me. She has sewn this poison in my mind.

I squeeze Henry's hand. "Thank you. You don't have to worry about me."

He grins, his dimple lighting his face. "I know."

Henry drops my hands and turns to make a bow to the three of us.

"I am overrun by women. What a pleasure. I will leave you to your entertainment."

Without any further comment, he takes the stairs two at a time and is gone.

111

I am left with Carmilla and Cora, nightshade and roses, two unexpected blooms that have taken seed in my expanse of moorland and are now mine to tend.

The workmen have begun an insistent hammering, the sound loud enough no quarter is unaffected. Already my head throbs, and I want to shut myself into my room and lock out the world.

"Let us walk," declares Cora. "I cannot bear this racket, and it was quite unkind of you to go without me earlier."

It was not for pleasure, I want to tell her—this wild land is my responsibility to tame. But I do not think she could conceive of such a struggle. "I apologize."

Cora laughs. "Don't be silly, I was only teasing."

I think, briefly, about slapping her across the face, and shock myself into silence.

Carmilla drifts forward. "Yes. Let us go outside. There is something I would see."

"A little air would be very beneficial for your health," says Cora generously, as though she is the one who has been tending to Carmilla.

"There is much left for me to do here—" I begin, but Cora cuts me off.

"Don't be silly. Henry is right—you work too hard."

I do not know how to begin to explain to her how risible it is for Henry to accuse me of working too hard when he is the one who has set my tasks, and instead I find myself turned around and directed back out of the house and into the blustery, wild day on the moors.

We set out with our hats pinned firmly against the wind and a cool breeze on the air. Carmilla seems more fragile in the daylight, and I realize I have not been outside the house with her before. It is as though she is a pencil drawing, so faint that the bright light all but washes her away.

Cora chatters as we go, swinging a little bag containing water and something Molly says is called parkin. "A walk can be most charming—I do love to walk. I would walk for whole days when I was a little girl, and I never once caught the sun. Isn't that something? I suppose I am naturally predisposed to a fine complexion."

As we pass the laundry, one of the maids is singing as she stirs the great vats of boiling cloth and water. A hymn, I think, but not one I know well.

Carmilla's face twists up in a snarl, her features suddenly coming into sharp definition. "What discordant noise. Make them stop it."

"I think she sings quite prettily," I say, taking Carmilla's arm to steer her away.

"It is foul. Sew her lips up."

I am so taken aback that I say nothing, and by the time her words have sunk in, we have moved far enough from the laundry that the noise has faded and Carmilla has returned to her wan, ephemeral state. Cora is far enough ahead, stooping to pluck flowers from the beds, that she did not hear us. Did I dream it?

We remain in silence as we follow a packhorse trail across the moorland towards Stanage Edge, Cora forging ahead, Carmilla lingering behind, and me in the middle, pulled between the two. In the distance, the thin pencil of Stanage Pole marks the parish boundary, the sole feature in this featureless landscape. No, perhaps there is some beauty to be found. When I look a little closer, I can see the grasses in the hollows are a patchwork of green and flax, blurring into the bristling buds of the heather; in the valleys between the peaks, forest pools like moss on stone, an uneven blanket of foliage that by some trick of perspective looks almost close enough to reach out and touch.

The track takes us along a limestone cliff I do not know the name of, then down through a gap between the rocks into the valley below. Carmilla carries a parasol of white linen with tassels that shiver with each step. I have only a straw sun hat that grows itchy where it grazes my forehead. The heat has begun to build, and steady movement under the sun works sweat into the backs of my knees and under my breasts.

I walk on, letting my mind imagine cool water glittering in the sunlight. I have read that Padley Gorge, which lies to the north of here, draws people from the steelworks and factories to paddle in the shallow river water. It is not something I could do as mistress of Nethershaw.

Beside me, Carmilla drifts off the path and darts down into a bush, her hand snatching something up. She turns to me, face shadowed by the parasol, and holds out what I think is the stem of a plant—but then it coils and flicks, and I understand what she has done.

"Isn't she beautiful?"

Carmilla brings the snake closer so that I can see the diamond cross-hatch of its pale belly and the black specks of its eyes. I expect to feel disgust, but I do not. Its tongue flickers, startlingly red against the white of Carmilla's sleeve. I am not sure I have seen a snake this close before—perhaps once in a glass case in London Zoo—and I lift my hand to graze my fingertips along its scales. It is cool and dry like leather, like stone. For a moment, I wish to be as cold and unmovable. I am too soft and vulnerable, as the past few days have shown, and it feels as though my life is slipping through my grip like sand: the harder I grasp it, the more my control slips.

I draw back. "No. It is not beautiful. Put it back before it bites you." Before Cora sees.

I walk past Carmilla swiftly enough that I do not have to see what she does, but when she appears again by my elbow, the snake is gone. She gives a small sigh.

"Do you like anything here?" she asks.

"What do you mean? Of course I do."

"It seems like it is all sour to you."

"If I am distracted by my responsibilities, it is only that they are so numerous."

"Oh yes, your responsibilities."

I let silence fall as we walk a little farther. Cora has stopped to gather a posy of purple bell heather, pink bilberry flowers, and yellow bog asphodel, and we overtake her, picking our way across rocky ground.

When we come to a fork in the path, Carmilla asks me which direction we will take.

"Whichever you like," I say. I have not ventured this far before, and I do not know where either road leads, but I can still see the cliff above us, and as long as we find another path back up, Nethershaw will stand out like a solitary gravestone against the moorland.

She leans against a boulder. "I have no preference. You choose."

My heart rate begins to pick up, and I do not understand why. "No, you are my guest."

Carmilla twirls the parasol where it rests on her shoulder, and the tassels dance around her head. "No. We will do what you want."

This again. I open my mouth to speak, but I cannot find the words. My tongue feels too thick, and there is something lodged in my throat, and I do not know if I will cry or shout.

"You must have a preference," says Carmilla, watching me so intently I cannot escape. "Why will you not tell me?"

It is a scouring gaze that fixes me in place and flays the skin and muscle from my bones until it is as though all the soft, intimate, raw parts of me are exposed for the world to peck out with its teeth and talons. I have kept myself so perfectly guarded for so long, learning

115

to strengthen my carapace against Aunt Daphne. I have had no home to be soft in, to want and need and to have those wants met. So what is the point in wanting?

"I do not. Why must I have a preference?" My chest is tight; I cannot breathe properly. What is happening to me?

"It is not so difficult to say what you want."

"I don't know what I want! I don't know."

I turn away from her, caught somewhere between tears and panic. Why does this affect me so?

"It doesn't matter," I say again, a talisman to hold. "It doesn't matter. You choose. Please choose."

Carmilla is unmoved. She does not come to my side to comfort me. She does not apologize for causing me distress. I can see her from the corner of my eye, lazing against the rock, drinking me in.

"No. You must choose. For once, choose what it is you want, and I will grant it."

There—that does it. The band of tension drawn tight around my heart snaps, and I cry into my handkerchief. It is stupid, and I am ashamed of myself.

"I want to go home." My voice is so soft I do not think she can hear me, but then breath tickles my throat.

"Soon, soon," Carmilla whispers, "I will bring you home. But we're not done quite yet."

When I uncover my eyes, Carmilla has drifted away, tearing fronds from the ferns as she passes.

I do not know what is wrong with me. She plants so many impossible, maddening thoughts in my mind. Cora and Henry, my passivity. These thoughts are hers; they are not mine. They cannot be mine.

Cora catches up with me and takes my arm, brows pinched in concern.

"Have you been crying?" she asks.

"No—no. I think I am a little sensitive to the plants."

With no thought at all, Cora chooses a path, and we wind down into the valley, where the sun pools rank and thick. In the distance, smoke rises from a stretch of moorland being burned by gamekeepers.

She pats my hand. "You poor thing, you're under so much strain. But you must think of how many people would give everything to have what you have. Even I envy you, Lenore—this is such a romantic setting. I wish I was the mistress of such a place."

I think about the bills piled on my desk for replacing rotting floors and replastering mold-thick walls. "It is an honor."

"So much history," she continues. "It is like something out of a novel—Walter Scott or a Brontë. Tell me, do you keep a madwoman locked in the attic?"

She laughs at her joke, and I force a smile, the memory of my strange dreams rising unwelcome in daylight. They seem so fanciful—the fears of a child or some disturbed individual. There is nothing wrong at Nethershaw.

"All we have in the attic is a leaking roof. It is all perfectly mundane and regular here. I am sorry to disappoint."

Cora isn't listening; instead, she is examining the set of her hat, though there is no one here to see her in it. We are quite alone.

I stop and turn, searching for a figure in a white cotton day dress, but I can no longer see Carmilla anywhere. Ahead and behind are only unbroken stretches of fern rolling towards pastureland; to our left is a drystone wall that I thought enclosed a conifer plantation, but I see now that it is in fact the land we stand on that is boundaried. Between the regimented trunks, there is a low stone building with smoke rising from the chimney.

A flash of white moving around one corner.

"This way." I draw Cora towards a stile over the wall.

"You think her lost?"

"I don't know."

"She can catch us up." Cora says. "I'd rather continue."

She does not like Carmilla; I can see it in the narrowing of her mouth. I find myself strangely pleased.

"I am not leaving anyone behind," I say firmly. "Perhaps there is something wrong."

Cora follows me through the woods to the cottage. It is plain, the same mossy gray stone as the drystone walls, with two mean windows set on either side of a door that is firmly shut. I follow around the corner where I saw the flash of Carmilla's dress.

There is a yard on this side, where the grass is trampled into submission, and a small cluster of outbuildings house pieces of farm equipment. This must be the farmhouse I can see from Nethershaw. Plantation pines separate it from the open moor where sheep graze. It seems so exposed from our vantage, but now that I am here, I can see how the trees rise high above the roof, making an enclosed world in the midst of wilderness.

There is a pigsty attached to one end of the building, from which grunting sounds emerge; a goat is tied to a post beside an unattended milking chair. Farther on is a chicken run, bounded with wire mesh. A henhouse sits to one end, and the dirt is scattered with feathers and droppings.

Carmilla stands before it. Her hair has come loose from its pins so that glossy chestnut locks hang around her shoulders like a cloak of bronze.

I stop.

There is someone else.

A girl crouches in the coop, hunched over so that her mousy hair covers her face. She has something in her hands.

118

There is a terrible sound, like flesh rending. A bone cracks.

"Hello?" I say to the girl's back, and it is a useless word, so small it is pulled away on the wind at once.

A hen lies dead in the dirt beside her, a tangle of wing and curled feet and glassy black eyes. A fox has been, I think, an intruder.

The girl shudders, head working at something I cannot see.

Feathers drift from her hands.

Cora shrieks, and finally the girl turns to us.

I cover my mouth with my hands in horror.

There is a dark light in her eyes when she locks onto me, as though I am the priest who can grant her absolution.

"I'm sorry," she says, mouth smeared cherry-red with blood. "I'm sorry."

The bird lies limp, chest cavity cracked open, and the pulsing slick mess of organs and muscle spread before her like a meal.

The girl looks at me, and it is as though I am broken open like the carcass in her hands, and every small, unspeakable thought is known.

All she says is:

"I was so terribly hungry."

10

I REMEMBER SCREAMING.

That is the abiding image I take with me: the screaming, and the blood.

It is Cora screaming, not me, as shrill and long as an actress in a melodrama, pigs' blood doused around the stage, the audience recoiling in shock and delight.

Bird blood, I suppose, is much the same.

I walk several stiff paces to the edge of the yard and empty my stomach onto the dirt.

Only Carmilla remains. Not unmoved, no—there is a curious look on her face that I cannot at first place, for it is so unexpected: an expression of rapture twists her cherubic features, a flicker of red tongue across her lips. It is Carmilla who bends to the girl and lifts the body from her hands, brings her to standing and leads her to the door of the farmhouse.

Cora's cry has brought a man from the house, older than any of us, and wiry from a life of work. He sees the girl—his daughter, I can only assume—and the mess of blood behind him.

"What is this?" He is frozen at the threshold, rough hands gripping the stone wall.

The girl cannot look at him, trembling at the horror of her own actions.

I think suddenly of Molly, knelt with Carmilla's hairbrush in her hands, sick with shock and shame.

I cannot bear to face it. Again, I am a coward.

"A fox," I lie without knowing I am going to say as much. It is too much to have the truth spoke and made real.

I am so good at dismantling the truth.

He looks at the blood around the girl's mouth and the feathers on her hands.

"A fox," he repeats, and looks over his daughter's shoulder to me pleadingly, as though I can undo what has been done.

I cannot give him what he wants. All I can offer him is this fiction, a place to hide.

Carmilla smiles at him, her mouth stretching wide. She pushes the girl into his arms, a fox to take into his home.

*

We have returned to Nethershaw, and Cora has taken to her bed. Henry, Carmilla, and I eat a stilted dinner together. My patience is worn to shreds, and Carmilla seems to know it, sitting peacefully, delicately taking small bites of the individual quail on each of our plates. Perversely, I am famished, and I eat everything placed before me.

It seems impossible, what we saw. The further I am from it, the more unreal it becomes. It is better to let it fade, to turn my mind away and close myself off to any pain, any horror. I know that too well, from washing my mother's blood from my hair, to hardening myself against Aunt Daphne's poisoned affection. No good will come from pulling at this thread: it is too easy for it to all unravel, and already I feel myself losing ground, the edges of me weakening and breaking open.

When we retire, Carmilla lingers at the entrance to her room. Cora's room is at the far end of the corridor. She has not emerged since we returned.

Carmilla turns to me. "I do not know how you can stand her."

I am tired. I cannot hold myself together every moment of the day. It is untenable. There are too many people here, worrying at the mortar of my boundaries, wearing me thin.

"I do not know what manners they teach where you are from, but it is not customary to insult your host's friends."

Carmilla lounges against the doorframe, something sultry in the way she looks at me from heavy-lidded eyes.

"You all lie to each other, then?"

"It is too easy to disguise cruelty as frankness."

Carmilla ignores me, studying me in that way that makes me feel as though I have never truly been observed before, and now someone has stopped to take in every guilty thought and fear that lies clear written on my skin.

"She is not your friend."

"You do not know of what you speak."

"Darling Lenore, you can be very boring at times."

I do not know why this wounds me so greatly, but it does.

Carmilla is wrong. I know the worst thing Henry has done, and it has only bound us together.

"Goodnight," I say crisply and go into my room, Carmilla's gaze lying hot across my back.

I think she might follow me.

What will I do if she follows me?

I shut myself in and am finally alone again.

But I do not lock the door.

*

Henry takes Cora and me into the city in his new gig, the roof folded away for the fine day that shines across the moors. I keep one hand on my hat as we rattle over the track leading through the wilderness. Far below, Sheffield is cupped in the twin valleys of the Don and the Sheaf, black smoke pooling across the rooftops like oil across water. The fires of the steelworks blaze among the pollution, sending great shivers of flame into the sky. The road works its way beneath the cloud of black, and we pass into the underworld.

Henry is at his best. He chatters cheerfully, talking of the investment he is courting for the works, the new hunting knives they intend to bring to market, and the successful opening of a new set of grinders' rooms. There is little need for me to speak; I relax in my seat, listening to the bright energy of his voice. Henry wants me with him today, and I fit myself to the shape he takes, his anticipation, his excitement. It is good to escape the damp and twisting corridors of Nethershaw and my two guests. I know who I am as Henry's wife. I am a master of this land.

Cora speaks little. She has said nothing of what we saw yesterday, for which I am grateful, but the shock has left her truly shaken, and she has concocted some visit she must pay to someone in town to avoid Nethershaw and Hungerstone Edge.

I find myself unshaken.

Perhaps my capacity for shock is diminished, having lived through the brutal death of my parents. There is only the problem and how to solve it. Aunt Daphne suffered no fools, and if I had taken to bed with my grief, I would have starved there. Weakness is for girls like Cora, who know they will be met with care.

Carmilla has been through much already in the short time I have known her, but she does not seem weak for it. She does not wait

123

for help to come: she *demands*. She has bent my household to her shape, and in some small way, I admire her for it.

Her need is not a weakness or a threat to her own survival. It gives her power.

We drop Cora near the town hall, before continuing past Kelham Island to the works.

The noise greets me first, an unbearable cacophony of metal striking metal. Then we turn, and the Ajax Works is a blot on the sky. The factories are all assembled along the canal, filthy water streaming past, but here is one vast building stretching unbroken as far along the street as I can see in the haze of smog. I think of the new prisons built on the outskirts of London that turn the land around inhospitable, a lifeless cavern to traverse. Coal smoke has blackened every wall, no tree surviving in the smog that rolls through the streets like the valley rivers. The gas lamps flicker, alight during the day against the dirty haze.

Henry drives the carriage through the arched entrance into the courtyard. The building engulfs us on all sides, a bristle of chimneys smoking across every roof.

Henry drops down from the driver's seat, casual in his familiarity with this place, then leaves the groom to find a suitable place to feed the horses. I take Henry's hand stiffly as I descend. His expression tightens as he notes the set of my shoulders.

"Is there something wrong?" But it is not a question.

"No."

"Good."

He drops my hand and sweeps towards the office entrance.

There is a neat lobby paneled in dark wood, where a man sits at a desk with a book to log visitors, an ornate clock hung on the wall behind him. I follow Henry up a sweeping flight of stairs to a narrow corridor of partitioned offices; there is more dark wood, with windows set high up to let through a weak light. At the end of the corridor is a grand door, with a brass name plaque.

Henry Crowther.

His position is not listed. Everyone here knows who my husband is.

As soon as we step inside, Henry's demeanor changes. He offers his arm, and I dutifully take it. Waiting for us are several men of varying ages, gathered around the leather armchairs and empty fireplace. They are well-dressed but a little rough, eyes lined, their facial hair coarse and full.

Behind Henry's desk is a window that gives a view across the works, smoking chimneys and sloped roofs, and at the center a great, monstrous thing that looks like a steel egg on legs. I cannot understand it; it is like something from a strange nightmare. Machinery cranks, and it tips over. I am frightened like a child, an unthinking, instinctual fear as the egg tips on an axis towards the scurrying men below. A red tide of molten metal slops out in a waiting ladle that is hurried to the next process.

The blur of red and orange is impressed upon my eyes even when I close them: a breaking down of order, steel, and strength made wanton chaos. It unsettles me in a way I do not understand, and I adjust the cuffs of my dress, smooth the buttoned front of my jacket.

"Gentlemen," Henry declares, commanding the space. "Welcome to the Ajax Works. What you see outside this window is the largest Bessemer converter in Sheffield. At work night and day, this plant produces enough steel to supply our manufacturers as well as three other cutlers around the city. This year alone, we have invested in new grinding rooms, diesinkers workshops, and filing rooms, and in each trade needed to control the whole manufacturing process from beginning to end. And all so safe I would bring my own wife along." Here is my cue to step forward, smile at Henry adoringly. "We are on the rise, gentlemen, and I invite you all to be part of history."

It is a pretty speech, and the men take it well. Henry moves me round the room, clapping hands on shoulders and making introductions. These are not the men who will attend the shooting party, but my purpose is the same: to reflect well on Henry to those whom he wishes to control. It is a collection of mill owners from the Lancashire valleys and minor railway owners planning lines between ports and factories. They are men with means, but Henry, with Nethershaw and a wife from the nobility, is something to aspire to.

Henry's charm is infectious. He calls me clever, tells them all how lucky he is to have a wife intelligent enough to understand his endeavors and to provide such gracious and insightful support. I understand what is truly important, he says. I am not like other women who demand flattery and coddling.

Essential, he calls me, and my heart rises.

We are to take a tour of the works, and as the men assemble into a party, Henry hangs back, his fingers tracing the nape of my neck.

"Did you ever think we'd end up here?" he asks.

He is so pleased I cannot help but match it. "Yes," I say. "I always knew you would do what you set out to. You were brilliant then, and you are brilliant now."

He swells under the praise, and I am satisfied to know I am the one to have made him feel that way. If he is changeable, it is because the pressures he faces are ever-changing. It is self-centered of me to assume that if he is short with me, it is because there is some matter wrong between us. Whatever foolish thought Carmilla has planted in my mind about him and Cora—it is all nonsense.

The tour takes us through a series of workrooms and factory floors.

There are grinding and polishing rooms, workbenches covered in molds for spoons and knives and files and every possible steel implement. There are vast warehouses hung with chains the size of my body, swaying walkways bisecting the inhuman space.

Henry moves between the men, speaking articulately about the process of gaining the purest steel, of the most modern techniques in grinding and file-cutting.

We come to a new room, with men bent over their machines, pushing blades against fast-moving grinding stones. Most wear handkerchiefs tied over the lower parts of their faces, and an extraction fan whirs in one corner, doing little to shift the haze of fine metal particles in the air. I can taste it in my mouth at once, like grit between my teeth, and I cover my nose and mouth with my own handkerchief. So many men are barely that: boys gangly and bent over by their trade.

I feel a strange guilt for being so ignorant of my husband's work. I have been happy to find security in his money, never thinking on whose backs such riches are made.

I turn away under the guise of fixing my hatpin.

An inhuman noise comes from behind me. A crack, then something wet. Glass shattering.

When I turn back, all is changed.

No one screams.

A man is flung back from his station as though shot, limbs splayed open and head tipped away. The grinders gather around and lift him upright.

Something has torn through his mouth like a hook through a fish, ripping open his cheek and jaw so that his skin and muscle hang in a loose flap over his ear, exposing the stumps of his teeth. The object is wedged under his cheekbone, and his tongue laps at the blood filling his throat. When they right him, blood pours from his mouth.

There is shouting, calls for a doctor. It is the grinding wheel that has broken and spun a shower of fragments across the workshop, smashing windows and lodging in walls. Henry is saying something, sending the gentlemen to another room on their tour.

I am frozen until his sharp fingers jab the soft underside of my arm; he guides me away, and I let myself be moved. There is something wet on my cheek. My fingertips come away red with blood.

I clean myself discreetly with a handkerchief as Henry takes us back to his office.

The men are unmoved by what they have seen, and I realize they are used to the cost of their industries. Henry is extolling the generosity of the compensation he is able to provide to injured workers because of the high profits his business generates.

All I can think of is blood. Fresh and red as it rose like a fountain in the man's mouth.

And yesterday, smeared around the lips of the girl we found with the chickens.

The crunch of bone and the tearing of flesh.

I think about Henry's wanton appetite, the works' great teeth tearing and rending flesh.

I am relieved I am not expected to speak to Henry's guests. I am here as a testimonial, an achievement displayed like the great Bessemer converter beyond his window.

"I end our tour today, gentlemen, with a great gift."

The word sparks something and the room comes into sharp focus.

The gift. That telephone call I overheard, the diamonds I found. My warmth towards Henry is fanned further. He has *not* forsaken me yet. I must only wait for his moment.

"There is something very special I would have you see."

Henry presses a button on his desk that rings a bell; the door opens, and two men wheel in something covered in a velvet cloth.

The cloth is removed. Beneath, on a circular wooden stand, is a cross, thick with blades. The upright and cross bar is made from an interlocking series of folding blades, showing files, corkscrews, paring knives, and any number of different blade types. The light glitters off the metal, moving from edge to edge as though something lives within.

It is an abomination. I look away quickly.

"One blade for every year of our beloved monarch's reign, each displaying a different technique from our master craftsmen. It is the apotheosis of the Ajax Works and our world-leading prowess. Gentlemen, this is the future. This is strength."

*

When the men have departed, Henry orders tea, and we drink it sitting on either side of the fireplace. He wishes to talk over the day, and I take it, echoing his words when he wants me to, confirming his opinions. I am a mirror for him, and I have learned how to show the desired reflection.

I have learned I am no more than that.

In my mind's eye, the molten steel from the Bessemer converter pours into the torn open mouth of the grinder, blood and metal merging.

"What will happen to him?" I ask, and Henry stops mid-sentence.

"To whom?"

"The man who had the accident."

Henry is bemused. "Did you not hear me earlier? We give good compensation, and just last month we installed new fans in several grinding rooms."

"Will he die?"

Henry loses his patience. "Men die, Lenore. We'll pay his wife compensation. Don't look so shocked—there is no such thing as a life without risk." He leans forward and pulls back his sleeve so that I can see the twist of scar tissue that connects the base of his index finger to his thumb. "You know this story. When I was twelve and visiting the old works with my father, I got in the way in the die-casting workshop and got burned. I accept just as much risk here as any of the other men. More. I have all their livelihoods on my shoulders—thousands of workers rely on *me*."

He is as insistent and passionate as he was speaking to his investors earlier, but I cannot swallow his words so simply. My mind snags on the newspaper article I read at the Royal Victoria Hotel just before he and Cora found me.

"I know that. But what about the journalist in London? He said there were rumors that safety at Ajax has been in decline—"

Before I can finish my sentence, Henry is out of his chair and standing over me, body vibrating as he holds himself back from whatever it is his anger wants him to do to me.

"Do not speak another word. Do not even *think* on it. You are out of your depth, Lenore—do not go any further or you may drown."

It is like a wave rising up on the seashore, cold spray speckling my face, then a great body of water bursting against me, lifting me up, and turning me over and over.

I am frightened of my husband.

I lower my eyes. "Yes. Of course. Forgive me."

It is not the first time I have felt blood hot on my cheek and buried my horror for the sake of my marriage, my future.

I should be better practiced at this by now.

He springs up, demeanor changing. "There's nothing to forgive. Don't be so silly, Lenore." He goes to his desk and opens several drawers. "The tour was only partially why I wanted you here today."

He plucks a box from a drawer and straightens. It is a slim box from a jeweler's. I recognize it.

"You didn't think I'd forget, did you? Ten years today."

"It is next week," I correct, but he carries on as though he hasn't heard me.

"I had to get you something. Just a token."

I come to the desk and take the box from him, heart beating faster. It is the box from his room; despite myself, I smile at Henry. Some part of me still wants to lap up these scraps he grants me, throw myself into his arms if there were not a desk between us.

"You beast, you made me doubt you."

"Never."

I am giddy, fingers fumbling as I open the box. Let him still be good; let me still believe the lies he offers.

Inside is a string of jet.

"Isn't it fine?" says Henry, lifting the necklace from the silk. "Whitby jet set in Sheffield steel. A true piece of Yorkshire."

"It is beautiful," I say. I am numb. There is something there beneath my tongue, beneath my breastbone, but I cannot let it rise.

Oh. I have been so naive. Henry promises much to everyone, but for whom does he deliver? Only himself.

"Let me help you."

Henry stands behind me to drape the jet around my neck and fix the clasp so snug it is like a hand around my throat. He turns me to the mirror above the fireplace; the necklace lies like chains, Henry's head above mine, assessing.

"Don't worry that you didn't get me anything."

My stomach drops. "I didn't think—"

"There's nothing I want, only for the shooting party to go well. Lenore, I must address it. I don't understand why Miss Kernstein is still here."

"The doctor has said that Carmilla is not yet well enough to travel."

"Then find a different doctor. For the right fee, they'll say whatever you want them to."

It is strange; I have heard Henry say all manner of things many times before, and yet it is only now that it strikes me as not only callous but underhand. He does not see why he should be limited, why he should not simply get what he wants. It is a cynical, selfish comment that casts the whole world to be as cynical and selfish as he is.

I am quite shocked by how these thoughts now rush into my mind, as though I have been storing them up for too long, and it feels as if Henry will be able to read my betrayal plain on my face.

"She must stay a little longer," I say. "There is nothing to be done about it."

Henry's mouth twitches. "Then while she is under my roof, control her."

Carmilla, whose will I cannot control.

The rocks on the cliff below me start to crumble; I feel the lurching vertigo of the drop—a hopelessness so total it is like a weight pressing me into the earth. I am not in the position I thought I was, and there is a sense of panic to it. A sense of threat.

I think of Aunt Daphne and her sharp eye, infractions I did not know I committed until her precise, shimmering anger took me to pieces. No matter how vigilant I was, my clumsy tongue would say the wrong thing or I would give offense by the tilt of my head.

Henry returns to the desk drawer and takes out a tin of pastilles to press into my hands. "Here. I thought you might have run out."

I look at the gleaming metal and the lettering painted upon it.

I feel suddenly so hungry.

He leaves me to attend to his business, and I am at my leisure now until Henry, Cora, and I return home at some later hour. I have an errand or two I could run, but it has been long enough since I have had time of my own to spend as I please, and I am quite lost in thought on what to do.

It is as the carriage turns into the street, I see Cora walking along the other side. Strange. She came into town to a call on a friend, but here she is, passing through the Ajax gates.

To where my husband is.

11

CORA IS WITH MY HUSBAND.

I know it.

It is not a wild thought now, some suggestion of Carmilla's. It is a fact.

I order the carriage to draw into Lyons Street near the works' entrance so that I can watch for Cora's departure. It is a minute or an hour later—I cannot tell which—when she finally reappears, walking swiftly down Carlisle Street towards the Wicker.

What should I do?

I know how to manage any social function, how to plan a dinner for fifty guests, run a house, direct staff, throw a ball. I know how to manage Henry's moods, how to school my own weak mind into order.

But I do not know what to do about this.

I am such a fool. Carmilla saw it at once, and yet I covered my eyes.

Henry will have exactly as he wants.

Perhaps, if I were a different woman, one who had not lost her parents as I had, nor spent the tender years of her life with someone like Aunt Daphne, perhaps that woman would be able to confront Cora and Henry, demand with clarity and courage to know the truth.

But I am not her. I am soft and bruised where life has landed its blows upon me.

All that is left to me is petty spite. I will not wait for her and Henry as agreed; instead, I take the carriage back to Nethershaw alone and leave them to their own resources.

*

I defied Aunt Daphne, once.

It was not long at all since I had arrived, and I went to bed one night with the clear and heavy sense of a prison door closing behind me. My parents were never coming back. I had seen them lowered into the clay-cold earth of their grave, overheard conversations about wills and bankruptcy. A small trunk of my clothes had arrived and nothing else. It had all been sold, I later understood, to pay my father's debts. I would soon grow out of the clothes, and then it would be as though my memory was wiped clean, the past snipped off like hanging thread.

Each day I spent sat at Aunt Daphne's feet on a footstool upholstered in carpet fabric, reading to her from the newspaper or old books with badly cut pages, or else I would stand at the window to narrate what my younger eyes could discern that she could not. A baker's boy pushing a cart painted a garish yellow; the cat's meat man with narrow-set eyes; a woman stood at the post box, pretending she was not crying. Aunt Daphne suffered from a nervous condition and a stiffness in her hips that meant she rarely left her chair. I was a medium through which she could observe the world but not participate in it. She locked herself in the mausoleum of a house and meant to keep me prisoner with her, if only to have company.

On my first week, I complained that my feet had gone numb and that I wanted to go outside. Aunt Daphne pinched the bridge of her nose as though her head pained her, and a few moments later, without answering me, she took herself to rest. I was confused by this response but happy in the freedom it afforded me. I wanted to go out into the garden in the center of the square, so I went downstairs to the kitchen, where our single servant, who did for both maid and cook, was sat at the back steps smoking a pipe. I took the ring of keys from its nail to let myself out of the house and into the garden. It seemed so simple, and I was pleased with myself to have met my own needs.

The garden was a carefully cultivated area of grass lawns, wooden benches, laurel bushes precisely clipped, and a stone birdbath blotched with lichen, all enclosed by a wrought iron fence painted black. I unlocked the residents' gate and crept through the undergrowth. I did not know what to do with myself now I had achieved my goal, and I felt cold with disappointment. There was no one here; I was more alone in this garden than I had been with Aunt Daphne.

I sat on a bench and swung my feet, mired in indecision. I did not want to go back and admit defeat, but neither could I see any point in staying. I realized then that what I wanted was for the mother who lived now only in my memory to alight upon me in this unfamiliar place, pluck me up and cover me in kisses and tell me how much she missed me.

But she never would. There was no one coming to rescue me.

A man sat down beside me and offered me a handkerchief to mop my fat, messy tears. He had moved so quietly I had not noticed him approach—or I had been too caught up in my own sorrow.

I took the handkerchief, because he was being kind and I knew I should be polite.

"Whatever could a little bird like you be so sad about?" His voice was low and rich, and for a moment it brought back the memory of my father in a way that was quite shocking, and I sobbed harder.

"Oh dear, oh dear." His hand rested on my knee. "Let's get you home, then."

He lifted me by the arm and led me from the park, as pliant as a lamb.

"I have a coach just here," he said as we came to the gate, and it was true: there was a gig and horse waiting, with an inviting traveling rug across the seat. "In you get."

I looked at the step, at the wheels of the gig that came almost to my shoulder, then to the man's face, his eyes so intently fixed upon me I felt pierced through.

He licked his lips.

Something tightened in my stomach, the sense of standing on the edge of a great drop, as though I had been climbing a staircase and not noticed a missing tread until my foot hovered over the void.

He hadn't asked me where I lived.

I twisted out of his arm and dashed down the pavement to the row of front doors, which were all so similar that for a moment I could not place which one was meant to be my home. I did not look behind me. I had not seen the man's face, and I could not bear the thought of seeing it now. In the row of first-floor windows, I recognized the spray of dried pussywillow that I looked at each day as I sat by Aunt Daphne's chair. I threw myself at the door of the house, and it swung open—I had not locked it behind me when I left.

No one had noticed me gone. I locked and bolted the door and slunk into the kitchens to return the keys to their nail. The servant still sat on the back step, facing away from me. I looked through a window, but the man and the coach were gone.

The whole episode had taken little more than twenty minutes, and all was back as it had been before.

The memory took on a dreamlike quality, and later I wondered if perhaps I had invented it all.

I never told Aunt Daphne. I never told anyone.

There was nothing to tell, I thought.

But perhaps the truth was there had been no one to listen.

*

I am grateful to be back at Nethershaw.

I did not think I would ever come to feel this way, but its twisted walls are familiar, the smell of its rot a balm to my feverish mind. Beyond Cora, I am disturbed how easily Henry cast off what we witnessed at the works, and I begin to conjure other horrors that may have come to pass under his watch. I think of the journalist at St. Pancras station and his questions, how violently Henry reacted when I spoke of him.

It is all revelation to me, but perhaps it has been on show for the whole world all this time.

I look at him differently, this husband of mine.

Carmilla waits for me, stretched across a settee in the drawing room, licking honey from her fingers. There is an abandoned tray of tea things beside her: tea, cakes, and sandwiches disassembled into their constituent parts and unconsumed.

"Lenore." She seems to move from settee to directly before me without any intervening motion. "You must taste this. Isn't it delicious?"

She places a finger inside my mouth. The rich, round sweetness floods my tongue, against the cold, clean taste of her skin.

I am mute with shock. This is a transgression so extreme I cannot comprehend it.

As quickly as it began, she removes her finger, sucks the last of the honey off it, and then strolls towards the dining hall.

"Come on, then."

I follow her like a dog after its master and hate myself for it. Is Nethershaw not my domain? Am I not mistress here?

I am hot with anger at Carmilla for her very nature as we wait for the first course to be served. She is the reason everything has unraveled since I came to Nethershaw.

Today is another test meal, and Cook presents curried lobster and fillet of duck, removed by leveret pie and a garnished ham. I do not know how or when Henry and Cora will return, and I do not care, so Carmilla and I eat without them, sat at either end of the dining table. I have ordered candles to be rationed until the shooting party, for I cannot risk us running low, and so only a few flames light the vast space. Beyond their weak sphere is darkness. There is no moon tonight, and the shutters have been closed tight against the cold moor winds.

"Is your health improving?" I ask, mechanically cutting up financier potatoes and placing forkfuls into my mouth. I am uncomfortably full; Cook presents each course with the variety needed for eighteen as she must when the guests arrive in one week's time. I cannot stop thinking of the horror of the accident at the works, of the girl knelt among feathers, rending flesh with her fingers. And Henry and Cora, so brazen they barely hide their stolen time together. It is as though reality has been put together badly, and the rules by which I know the world to operate are losing their power. The only solid thing is my body and the sensation of fullness like ballast against a storm.

"Tolerably," replies Carmilla.

She does not eat. She never eats. Neither does Cora, but where Cora takes a little soup and makes sure all at the table know that her petite appetite could not tolerate any more, Carmilla ignores her food as though it is slop put before a queen, a meal that has no capacity to satisfy.

"Though it did not do me good to be left alone all day, Lenore. I am neglected." In the low candlelight, Carmilla is half cast in shadow; the curve of her eye socket and the full line of her cheekbone stand out like the skull beneath.

"Henry needed me at the works."

Carmilla sighs, elbow on the table, chin propped in her hand. I have bored her again.

I am such a disappointment to everyone.

"Don't let's talk about my health. I know you do not want me to leave. I will tell you what I think you want but will not say." She leans forward, and the tight bodice of her dress spills the milky tops of her breasts over the top. Why do I not look away? "I think you want to throw Cora out for good, and tell her she is a self-involved, smug little bitch."

I drop my fork in shock. "Excuse me?"

"I think you want to slap Henry for all the ways he has hurt you and made you say thank you for it."

"Stop it. This is too much."

She pays me no regard. "I think you'd like to set this house on fire and take Henry's money and never see him again. I think you are *hungry*."

"What is wrong with you? Stop this at once."

She sits back, head cocked. "No? My mistake."

I am breathing too fast, that sense of panic I felt when Carmilla demanded I choose our path on the moors is rising again, and I do not understand it.

No, that is a lie. I do understand it, but I am not willing to accept what it means.

I stand abruptly, dropping my napkin on the table.

"Please, Carmilla. Please leave me be for one night. I cannot take so much."

I flee, taking the stairs almost at a run. I am shaking too hard to catch my breath. I think I might cry. I hate this—what has she done to me?

She is wrong. She is completely wrong. I would never want such things. I do not get angry; I am not some hysterical, selfish child. I can cope with this. I can cope with all of it. Henry, Cora, every betrayal, every abandonment—I will swallow it down, all the pain and anger and grief, and I will survive a hollow, cold, hard creature, because what else is there?

In my bedroom, I hold the tin of pastilles in my lap, and one by one place them into my mouth, cracking them between my teeth to consume them faster. A flood of overpowering sweetness coats my tongue and teeth.

There is something empty in me. I can feed and feed and feed it, but somehow, I am never satiated.

There is one way in which Carmilla is right: I am *hungry*.

*

A weight depresses the bed on one side, and I wake with a lurch of fear. A hot hand presses my shoulder into the mattress before I can struggle up.

"Shh, shh."

"Henry?"

It is my husband, climbing into my bed in the darkest shadow of night, no candle to light the room or moon to look in upon us.

"What are you doing?"

He sinks down beside me, suddenly large and solid now that he is closer to me than he has been for a long time. His breath is hot on my cheek, the muscled bulk of him raising the covers. I feel the press of his thigh against mine, the firm angles of his chest and shoulders. I am unused to this physical intimacy, and I cannot shake the tension with which I woke.

"Did I wake you?"

I resist the compulsion to wriggle away and put a safe gap between us. This is my husband. A week ago, I would have thrilled at his touch.

"No," I lie.

"I had to come home in a hired gig. What happened? You left town without us."

His hand presses more firmly on my shoulder, his thumb digging into the flesh below my collarbone. I am on my back, my soft belly showing.

I swallow, deciding my story. "I am sorry. I felt so ill again I had no choice."

Henry lifts his other hand to my jaw to trace his fingertips along the line of bone, down the bared column of my throat.

"Poor Lenore. You have worked yourself half to death."

He rests his hand across my neck, which rises and falls with my hectic breath.

Then he leans in and places a gentle kiss at the corner of my mouth.

"What a wonder." His voice is a whisper against my lips.

He kisses me again, fully now, taking his hand from my shoulder to brace himself.

It is shock that holds me still, opens my mouth to his tongue, mirrors his movements. My yearning, hopeful heart wants this to be real, to be true.

When he pulls back, he says softly, "It has been a while."

"It has," I murmur.

"Cora stayed at the hotel in town. I think she was a little hurt."

He is reproachful, and again I am on the backfoot, unsure how to navigate this encounter. "Oh. I didn't think . . ."

"Look at it from her perspective—she must feel as though you have replaced her with Miss Kernstein."

I could laugh. It is not possible he has spoken these words to me. *Cora* feels replaced? Did she tell him of this hurt when she came to him at the works? At the Royal Victoria Hotel? In his study at Nethershaw? All these times they have found to be alone together, and *I* am at fault?

I have lost my words. What could I possibly say in response? I could fling at him everything I have seen, but I am too frightened that he will behave as he did at the factory, and I lie beneath him defenseless.

Or, worse, what if I screw up every ounce of courage left to me and speak truly, and he acts as though I have said nothing at all. Denies—no, ignores—my reality, and bends the world to fit his will. In that, I would disappear entirely.

So I say nothing.

As always, I am nothing.

"She said she will take the train to Hathersage tomorrow, if you care to meet her. I think it might do well for you to do so; it will go some distance to repair things between you two."

"I'll go."

"Good."

He strokes my hair from my face, and beyond the unshuttered window, the clouds have shifted to let a little starlight stream in, lining his face in silver at cheekbone and temple. A curl of blond hair falls across his brow, and his cupid's-bow mouth is slightly parted. This face that I have known for all my adult life. This face I loved once, love still, I think—as best I can love the place of my deepest disappointment.

"I think I scared you today," he says.

I nod.

"I am sorry, Lenore. There is so much demand upon me, and it has been affecting me more than I realized. I must apologize for all my behavior, really, since we arrived at Nethershaw. I cannot truly say I do not understand why you wish to keep Miss Kernstein, to have a little friend so much at your bidding."

At my bidding? He sees nothing, understands nothing.

"So there, you have them—all my apologies, for whatever little they are worth." His mouth widens in a rakish grin, dimples forming on either side, and still now after ten years, I am a little breathless at how handsome he is.

Before I can reply, he takes up my arm, presses an open-mouthed kiss to my palm, the inside of my wrist.

"You know I think very much of you." His tongue draws a line to the crook of my elbow, where he places another kiss. "Say you forgive me."

My heart is racing. What is he doing? Has some memory of our past passion awoken in him again?

"Say it." His voice is a low growl.

"I forgive you," I whisper, for what else can I do?

Henry wraps his arms around me and pulls me into a deep kiss, crushing me against him. I can feel that he has become excited, from the hectic pace of his breath and the way he moves against me, urgent and insisting.

"This will all be over soon," he mumbles into my mouth. "Let's go away after. The continent. Vienna, Paris, Prague—wherever you like. Only name it."

"Truly?"

"I promise."

I am so tired. I am so tired of struggling, of vigilance, of hopelessness. It would be so easy to believe him, to take the fantasy that he sells me and hide within its pretty walls. So easy. I miss when I thought it all possible. That I could master all my disappointment and vulnerability, and walk steel-plated and invincible through the world. I miss when I thought Henry was part of that mastery.

I kiss him in return, shifting to allow him to pull up my nightdress and put his hand between my legs.

"Do you like that?"

I nod, though his movements are too rough and firm and abrupt to spark anything within me. I have become used to my own ministrations, and Henry lacks that subtlety.

He stops too soon, nudges my legs apart and mounts me, taking up an impatient, urgent pace with his hips. Whatever heat had been building in my belly dies quickly, and I turn my head to one side to avoid his hot, panting breath.

Does he fuck Cora like this?

The thought arrives like the cut of a knife, and I come back to myself with a sickening feeling.

Maybe she likes it like this, and he has forgotten that I am a different woman.

Henry's pumping hips, the slap of skin and sheen of sweat all feels at once so sordid and degrading.

I am being bought off.

This is what Henry thinks I want. Jewelery. His attentions.

Today, I unsettled him, and he is here to pull the blindfold over my eyes once more.

He finishes with a grunt and rolls off, breathing hard. "You were wonderful."

It is all I can do not to snort with laughter. The voice in my mind is tinged with Carmilla's tones when I think, *wonderful? I simply lay there.*

After a moment, he rolls over, pulls me into his chest and pins me within the prison of his arms. It is stiflingly hot in the room already, and he is like a furnace against my back. I want to go and clean between my legs, change into a fresh nightdress and breathe the moorland air.

Henry stills behind me, body slackening as he falls asleep.

Oh, my husband. I am not buying what you are selling.

I have seen him be brilliant, charm everyone in a room; even today at Ajax, I witnessed him at work.

I am only another mark to him.

Though I hold such power over his life, he still thinks he can pull all the strings.

There is something deeper working inside me, some too-close pressure like the movement of rocks within the earth. I wonder when it was Henry's stoniness towards me first set in, when my once-loved face became his Medusa, and the sight of my unwilling body made him cold and unyielding. He has come to me tonight, but how long has it been since we have truly been husband and wife? Sometimes, I still catch Henry looking at me in disgust and desire, as though I am rotten meat in the butcher's window dressed in fresh fat.

There was never a child for us, never even the inkling of one. Never the pause, the bated breath and the hand on the stomach, nurturing something new—never any of it. In the days when we still lay together, my body moved efficiently from month to month, paying no attention to Henry's ministrations. I wonder if this angered or frustrated him most—that for all his effort, his mighty, noble will, my body remained an uncracked fortress, the chilly mistress who cut him dead in the street. He could bring any manner of action to bear upon me, and yet it would not make my body bend to his want.

Perhaps he did fear me a little, even then.

*

This time, I wake with a pulsing headache, a matched nausea rising in my gullet. This illness that hunts me like a predator, this curse that lays me low. My body gives me no quarter and I long, not for the first time, to step outside it, to shed my skin and float, formless and unfeeling through the world. It would be to die, I realize abruptly, without this body I would be dead. What an unnerving, new thought.

There is something in my room; I know it with an icy certainty. The hairs on the back of my neck prickle, and my body hums with tension.

I cannot move.

Henry is still beside me in a hot line, breathing softly, but I cannot reach out to alert him.

A darker stretch of shadow detaches itself from the inky corners, and begins to pace before the window overlooking the moor. The shutters are still open, but there is only a blank, black view like a stage set.

The cat paces closer, eyes flashing with some strange, dark light. She is monstrously long, and I know this is the creature that has sat upon my chest when I have woken before.

Am I awake?

I cannot be sure. I am cold, so unbearably cold, save where Henry brushes against me.

The creature bounds upon the bed, and I am terribly afraid. Surely Henry will wake.

But he does not. The closer the cat comes, the more indistinct it is, only the sense of weight on my breastbone, and then that hot tongue rasping at my neck. Twin pricks of pain pierce my skin, and it is too much. I cannot bear it, not again.

Against my paralysis, I force out a cry, and the weight vanishes from my chest in an instant. There is a shifting in the air, and the shadows are replaced by a vision of Carmilla at the foot of my bed. She is dressed in white like the day we found her in the carriage wreckage, but she is drenched in blood from her chin to her feet.

I think she is smiling.

I cry out again, and this time it is as though a bell has been rung. The vision is gone. The light has changed, coming soft and gray with the first notes of dawn, and beyond the window, there is the shape of heather and limestone, of a bleak vast moor so wild and alien.

At once, I scramble from my bed. Something is wrong—I can feel it.

I touch a hand to my throat, but it comes away clean.

It was a dream. Yes. I have been unwell; it must be a product of my exhausted mind.

Or perhaps it is something more.

I think of the girl and the chickens. The terrible light in her eyes.

It is as though there is something infecting us.

Wind rushes the glass, rattling the panes in their ancient frames and sending a gust to lift the sleeve of my silk housedress I had lent—

Carmilla.

Guilt floods me. I wanted her gone, and it is as though my dream presented the fruits of my anger: a vision of her come to some great harm that I have wished upon her. I cannot but feel it is a portent, and I fumble to light the oil lamp on my bedside table.

"Henry," I hiss. "Henry, wake up."

He stirs at my voice, opens his eyes and frowns at the light. "What's going on?"

"There is something wrong—I know it. We must go at once."

"What are you talking about? Did you have a nightmare?"

"It is Carmilla. Something has happened to her."

He sits up, rubbing the sleep from one eye. "What?"

I do not wait for him to follow my meaning. Instead, I go at once to her room opposite mine. I knock softly and call her name, but there is no response. When I try the handle, it is locked. I try to rouse her again, and when there is still no reply, my sense of trepidation grows to fear.

In my nightdress, oil lamp in hand, I stumble downstairs to my bureau in the drawing room to find the ring of keys that should open most doors in Nethershaw. It is bitterly cold with my bare feet against the flagstones, and my skin prickles at the shadows that surround me on all sides. My dream is not so easily shaken off, and I feel acutely aware of how exposed we are in our position in open moorland, so far from any other living thing.

I search but cannot find the keys. Have I misplaced them? Did I give them to the housekeeper?

A floorboard creaks, and I am so startled I nearly drop my lamp. A figure stands in the doorway.

"My lady?"

"Molly. You gave me a fright."

"I'm sorry, my lady. Is all well?"

"I was looking for—no. Come with me. It is Miss Kernstein—I cannot rouse her, and I fear something terrible may have happened."

I am thankful to Molly that she does not question my wild notions, only returns with me to the corridor upstairs. This time, we both knock and call Carmilla's name, but still there is only silence within.

Henry comes to my bedroom door in his nightshirt, hair tousled and wild.

"What on earth are you doing?"

I explain, and Henry's face crumples in irritation.

"For goodness' sake," he says, sizing up the door. "Move out of the way."

I realize what he means to do only a moment before it is happening. Henry throws his weight at the door, rattling it in the frame. It does not give, and this lights some stubborn fire in him; he repeats the action once, twice more, before the worm-eaten wood fractures under his assault and the door bursts open.

There is silence within.

I think of the girl hunched over the chickens, smeared in blood; Carmilla at the foot of my bed, drenched like my parents in their moment of death.

But there is nothing to see.

Carmilla is gone.

12

"IMPOSSIBLE." HENRY STALKS ABOUT the room as if every article of furniture offends him, each empty corner that does not conceal Carmilla. "Impossible," he says again.

For it is. There is only one door into the room, and it is the one we have just now forced open. The windows have been long painted shut, and I have yet to have them seen to. I press my hands against the catch in case it has somehow come loose. It has not.

The key to her bedroom lies on the bedside table, as though placed there after locking the door before sleep. Her sheets are rumpled but cold.

We move through the room, checking inside the clothes press and beneath the bed. There are clothes lying rumpled over the back of the chair, a book open on the bedside table, a still-burning candle, a mess of brushes and cold creams across the dressing table— all borrowed from me but scattered so thoughtlessly it is as if she could walk in at any moment and resume her toilet.

But there is nothing. No hint, no trace of what could have happened to my strange friend. I feel the weight of my nightmare like the albatross around the neck of the ancient mariner: this is my fault. I wished her gone, and now she is.

"I do not understand. Why would she play such a trick on us? How has she done it?"

"If it is a trick, it is in poor taste," snaps Henry. "She does not have supernatural powers—she must be somewhere."

It is as though her disappearance is a personal affront to him. Order and logic have been upturned, and my husband cannot stand it.

"We will find that woman, and when we do, we are throwing her out." He rounds on me. "I'm sorry, Lenore—I said I understood why you wanted her here, but this is too far. Put her in a hotel in Sheffield, visit her if you will, but she cannot be here when our guests arrive. Do you understand?"

His words hammer into me like bullets. I rarely face his rage, and it unmans me.

"Yes. As you say."

We search the rest of the house, but it is just as empty. When pressed, I cannot explain why I am so fearful for her. The dream is not something I can share with anyone; it is too bizarre.

Dawn rises weakly over the high moorland, and my carefully guarded candles are used by the fistful as we send servants through every room and corridor, every cupboard and attic, in search of Carmilla. I open up the room with the collapsed floor and the room with the smashed window; Henry crawls through the waterlogged attic, growing sharper and sharper in his anger. In the warren of cellar rooms, we discover a covered-over well that, when we lower a candle into its depths, is mercifully empty.

There is only one place left.

As the first swell of pink crests the horizon, I greet it from the entrance of Nethershaw, a light cloak around my shoulders against the cold morning dew. I think of that speck of white seen from my window—Carmilla walking at night. Open moorland lies in all directions, a sloping stretch of purple heather and green thistle, thrown across its limestone boulders that mass along the cliff line,

Stanage Edge in one direction and Burbage Edge in the other. It seems impossible to think someone could hide in this barren place, but I know the ground is treacherous, hiding hollows and ridges where a body could easily lie unseen.

The servants scatter in all directions, and I join them. Henry thinks it mad, but he has lost patience with my concern already, returning to bed with muttered words about the mad impulses of irrational women.

I do not regret it. After last night, I want him as far from me as possible.

Tramping the pit-pony paths as the sun breaches the night sky, flooding the heavens with pale light, I call her name. The moon lingers, a sliver low over Kinder Fell. I am alone. From this bleak hilltop, I can see no other house, no farm, no grazing flock of sheep. There is nothing but Nethershaw and my deep, riotous dread.

Yesterday, I would have sided naturally with Henry and been ready to throw Carmilla out. Now that the prospect of losing her lies vivid before me, I find myself seized with a panic, as though I am the one lost.

I return to Nethershaw, sweating beneath my cloak, to dim faces and shaking heads. Henry is in the kennels, barking orders at the gamekeeper, his mind already on the shooting party.

At the door to my bedroom, I am stopped by a sound: the gentle hush of fabric on fabric.

It comes from Carmilla's room.

Hardly daring to hope, I push the door open to discover her sat before her dressing table, the long stretch of her chestnut waves hanging glossy and lustrous down her straight back.

I give an involuntary cry and kneel beside her. The hem of her nightdress is filthy and wet, her feet smeared with mud.

"Where have you been?" I mean to be scolding, but the twin fear and relief make me only craven, like a child who has been briefly abandoned.

She takes my head in her lap, stroking the hair from my cheek, but gives no answer.

"Where do you go at night, Carmilla?" I speak softly. Then, after a moment's courage-gathering: "Did you do something to that girl at the farm?"

She presses her cool palms to my cheeks, and draws my face up to regard me.

"Do you really want to know, Lenore?"

"Yes. Tell me the truth."

"I have been trying," she says. "Open your eyes."

My mouth trembles. "Tell me the truth about *you*. Who are you?"

"Does it matter?"

I bite the tip of my tongue. "I saw you in a dream, the night before we found you. I put it out of my mind, but it was real. It was you."

Her mouth breaks open in a smile. "Your pain was so loud it was a beacon that called me. I found you so easily."

"What for?" I whisper.

"I am a mirror to those who need it. To those who hunger but deny themselves."

I cast her hands from me in frustration. "Stop it. This is too much. Do not speak to me like that." I am breathing hard, and I work to steady myself to regain control over my hectic emotions. This is madness. I must master myself, school my wayward mind. "I am sure you understand that we will be quite at capacity when the shooting party begins, which is less than a week away now. We will arrange your onward travel before then."

It is the only way I know to hurt her, but as I take my leave, her expression does not change: the small bud of a smile, a knowing look that makes me want to slap her.

*

I feel a bout of nausea coming on, the slow knot of cramps forming in my stomach.

I make it back to my room in time to empty last night's dinner into my chamber pot, specks of pink lobster among dark claret wine. Something deep and sour within me twists tighter and tighter, bringing with it fresh waves of agony as I empty my stomach and bowels.

Something is wrong with me.

I think, if I let myself linger on it, I am quite frightened.

I retch twice more, and by the time I am able to dress and begin the day, I am too late to attend church, and I am sure Henry will be displeased with me for it. I am faint with pain and lack of sleep, and my hands tremble so badly I draw blood with my hairpins. I am the only one at breakfast, and I attempt to smother my nausea with kedgeree and toast with jam, as though I can insulate myself from each repulsive feeling.

Carmilla keeps to her room for once, and Henry to his study. Cora is still in town and will not arrive at Hathersage until this afternoon. I am left alone with this wreck of a house to salvage.

No matter how much work I have done already, somehow the list of tasks waiting for me at my bureau is overwhelming. I snap at Molly, who brings the wrong menu cards, and write a terse note to the builders, who have failed to return to repair the hole they splintered into the floorboards of one of the bedrooms. My headache builds like a warning, and I only just make it in time to thrust my head through a window and empty my guts onto the path outside. I am too ashamed to own it, and instead tell the housekeeper that one of the workmen must be a drunk.

Despite it being Sunday, a man arrives driving a cart loaded with books—a complete library Henry has ordered without informing me—and I am overwhelmed by a moment of panic. Has the library been checked for damp? Is it cleaned? Are the bookshelves solid? Will there be time to revarnish the wood? Do we need to replace the moth-eaten rugs?

Everyone about me seems slow and stupid, and if I am not in every place at once, ensuring each decision made is the most rational and logical, none of this will come together. The shooting party will be Henry's moment, but it will be also mine. If there is one thing I can do perfectly, it is this, and so perfect it must be.

If I am unwell, it is no matter. If I am weak, I must supress it. I have come this far through strength of will alone. I cannot fail now.

But it seems failure stalks me whatever I do. The library is too dirty to install the new collection, so I set a team of maids to cleaning, denying them their half day off, but the bookseller is angry at the delay and threatens to return to Sheffield with his load. The more I offer him sweetness, the more sour he becomes, and abruptly I turn him over to the butler.

In the kitchens, the dogs have broken free from the kennels again and gorged themselves on meat hanging in the cold room. The leak in the dining hall has grown worse, and a piece of plasterwork the size of my torso crashes into the floor just as I am passing by, covering my skirts in a fine powder and causing me to cough so violently I am ill again.

When Henry is returned from church, he stops long enough to push his correspondence into my hands, instructing me to have it in the post this afternoon, and then he is gone again, taking his new carriage out.

The post is ordinary—to his solicitor, his banker, his club—but there is one local address, in the village of Hathersage, where Cora will be arriving by train in a few hours' time.

I decide to deliver the letter by hand; Nethershaw is full of demands, and I am in desperate need of the quiet of the walk. And if I see Cora and am able to smooth things over, then all to the good.

"Where are we going?" Carmilla appears at the drawing-room door, wearing a green cotton day dress of my own that looks much better on her, and rubbing the sleep from her eyes. It is well past noon.

"I am going to Hathersage," I say, pinning my hat in place. "You will wait here."

A dark light flares in her eyes. "No. I think I will join you."

I want to tell her *no*, but she has already gone through the front door, sending a coy glance over her shoulder.

I cannot read her expression under her heavy-lidded eyes, and I turn before our gazes meet. It is too late for me to say anything more; I cannot make any strong objections where the servants will hear.

Carmilla waits for me outside.

"Will you forgive me for worrying you?"

"You did not worry me." It is a lie. She knows it and looks almost pityingly at me, but I do not know how else to speak. "It is true we will lack space for extra guests when the shooting party begins. If you are not ready to travel on before the twelfth, we can arrange a stay at a hotel—"

"Do not fear," she says, her voice low and sensuous. "This will all be over by then."

Something cold prickles across my skin, and for a moment I am rigid, unable to move. Carmilla's smile is too wide, and her eyes hold me fixed.

She takes my arm proprietorially, and we start the path down into the valley.

*

We follow an ancient right of way that snakes across the moor and between the sharp outline of the limestone edge into the valley of the Derwent. The day is muggy and close; the gray skies fooled me into overdressing, so I am slick with sweat between my thighs and under my breasts by the time we wind towards the outposts of Hathersage. We have, unspoken, avoided the path that led along the conifer plantation and the farm. I see it in the distance, the dark thatch of branches and the stone house within that seems like a toy this far away.

Our route takes us through a churchyard, and Carmilla begins to flag, stopping at the lych-gate. The graveyard is bounded by a drystone wall; in the center is a low stone church with a tower so squat and weathered it could be Norman, and crowding the clay cold graves are broad-trunked yew trees, twisted and split open like doorways.

"Do you need to rest?"

Carmilla is as pale as the fleece snagged in the crook of wall-stones, her mouth drawn tight. "Not here," she sneers.

"There is a bench," I say, indicating a place a little farther along. I try to draw her in, but she pulls back.

"This place is ugly." She looks up at the bulk of the church, its sharply gabled roof and the ivy creeping around its windows. "I hate it. Lenore, we must leave."

I am perplexed by her outburst. "We are nearly at the village. It is only a few minutes through the churchyard."

"Not that way."

Before I can speak, a blot of red appears above her lip.

I frown. "Your nose is bleeding."

Carmilla does nothing to stem the flow, letting it cut a slow course over her lip. I try again to draw her to the bench so I can tend to her, but she struggles out of my grip.

"Very well." I concede defeat, and we leave the churchyard, skirting its borders to where the path emerges on the other side.

Carmilla does not take my handkerchief when offered, only licks away the blood.

The village is not far, a winding road along the hillside banked with stone cottages and the occasional larger Georgian or newer house. There are small outposts of the great Sheffield works, grinders and polishers and cutters taking piecework or finishing.

The brand-new station sits on the far side, its wooden buildings fresh with white paint, and the platform boards sticky and bright.

I see Cora from a way off, wearing sprigged cotton and reading a small novel, leaning picturesquely against a wall. Aunt Daphne would have called her a whore to loiter alone in public.

"Interesting," says Carmilla, lingering behind me. "You welcome back the cuckoo into the nest."

"Cora is a friend, and it is not necessary to cause a public rupture over wild suspicions."

Carmilla is too close to the mark. I am tight as a bowstring on seeing Cora again, humiliation and anger flaring hot in my stomach—but feeling is a luxury I don't have time for. I would be foolish to think that Henry has not strayed before; I must hope that he tires of this dalliance before long, and then I can cut Cora from my life like a canker.

"Not *necessary*," scoffs Carmilla. "Life is a sterile thing in your hands—all necessity and obligation. Do you *want* to see her again?"

I feel the bead of panic take form under my diaphragm. I cannot have such an exchange with Carmilla again. Not here. Not in public.

"Lenore!" Relief floods Cora's face when she spots me, mercifully cutting Carmilla short. She kisses my cheeks and squeezes my hands. "How glad I am you came." Cora's expression falls to see Carmilla. "Oh. I had thought we might spend a little time alone."

Carmilla drifts into our orbit, her complexion washed gray in the sun, despite the parasol she keeps carefully shading her face. "I would not miss this for the world," she purrs. "Things are becoming quite thrilling."

Cora smiles uncomfortably. "I thought perhaps we could visit St. Michael's and see Little John's grave."

I nod my assent. "I have an errand to complete first."

We find the address on the letter without too much trouble: it is one in a line of cottages, the slate roof dull and furred with moss, the doorway so small even Cora would need to duck her head. There is no letterbox, so I rap my knuckles against the wood.

A woman answers, drying her hands on her apron.

"Can I help you?" She is tense in the presence of three strangers in fine dresses.

I hand over the letter by way of explanation. "My husband intended to post this, but I thought to bring it by hand as it is a pleasant day."

"What is this?" She takes the letter cautiously and opens it, running a finger laboriously over the words as she reads. I am embarrassed to think she might not be literate.

As she reaches the end, her face drops, and an absolute, radiating coldness takes the place of her caution.

I smile. "I hope no bad news?"

At that, she looks at me with such disdain I almost recoil. She balls the paper up and throws it at me before slamming the door in my face.

"How rude!" says Cora, mouth open. "How utterly shocking."

Carmilla says nothing; she leans against the wall, face lost in the shadow of her hat brim.

I pick up the letter from the ground and smooth it out.

It is short: a typewritten letter to which Henry has put his signature, explaining that the death of Alexander Whitmore following injuries sustained in the grinding room of the Ajax Works has been found to be caused by an error on the part of the grinder, and not the machinery, and as such, no compensation is due to his wife.

Without thinking, I crumple the letter back into a ball and drop it on the ground.

"What did it say?" asks Cora.

"Nothing important."

I start walking with no direction in mind, only knowing that I must get away from this house and the woman within. I saw the accident in full: the grinding stone that had exploded and thrown shrapnel around the room. There is no way a man could do that to himself.

The journalist. Stories of safety declining. Yet Henry touts his exemplary treatment of his workers, the compensation he promises, the lies he spins to his investors. To me.

I think of Henry rising in anger when I spoke to him about it at the works, the taut, simmering violence in the hand he began to raise as if to strike.

"Slow down!" Cora hurries after me, but I am walking quickly, and soon I hit a crowd that has gathered in the street. I do not understand what it is for, but I edge my way through it, wanting

161

only to increase my distance from Henry and the callousness of his appetite.

What has Henry *done*?

At the front of the crowd, a woman has fainted into the arms of a man wearing a baker's apron. Behind her, the door to another cottage stands open. People bring her water, a chair.

Something about the open door draws me like a hook in the pit of my stomach.

I slip past the crowd and come to the entrance.

A wave of dread moves through me. The interior is smoky and dark from badly cut tapers, and there is the sound of someone groaning in pain. I do not want to see what is inside, but I know I must find out all the same. I cannot stop myself. It is as though this place has been waiting for me, just as the girl with the chickens, just as Nethershaw has, just as my nightmares wait for me to close my eyes.

I step inside.

There is a man at the kitchen table, slumped forward with one arm hanging loose. He is the one groaning. His slack arm is in a darker sleeve than the rest of his shirt and misshapen—and then I understand.

It is soaked through with blood, and there is a fist-sized divot carved out of the muscle of his bicep. The scent of blood hits me, and I think I should retch, but I do not.

There is another smell, more movement, coming from the range. A woman stands before it. A rich scent of cooking meat joins the blood, and the strange combination is not entirely unpleasant.

"Excuse me for intruding," I say as I take another step across the flagstones.

Has this woman not noticed the injured man at her table? Distantly, I think I should help him, but I am captured by the gently swaying back of the woman at the range. It is as if she is moving to music I cannot hear.

When I come closer, I see that she has a piece of meat in the pan, frying in dripping, and she is cutting slivers from the joint with a knife and placing them into her mouth.

I go to speak again, but between one breath and the next, everything comes together, like the tightening of a noose.

The injured man. The wound in his arm.

The frying meat.

The woman eating.

As if noticing me for the first time, she turns to me, a piece of flesh skewered on her knife, from which she pulls a strip with her teeth. Her eyes are sunken and hollow, but a dark light shines within.

Everything telescopes, becoming distant and close at once. I am dizzy. I should be screaming, but I am not. The tug in my navel, the dread, the sense of something waiting for me.

It feels so obvious.

Licking her grease-stained lips, the woman looks at me.

And simply says, "I was so terribly hungry."

13

THE POLICE ARE SUMMONED.

The woman keeps chewing as the men draw her outside and place handcuffs around her wrists. I cannot bear to look.

There is nothing I can say to make this not have happened— no quiet word and careful look that will allow us to flee back to Nethershaw, as with that poor girl and the chickens.

Anger flares in me, and for a moment I am furious at this woman for doing this to me, for bringing more chaos and horror into my life when already I feel torn to pieces.

No. That is selfish. These strangers are the ones who have had the most horror visited upon them. I did not have to come into their house; I did not have to witness their destruction.

I do not know what is happening to me lately. My thoughts pupate and shift as I try to grasp them, becoming something different and new, but not alien. No, I feel these thoughts as though they are plucked from the marrow of my bones, some sickness that has lain within me all along.

Aunt Daphne saw it in me. She knew there was something wrong with me—why else would she have treated me so?

I stand somewhere beyond the crowd, shaking uncontrollably. I do not know what to do with the images in my mind, these things I have seen that will live with me forever, with the blood of my parents' death across me, all these moments where the world has been rent open and shown for the sharp-toothed, raw place it is.

I am questioned by the police. It is quite strange. There is a man with a bristling mustache and an egg-shaped helmet asking me the most peculiar questions I do not know how to answer. I have seen a man eaten like a piece of steak. It is all madness. What sense can I give him? Sense has fled the world.

In the crowd behind him, I see Carmilla.

She stands at the back in her pale dress, her dark eyes fixed upon me with such a look I feel quite unmanned.

She knows something. I feel sure of it. All of this comes back to her.

The police do not keep me long.

A carriage is found to take the three of us back to Nethershaw, and I take care to sit beside Cora, who clutches my hand in silence. It is a shock beyond what any of us can articulate.

Except perhaps for Carmilla.

She leans back in the carriage, watching the world go past with those lazy-lidded eyes. Her skin seems to shine like pearl, and her lips are shockingly red.

Henry is angry upon our return, so late in the day. I have no option but to tell him what has happened and why we were there. Cora will say, even if I do not.

He is chalk-white with rage. "You took my letter?"

"I thought I could be helpful—"

"You meddled with my business correspondence?"

"All I did was deliver it."

"Why must you always put your nose where it is not needed, you empty-headed, self-involved fool?"

There is a bolt of shock that passes through the entrance hall. Cora and Carmilla have come in behind me and are removing their hats and gloves. Wordlessly, Cora guides Carmilla by the elbow into the drawing room.

"I'm sorry." The words are barely more than a whisper.

Henry is breathing heavily and runs his hands through his blond hair, sending it into disarray. "What did the police say? Did you tell them your business in Hathersage?"

I hold on to the newel post of the staircase like it is a tether.

"No. They don't know about the letter," I say. "They don't know you denied that man the money he is owed."

He laughs, a brutal thing. "Oh, you had to read it, didn't you? I am sick of your sanctimonious opinion on everything I do. This is *my* business—you have no conception of the sort of decisions it takes to run the Ajax Works."

I think of the man in the grinding room, the lower half of his face blood and gristle.

"I'm sorry."

It is our conversation in his office again. I have taken a wrong turn. No matter how hard I try, I cannot keep everything under control. I cannot master it all. No, there is always something I have done wrong, some fatal flaw in me that makes it all mean nothing.

My heart is beating too fast. I can hear it like an urgent drumbeat inside me, the lockstep march of panic as it takes over.

"I'm sorry," I say again.

Henry is breathing heavily as he straightens his waistcoat and smooths back his hair. "What a waste of my time."

He returns to his study, the door slamming.

There is too much emotion flooding through me; it is like a fast-running river, alive and unrelenting. I stumble up the stairs, eyes blurred with tears.

Behind me, I hear Cora's voice addressing Carmilla. "Leave her be—"

I sink to the floor at the top of the stairs and hide my face in my hands like a scolded child. I cannot breathe; my chest is too tight and my heart hammers so hard it is painful. I don't want anyone to see me brought so low.

If I lie down here and never moved again, it would be better than facing my life.

From below, I hear footsteps, the murmur of voices. A maid will come past soon, I am sure, or a workman. I can never truly retreat.

I need to fix this.

I need to at least try.

I scrub the tears from my eyes, smooth my dress and wait until I am sure the hallway is empty before I descend. Henry's study is to the left, and I approach the half-open door, still unsure what I will say to disarm his anger.

It proves unnecessary.

Henry is not alone.

He has his back to me, and before him is Cora, standing so close that her skirts brush his shoes.

The ground drops from beneath me.

Oh, I suspected. I feared it. But to witness them, intimate together—it is like a slap.

Then Cora's eyes flick towards me, and though her expression only changes but a whisper, I know she sees me.

I need air. I need out, away. I cannot breathe.

I dash out of the house, breathing shallow and fast, body so light and cold I feel as though I may float away. All my courage has been used up, and I want to run barefoot into the moors, as far as I can make it before I collapse, so far that I cease to be, that Lenore Crowther is no more, and I am only animal muscle and blood, instinct and adrenaline, and I need feel this shame, this humiliation, this abject despair no more.

At the boundary wall where the formal gardens dissolve into open moorland, a set of steps sinks into the moss and heather. Blotches of white speckle the stone balustrades, and the heather is brilliant purple under the long summer sun that still sits low in the sky. Streaks of pink and lilac spread out from the west, and at last I am in the vast, unpeopled wasteland.

"Lenore!"

Cora's voice rings out behind me, and I run farther, stumbling on the uneven ground.

"Lenore, wait!"

She is gaining on me, and a moment later, a hand snags my elbow and spins me around.

"Please. Let me explain."

I yank my arm from her grasp. "Do not speak to me."

"It is not what you think."

"Do you suppose me a complete fool?"

"You think I have seduced your husband," she says plainly.

I sink down onto the loamy earth and turn away from her. "No."

She sighs softly, as if coming to a decision, then sits beside me.

I think I might vomit. My stomach is in knots, as though my illness is about to overcome me again.

"I am so ashamed." Cora's voice is low and tremulous. "I never thought I would keep such terrible secrets from a friend, but I have become quite a stranger to myself."

I think about pushing her into the gorse, letting the thorns rip open her pretty skin.

What is wrong with me?

I manage the words: "How long?"

Cora stops suddenly and gathers my hands in hers. "You must not believe your worst instincts. I swear it is not so. It is true I have visited Henry in secret, many times, but it is not for the reason you think."

I choke. "What other reason could there be?"

She closes her eyes as if pained. "I swore I would never speak of it—it could get so many people into terrible trouble if the truth comes out. But I cannot let you think this of me."

She takes another deep breath, and I want to slap her. This isn't difficult for *her*. It is difficult for *me*.

"Henry is in trouble," she says. "Or the Ajax Works are, at least. They have promised great packages of compensation to injured workers, and Henry has used this when raising investment funds as evidence of his modernization."

"I know that. And he has denied it to a worker I saw injured."

"It is worse than that. A party of workers have gone to a journalist at the *Manchester Guardian*, claiming that he has never paid out a *single* compensation case and that their demands for fair treatment have gone ignored."

I think of the journalist who approached me at St. Pancras station. Henry's fury—and fear.

Cora continues, "No one wants a repeat of the Outrages back in the '60s, but that is what they are threatening. Henry came to me with it because he thought my father, being a minister in the Home Office, might be able to help. Henry wants the journalist discredited and the workers arrested for blackmail—but the problem is that they are right. Henry has *never* paid out a single penny in compensation. He swore to me that this is because every case brought to him has been unjustified, and I believed him. I knew you would, too."

Would I? Yes, perhaps Cora is right. I have swallowed so many lies already to preserve this life of safety I thought I had built with Henry.

"So of course I agreed to help him. Oh, Lenore, I've hated keeping this from you, but he made me swear not to tell a soul, and you can see why, can't you?"

She squeezes my hands pleadingly, and I want to laugh.

"You swear there is nothing between you?" I say, trembling.

"Nothing."

I nod, neck stiff, legs aching from the tension I have held. "Very well."

It feels a risk to believe her, but it makes a sick kind of sense. I do not know what is more humiliating: that Cora has seen me brought low by my fear of Henry's betrayal, or that Henry would not trust me with this secret. Have I not supported him loyally for ten years? Have I not shaped his life, built his fortunes?

Why would he keep this from me but trust Cora?

Cora does not let go of my hands. "Tell me that all is mended between us. Please."

She cannot bear not to be liked. I see that now. Her weakness.

I remove my hands. "It is mended. I would not speak of it anymore."

Cora nods. "Please don't tell Henry."

"I am his wife. He can trust me."

Though he doesn't.

I begin to think my husband a total stranger to me.

"Lenore."

"I won't tell."

She sags in relief and presses a kiss to my cheek—then hesitates. "If I could say one more thing."

"Yes?"

"The girl we saw . . . on the farm . . . And that woman today, doing such an awful thing . . . What do you think was wrong with them?"

"I don't know. I do not care to dwell on it."

Cora looks at her hands, chewing on her rosy lips as she thinks over her next words. "Your guest is quite peculiar," she says. "I do not think you should allow her to stay in your home much longer."

Though I have felt the same way, I do not like Cora telling me so. "I understand your concern, but I do not need your advice."

The set of Cora's jaw tells of her displeasure. "Do you not think she perhaps takes advantage of you?"

"How so?"

"She claims to be an invalid, yet she seems quite well enough to wear your gowns and follow you about the place. There is something I mislike about her." Cora licks her lips. "I saw her, once, at night. She was outside in her nightdress, walking away across the moor."

"I don't know what you're talking about."

Of course I have seen this, too, but it seems stark to me now that Carmilla, strange as she is, may be the only one at Nethershaw who is on my side.

"Perhaps I dreamed it. But the way she reacted at the farm—it was quite unnatural. Any normal woman would have been quite horrified. And today—she hardly seemed shocked at all when you told us what you'd seen. And yet she lounges around your house like a cat before a fire, quite content and unperturbed."

I stumble at her words. *Any normal woman.* I did not react as Cora did either. I was shocked to see a girl with her mouth bloodied, eating a chicken as though she were a fox, but I did not fall to the ground in a fainting fit or scream myself hoarse. Even today, I did not faint as that woman outside had.

I think of what Henry so often says to me, that I am not like other women. Cora wears her womanhood so easily. Perhaps she scents my failure on me, as she does Carmilla.

171

"Carmilla has been through her own trials," I say. "We cannot judge how others react."

"You are right. Forgive me."

"Please, leave me to my own company."

"Of course."

Cora goes, and I wrap my arms around my knees to watch the sun sink towards the horizon.

I believe Cora, because I know exactly how Henry is using her. I know he is capable of manipulation, of twisting the truth until it suits him. I am sure he is quite convinced that none of his workers are due any money, that all his actions can be justified.

What I do not understand is why Henry has not tried to use me, too. I have connections; I have proved myself to him from the first days of our marriage.

He holds me at a distance for some other purpose.

I understand something now: I hold more of Henry's secrets than he does of mine. I have a power over him of a kind that he cannot wield over me.

He does not want me to have anymore.

*

When I do not come downstairs, Carmilla finds me in my bedroom. I have laid myself on the bed still dressed, collapsed on my side, all the fight gone out of me. Everything I have worked for: escaping Aunt Daphne, building a safe fortress for myself—all of it is coming apart. Henry risks my future with his selfish actions, and now I may be trapped on a sinking ship when all I have ever done is work to keep afloat.

"Lenore?" asks Carmilla. "Are you ill?"

"I'm not good company at present."

There are footsteps slowly circling the room.

"You think you must be good company for someone to come to your side?"

I will not be drawn into another of her maddening arguments. "Please. I will come down later."

Her arc ends, and she stoops before me so that I cannot help but look at the lovely heart of her face.

"Why do you let him talk to you like that?"

The panic is too much, and I feel blank, a haze passing over me like a fog, reducing the world to the ringing in my ears.

My words are mechanical, a reflex. "I don't want to talk about Henry."

Carmilla is still talking to me. It is as though I have been struck mute. I mean to speak, but I feel too heavy. The outside world is too much, and my body is protecting me from being part of it.

There is a weight in my pocket. I brush against its shape.

The pastilles.

Here I always am.

Mechanically, I take them out and open the tin. There are five left, round and lightly colored, glowing from beneath the powdered sugar. They hypnotize me like lights in a window, a compulsion that lives its own life within me.

In the sharp smack of her hand, Carmilla knocks them from my grasp and the tin goes clattering to the floorboards.

"Stop it. You are feeding the wrong hunger."

I am too shocked to say anything. She bends and plucks up the pastilles and throws them out the window.

I am crying again. Carmilla sits me on the side of the bed and draws me into her lap, stroking my face with her soft fingertips.

"My dear Lenore. Do not give up."

At that, I sob harder. There is some kindness in her that is brutal and unrelenting, and it confuses me more than I can bear.

"What are you doing to me?" My voice cracks. "What did you do to those women?"

She does not deny it. There is no point.

"I don't understand. Everything has gone so wrong since you came."

"No. I am not the beginning of it." A cloud passes over her face, her features for a moment stormy and jagged. "I am the end."

*

When Molly comes with a tray of tea, I tell her I am sick.

I am.

My head is pounding, and I feel so weak it is all I can do to peel the dress from my sweaty skin and slip between the covers. My mouth tastes like copper.

Around me, the vines of my wallpaper seethe like snakes.

Am I dying?

Molly presses a cold flannel to my forehead and feels for my skittering pulse.

She leaves me for a while—at least, I think she is gone, but I cannot be sure. I sleep fitfully, scraps of horror passing through my mind: the girl with the chickens, the man in the grinding room, the beast upon my chest, the woman at the stove.

It is a wonder that I sleep at all.

The light is fading over the moors when I feel strong enough to rise. The sky flares red and orange like a warning fire, spread above the distant, ill-defined shapes of Kinder Scout and Mam Tor that rise like tooth-stumps.

I fold a wrapper over my nightgown and step out into the corridor. I can hear soft voices from below, the tinkle of glassware and cutlery.

I lose my courage and return to my room. It is easier to be alone.

At my dressing table, I repin my hair at the nape of my neck and put a little cream on my flushed cheeks.

There, nestled amongst the perfume bottles and sticks of rouge, is the jet necklace. Henry's gift. My gut twists again, this time in disappointment and dread. He was so very angry that I knew the truth of Ajax.

He buys me off, lies to me. Fears me.

There is something not right here.

I run my fingers over the glossy, angular-cut stone.

I thought it was Carmilla.

But perhaps I am looking in the wrong place.

What happened to the diamonds I found?

I make soft noises outside Henry's room, letting my tread fall heavy on the boards to alert anyone inside to my presence. No one comes to the door, so I knock lightly, then open it and let myself in.

The room is as badly organized as the last time I was here; all my work bringing his possessions into a pleasing arrangement was for nought.

I close the door.

The clothes press hangs open, and it is the work of a few moments to shift aside the hat boxes and crumpled shirts to find the space where once the jewelry box lay.

I sit back on my heels, frowning. Did I dream it? Surely not. There had been a box, and there had not been jet inside.

Henry bought diamonds for someone who is not me. If not Cora, then who?

No, I cannot condemn him so quickly. Perhaps he has moved them somewhere else.

Have I been wrong about Henry from the start? Or has he only become this monster by slow degrees as life worked its subtle cruelty on him?

I did not marry happiness. I married the shape of something that could look like it. But I knew its bones: security, certainty, mastery. Whatever the cost.

It is only that I do not want this to be true.

I work through the room, turning out drawers and traveling bags, and even holding my lamp to the dark space beneath his bed. There are empty Egyptian cigarette tins and soiled handkerchiefs, a comb with snapped teeth, a half-used pot of hair oil, crumbs from something I cannot identify, bent collars, and one of a pair of cufflinks that I place onto his dresser.

No diamonds.

With some effort, I pull his trunk down from the top of the wardrobe; it is the only place I have not looked, and it is heavy enough that there must be something still enclosed within. I am hot, and my head swims, a band of sweat around my hairline.

The trunk is not locked. Inside is a folded coat, which, when lifted out, exposes neatly stacked tins of pastilles.

I pick one up to confirm it is the same brand I always take. The enamel is the same, the same smiling woman and pink-cheeked child, the curling green letters. There must be at least ten tins.

I do not know what to think.

Next to them is a palm-sized paper bag, something like a packet of flour or sugar from the grocers.

I open the tin, unable to understand what is before me. Inside are the same pastille sweets I know.

Odd—they have no powdered sugar.

I put the lid on and put it back into the trunk. The memory comes to me of Henry handing me a new tin after our uncomfortable conversation in his office. I know I should find this touching, but there is some slant to the picture that unsettles me, as though some warning bell is sounding in the far distance.

I think of Carmilla's eyes, always watching.

I lift the paper bag. It is lighter than I expected, half empty. There is white powder around the creases, and on the front, the name of a chemist is stamped in black ink.

I think again of Carmilla snatching the pastilles from my hands and throwing them from my reach.

You are feeding the wrong hunger.

The warning bells grow louder, a ringing in my ears that shuts out any thought.

Only this image remains: the pastilles I have opened a hundred times, covered in white powder, and a paper bag with the mark of a poisoner.

14

I HAVE CARRIED HENRY'S secret for so long, it has become like a fiction to me. My memory and the story we wove afterwards blur together, winding the threads between reality and falsehood into a knot. He is innocent; he is guilty. I saw nothing; I saw everything. It is all as one.

Henry's secret is this: I have helped him kill.

Shortly after the first anniversary of our marriage, we attended a shooting party at an estate in the Pennines. It was the jewel in a crown I had constructed, a perfect debut into married life. As soon as I was out of mourning for Aunt Daphne, I made it my mission to become the indispensable wife I had promised Henry. With my ranked books of etiquette and household management, I studied society in careful detail, alert to every shortcoming in Henry's and my pasts that must be covered. I was wildly out of my depth, but I could not allow anyone to see it, not Henry, not even myself. I had learned upon the death of my parents that to be exposed as vulnerable, as not-knowing, was the greatest danger possible; death, at least, offered certainty; to be vulnerable meant being at the mercy of others, one's whole selfhood at risk.

A carapace suited me better than soft skin, and I found it powerful to want nothing: for then I could never be disappointed. For then no one could ever see the ways in which I lacked. I had mastery over everything, even my own wayward heart, and Henry loved me for it.

I arranged whist drives, parties and balls, seances and charitable luncheons, and at all of these events, I took it upon myself to befriend every person I could. I had passed too many years of my life in monstrous isolation, and I knew that one way to ensure my future was to populate it not with people who cared for me but with people for whom it would be deeply inconvenient if I were to be absent.

Of course, I counted Henry among these people, at once learning his peculiarities of appetite and dress, arranging a menu perfectly suited to his palate, and standing orders of collars and cuffs so that he would never risk looking unpresentable. I read tiresome books on steel smelting and industry in the Don Valley, newspaper articles on industrialists and bankers, financial planning and loan terms. Henry did not want me at his side in his business, but when I took his arm at a gala or assembly, I would be impeccably informed on any topic that arose, and he was happy with the way it reflected on his own prowess. If he canceled a trip to Berlin to see the art galleries I had read about, then it was only because his business was urgent. If I ate dinner alone most nights, it was only because it was the sole time he could relax. These were the rules I set for myself: no tears, no weakness. I would master it all.

It was I who secured us the invitation to the shooting party.

It was a gathering of the brightest and best of the aristocracy, politicians, minor royals—the oldest of old money. I had worked connection after connection, ingratiating myself with wives and sisters and mothers-in-law, flattering Henry and drawing him into grander and grander circles with me, until finally it arrived: the cream card with gold leaf inlay. The invitation.

This was the moment of our ascendancy, our youthful beauty and vigor welcomed in as novelty. A hand held out, the door open, and a bright light shining through.

We traveled in a private train compartment to Penrith, then by coach to Garrigill Lodge in the foothills of the Pennines. It was a beautiful place with a neoclassical frontage completed last century and well-maintained Capability Brown–landscaped grounds. I saw the joy and wonder in Henry's eyes as he took in the rococo drawing rooms and well-stocked libraries, the billiard room, the long gallery and the Canaletto sketches and Gainsborough landscapes. Truly, I marveled alongside him.

Finally, for the first time in so very long, I began to relax. Henry was in good form, joking easily, and letting his charm and good looks buoy him through card game and breakfast table. He took my hand and pressed kisses to my cheeks, and became attentive at night where once I had accepted his ministrations as no more than my wifely duty.

Now, I thought, perhaps, I could learn to enjoy myself.

Shooting took us out on dog carts and landaus, past tarn and burn and force, into the moors. With heather and gorse catching my skirts and a baked, broad sky, I let myself be drawn along in the ease of chatter, the bounding spaniels, the picnic blankets and hampers, the men with guns broken open in the crooks of their elbows. It was beautiful and uncomplicated and mine for the taking.

When the men left to shoot, the women ate a little lunch, and I slipped away to find a quiet place to relieve myself. A copse of trees clung to the meandering banks of a valley stream; I picked my way to the hidden heart of it and was about to do my business when I heard voices abruptly close.

"You've had your fun—stop it."

"Lord, you do go quite red when aggrieved, Crowther."

It was Henry, upset, and another man. Between the branches, I saw them so close I could have reached between the dense leaves and touch Henry's arm. It was only the shadows and my low crouch that concealed me, and I hardly dared breathe. They were in the midst of some heated debate. I recognized the second figure as Lord Abney, someone from our party whom I had spoken to little but who seemed a great friend of our host. He was tall and sandy, with the pink cheeks of a perpetual schoolboy and the snigger to match.

"Look," Henry said. "We're both men—I can take a good-natured joke as well as anyone, but you go too far."

I had never seen Henry so angry before. His cheeks were pink, and his hands twitched into fists by his side. The men's guns were propped against a tree with their bundled jackets.

Abney snorted. "Don't be so touchy. Surely you must have heard it all before with *that* accent."

"I don't *have* an accent."

"If you say so. Listen, my lawyer is looking for a new set of cutlery—do you think you could set him up?"

"That's enough!" Henry's fist smacked into a tree trunk, splitting his knuckles red.

Abney laughed, an uptilt of his head. He stood so at ease, hands shoved in his pockets and shoulders low. I bit my lip, unsure. One part of me wished to intervene and cool Henry's temper, while another knew he would be only angrier at being witnessed in his humiliation.

I had noticed Abney's jokes during our stay: sly jabs about Henry's work, the newness of his money, the baseness of his roots. Abney seemed the kind of man who dealt out insults easily, but took them with little grace, throwing a game of cards in spite or storming out of breakfast with a flourish. Henry endured his own taunting with a forced laugh in company, and several smashed cups in the privacy of our own room.

181

I had thought it only the cruel humor of all the society men I saw around me. My mistake.

Abney began to leave, and Henry grabbed his arm, before being shaken off. Abney's expression dropped, his anger rising to match Henry's, and I thought I was about to see a fistfight.

I wished I had.

"Get your hands off me, you dirty little commoner. We let you hang around like a stray dog, because it's fun to give you a kicking. You'll never be anything more."

Henry moved first. Abney spat something at him I could not hear—their words turned dark and low, then Henry's hand darted out for the gun before Abney saw his intention. I thought he would only threaten him, but it happened in one motion. The gun rose, Henry's finger finding the trigger, Abney storming towards him, outraged.

Then the shot.

It was loud enough that my ears rang, my body shivering in shock.

Smoke in the clearing, the scent of gunpowder.

Abney lay limp among the understory, the meat of his head blown open: white shards of skull, gouts of blood, a porridge of brains, strips of skin dangling like fern fronds.

Henry stood over him, gun still held in a white-knuckled grip. His face was splattered with red.

I made a noise—I do not know what—some keening sound that drew his gaze. There was a wet mist of blood across my cheeks, my cuffs, my skirts.

My husband looked at me, blank with horror, and I stared back, this tear in reality stretched between us.

My husband, a killer.

In the distance, the guns of the shoot sounded, the yip and howl of dogs. They had not noticed Henry and Abney gone yet, but it would not be long.

There hung in the air a sense of the future rushing to meet us. We had been working to build one path, but another now fell over it.

I could not allow it.

This could not be. This path was not mine.

I had not survived everything I had to end here, with the stupidity of one man. I would wreck on the rocks of his downfall as surely as blood was hot.

A sob rose in my throat, and I swallowed it down.

No. No tears. No weakness.

I killed my heart, the raw beating thing that cried in horror at the monstrousness of what had just occurred. I drove a nail through it and buried it in unhallowed ground.

I could master this, too.

While Henry still gawped at me and the destruction that lay at his hand, I moved to the other gun and emptied it, dropping the cartridges into my pocket before replacing it.

"I was here the whole time. I saw everything."

He regarded me warily, the question unspoken.

"It was an accident," I said.

"An accident," he repeated, unsure.

"He handed you the gun—you thought it was empty like yours. He must have mixed up the two. There was a scuffle. It went off. Everyone knows he pushes things too far."

"An accident," he said again, warming to the word.

"A senseless tragedy. There will be an inquest, but we can pay the coroner. An accident is better for everyone. No one will want a murderer among them."

He flinched at the word.

Power shifted between us in that moment. We had held the shame of each other's pasts as ballast on the swaying ship of our marriage: now we were overweighted to my side.

So I made a promise to him there: the fiction I wove would become truth. For us both to survive, I would let him use me to launder his appetite for violence. I would testify his innocence, soften his edges, carry his guilt for myself.

He accepted—and spent me like coin.

Fool that I was, I thought it bonded us unshakably.

I think I have been wrong about everything.

*

The world lurches around me.

I stumble back from Henry's trunk, brushing the residue of white powder from my hands. I must wash them.

I stand in the middle of my husband's room and laugh.

Why bother washing them if I have willingly eaten this poison for months?

Everything looks so strange to me, as though it has been picked up and shaken until all the meaning has come loose.

This cannot be. Henry cannot be poisoning me.

But there is poison among his things, among the silly bon-bons he plies me with.

These two thoughts tilt and sway, their weight destabilizing.

I called Carmilla's words poison, but I have been so wrong. So very, very wrong about everything.

No. I will not allow this to be happening.

I repack the trunk, put it back on top of the wardrobe and quietly go downstairs to the new library. I will look up poisons and prove to myself that my recent illness is not caused by such a thing. From the dining hall, I hear nothing, and I mislike it. Where are Cora and Carmilla?

The library is quiet and cold, the shutters folded back so the blank expanse of moor is visible, purple heather turned gray in the dusk. I light an oil lamp and move along the shelves until I find a medical compendium. *A Dictionary of Practical Medicine* with the logo of J&A Churchill on the spine. Its pages have not yet been cut, so I fetch the scissors and work my way through the index, then begin to clip each page free in the right section.

Aconite, antimony, arsenic.

I read as though from a great distance, the page swimming away from me.

. . . a white crystalline or powdery substance . . . nausea, vomiting . . . cramps, tremors . . . faintness.

Frequently administered in small and repeated doses. The chief symptoms then will be the severe and continued ill health for which no cause can be assigned, a liability to vomiting . . . especially after a particular meal each day . . . patients are irritable and depressed.

The book falls from my hands. I do not hear it hit the floor, for the ringing in my ears has grown so loud it is as though I am a bell that has been struck, trembling through with the horror I can no longer deny.

I am poisoned.

Mechanically, I replace the book and the scissors, douse the lamp and walk back to the staircase. There is no light from beneath Henry's study door.

I look at my hands in the dark. Are they too pale? Is the poison on my skin where I touched the pastilles? In my mouth? My teeth?

In my mind, a white rot spreads through my body like mold, the meat of my organs and the red spill of my blood turned powdery white, corroding like acid. It is *in* me, in my bones, my gut, my lungs.

I double over and vomit onto the flagstones. Trembling, I wipe my mouth on my sleeve.

How long? When did Henry first give me a tin of pastilles? Weeks ago? Months? I cannot place it. Have they always been tainted? I imagine asking him, and, craven thing that I am, I recoil. Henry's anger flares bright in my mind, and I can hear his denial already. I am mad—I am wicked—I am heartless. There is no proof—how cruel I am to think such things of the man who took in a girl with no family and no money. I forget myself.

As I climb the stairs, I feel heavier and heavier, as though I am sinking deep into the peat beneath Nethershaw, down to the limestone bedrock.

I am being murdered, and I am too frightened to do anything about it.

In the corridor, between the door to my room and the guest room, stands Carmilla.

All the lights have been doused. At the far end, a window overlooks the limestone crag of Hungerstone Edge, a pale slash against the velvet darkness of the night unlit by stars.

Carmilla alone holds a flame, a candle, its pale glow gilding the jaw, cheekbone, and eye socket of one side of her face. Her chestnut hair falls free about her shoulders, and the white nightdress she wears is thin enough that I can see the dark circles of her nipples.

You are feeding the wrong hunger.

I take a step towards her, then another and another.

"Did you know?" My voice is a trembling leaf.

She cocks her head, a feline smile across her obscene mouth.

"About the *poison*," I hiss, and the word on my lips is a shock like a slap.

Carmilla goes into her room, glancing at me over her shoulder. I follow her.

I have not come into this space for many days now, and it is transformed, candles and oil lamps lit on the mantelpiece and the dresser, the shutters folded back to expose the slope of gorse down to the tree line. The atmosphere is close and exposed at once, strangely intimate, as though I am seeing her naked.

"I have been trying to tell you," she says.

"But you didn't. You knew, and all you did was torment me with it."

"It was obvious to anyone who truly sees you. But no one does, do they?"

"Stop speaking in riddles."

She has set down the candle and now reclines on the bed, propped up on her elbows, the nightdress riding up her thighs. It is obscene. "Very well. I shall speak plainly. You know the truth now—what will you do about it?"

She takes the wind from me in one breath.

I feel my cheeks flush in shame. It is as though she has looked into the core of me and found me wanting. "I don't know."

"Yes, you do." Her eyes watch me so keenly I feel stripped bare. "What do you want to do? Tell me."

"I don't know!" I say again, this time feeling the desperation of it. "There's nothing I can do."

She sneers. "So sad. Poor, poor sad dead girl."

"Stop it. I know now—I will stop eating the pastilles. What else do you want me to do?"

"You think he won't notice? That he won't find another way?"

"So tell me! Tell me what it is you want me to do about it?" I am frantic, my stomach a tightening knot.

"What I want has nothing to do with this. What do *you* want?"

"Stop asking me that. Why do you always ask me that? Why do you want me to be a selfish person?" I am crying now, short, staccato gulps of air into lungs that will not fill.

"Wanting is not selfish, Lenore."

I cover my face with my hands and sob, all the horror and exhaustion wringing out of me.

Carmilla sits up, fixing me with eyes as dark as the ocean depths. All the light in the room cowers from her, wild shadows leaping up the walls. I feel my blood run hot in my veins, the pulse in my throat an insistent drumbeat.

"The man you take to your bed wants you dead, and you will let him kill you. Only, no—he does not come to your bed anymore, does he? He is done with you. Aren't you *angry*?"

"Yes. No. Maybe. I don't know."

"*I don't know.*" She mimics me and leaps up. "Poor Lenore Crowther, so terribly sad about the inconvenience of her own murder." Her mouth pulls into a cruel laugh.

"Why are you like this?" I whisper.

"Because you won't *listen to me*," she snaps. With a finger like an iron bar, she jabs me in the shoulder. "I see you. I see everything in you that you will not admit, and I want *more* for you."

I take a step back, towards the door, pulling my wrapper closer about my chest. "You know nothing about me."

"No. You know nothing about *yourself*." She stabs at my shoulder again, pushing me off balance. "Aren't you *furious*?"

"Leave me alone."

"Why? You don't want anything. You're so happy to oblige. What if *I* want to push you?"

She pushes me so hard I stumble into the edge of her dressing table, the corner jabbing a bruise into my thigh.

My tears are gone in an instant, my mouth an O of shock. "What are you doing?"

She goes to push me again, but I duck out of the way, and she crows with enjoyment.

Finally, my anger rises, like a fossil emerging from the deep earth, something old and barely understood. "I mean it. Stop."

"Make me." She darts in and yanks my hair. "You don't know your own appetites. You don't know what you *want*."

This time, I am ready for her. Anger is like a heat beneath my skin, sharpening the gloss of her hair and the dark frame of her lashes, and when she gets close, I shove her first.

"Get *off* me."

Carmilla laughs in delight. She shoves me back as though we are playing. "Are you alive, little Lenore? Does your heart beat still?"

It is as though she has made mobile some long-calcified element of my soul, a great crack of a landslide within me as something shakes loose—something buried by death and blood and fear.

The curl of her lip incenses me, and I push her again. I am being murdered. There are no consequences to my actions anymore.

Carmilla falls back hard, not anticipating my violence, and the back of her head cracks against the bedpost sickeningly loud. She slides sideways onto the counterpane, panting, her eyes glassy.

I feel a spike of worry, some rote instinct to mend and master. I come to her side, looking for blood darkening the rope of her hair, but there is none.

A hand darts out and tangles itself in the lapel of my gown. Carmilla yanks me in quickly, so close I can feel the bright, radiating tension alive between our two bodies. It is something alien and sharp, intoxicating and repellent at once.

I want her.

It is simple, and it is impossibly complex.

189

In this brief moment, I know what I want, and I understand how completely that terrifies me.

Because to want is to risk disappointment. And life has so bitterly disappointed me.

I kiss her, and she kisses me at once, and all the acid panic flooding my body threatens to take me out, a feeling so potent I might scream or faint—I do not know what to do with it. But there is excitement there, too, in the softness of her lips, the warm flick of her tongue, and in the pure pleasure of pursuing what sparks a need in me.

The kiss is soft at first, as though Carmilla knows not to frighten me—and of course she must: she has seen more of the truth about me than I ever have. I should pull away—I can only take this in small sips—but then what other time am I waiting for?

I am here, now, and I want this.

So I kiss her back. Henry is the only person I have ever touched like this. It is quite different, not only in the softness of her body against mine where his was hard and coarse with hair on his chin and chest. No, the real difference is this: I see now that I wanted with Henry only to accomplish what I knew was expected of me. There was no heat, no hunger.

Carmilla sucks my lip between her teeth, and a bright pain lances through me. I draw back, putting my hand to my mouth.

She has bitten me.

My fingers come away red with blood. She takes them and one by one places them into her mouth and licks them clean. I do not know what stirs in me, but it is beyond words—only a feral, urgent instinct.

I push my fingers into her mouth as she meets my eye, and I understand her message.

"What have you done to me?" I breathe.

She bites my fingers in return, and I revel in the intensity of the sensation that pins me to the present, takes me from my mind and into every inch of my body.

"I have set you free."

Carmilla yanks my gown, and it falls from my shoulders, leaving me exposed to her gaze. If she were anyone else, I would feel ashamed of judgment, fear that my nakedness would be found wanting.

But not Carmilla.

I know she has no interest in flattery or lies. The hunger in her eyes is the truest compliment I have ever received.

I pull her up by the hair and kiss her again, the contrast of soft lip and sharp teeth driving me to kiss her harder, deeper.

She still wears her nightgown, and I tear at it until the fabric rips, and I can place my hand on the silk of her skin, feel the curve of her waist and the blade of her shoulder. She laughs against my mouth, and I am glad to please her.

We find our way onto the bed.

"What do you want, Lenore?" she whispers in my ear.

And I show her.

In the candlelight, I take her hand and show her how I touch myself. I am wet already, and it doesn't take much to make the pressure between my thighs build, so I pull her hand away. I do not want this to be over so quickly. I lead us back to our mouths, putting my tongue against the peak of her nipple, the hollow of her throat, and she does the same, nails digging into my back, teeth grazing over the sensitive skin of my breasts.

She stops at my throat, biting and sucking a mark into the place where my shoulder meets my neck; the pain grows sharper, like the slice of a knife. She has broken through the skin and is lapping at the wound she has made. It frightens me, but I do not want her to stop. Every rule I have ever laid down for myself is gone, and it is exhilarating.

I push the hair from her neck and bite her in return, marking her as she marks me. She makes a noise, high-pitched at first, as though in shock, and then something low and rumbling, like a purr of pleasure. Her blood is coppery and rich, salty and thick as I swallow.

My hunger builds, and I pull her from my throat and push her down my body, in between my legs, with the idea of something I have never experienced.

Of course, Carmilla understands. She nestles between my thighs like a cat curling in a patch of sun, the red line of her tongue flicking over her lips. I think of my nightmares, the weight on my chest, and my inability to move. I thought something terrible had been haunting me, but perhaps I have been haunting myself: Carmilla has but given it form.

I push her head down to the apex of my thighs.

I am hungry.

She works her mouth and fingers in tandem, and I am undone. I cannot think or breathe or hold any space for fear or shame. There is no control in this place. I cannot master it. The boundary between myself and Carmilla is gone, and when she sinks her teeth into the soft skin of my inner thighs, it only feels right, this transgression.

The tension builds and builds, and I know I am making a terrible keening noise, but I do not care who hears. There is only this moment, Carmilla, and everything she gives me.

The peak comes, so much more acute than when I have brought myself to climax, and every muscle in my body locks tight, a starburst of pure pleasure radiating through my body.

It is too much.

I am crying as soon as the wave of pleasure recedes, as though the sorrow has been drawn behind it like dusk pulling night across the sky.

Carmilla sits up from between my thighs, her mouth sticky with blood and fluids, and I roll into the pillow to hide my face, throat clenching, ribs shaking.

After a moment, I feel her settle behind me. She draws me into her arms again, this time with the softness of a lover.

"Oh, little Lenore. It is terrible to be alive. But it is worse to be dead to ourselves."

I curl into her side like a child and bawl, every tear I have ever swallowed down ripping its way out.

"Why me? Why me?" I am hoarse, my cheeks stinging with tears.

Carmilla holds me like an anchor as the storm of grief moves through me.

"I found you because you needed me," she says into the shell of my ear. "You were calling to me, dear Lenore, and I came."

I sob for every day lost before she found me. I mourn for the shallow grave of my dead life.

The poison I have fed myself, years before Henry and his arsenic.

I am dying. I am dying.

I do not know if Carmilla has come too late.

II

It is the living

15

I SAT AT AUNT Daphne's feet at twelve years old and did not grow since.

I think now how odd it was that I fitted so neatly into her life when I had been such an unexpected burden. But once I was there, I was almost always at her side. We ate meals together; I taught myself from lesson books beside her. While I embroidered, darned stockings, studied my writing and arithmetic, she would work through stacks of interchangeable books from the circulating library or simply stare out of the window at the dancing leaves or at the people below—or perhaps at something more that I could not see. I would borrow the books after her, and let myself die for several hours at a time, expunging any trace of my existence by remaining as quiet and abstracted as I could.

In truth, I craved it, for I was either at her side or I was alone.

The shock of the accident had shaken loose my memories of my parents, of my life before. I had a sense of two elegant but distant figures, a grand house and garden, changing ranks of nursemaids and governesses. I think I was alone then, too, but it was a place I was, at least, welcome.

I did my best to never think about any of it. It was easier to avoid the pain when there was nowhere for it to go.

On a dreary afternoon when I had quite lost track of the days of the week, I found, tucked between ancient copies of *The*

Athenaeum and *The Englishwoman's Domestic Magazine*, a faded penny dreadful. On the cover a young girl in short skirts, in the full style of twenty years ago, recoils in horror from a carriage rearing out of control.

I glanced up at Aunt Daphne, struck with the sudden fear she would spy my discovery, and watch me read something that felt so immediately personal and close. She always watched me, as though I was a performance for her own private audience.

But she had not seen me, so I turned the page in breathless anticipation.

The story told of a girl, an orphan from a carriage crash. I read hungrily, eyes drinking in the uneven print. Had I found myself? Would this show me a path forward? I was so lost and so hopeless it was like rain on my parched heart.

There was no great substance to the work, the kind I now know is churned out for a shilling at best. A heroine, a wicked plot against her, a standard villain, a moral lesson. The girl loses her parents and is sent to a horrible school, but there she finds fast friends. A wicked uncle has designs on her fortune, but he is thwarted by some good Christian. She is alone in the world, but ah, there, a long lost, loving relative alights upon her with a warm embrace. She is so good and innocent and brave, and all who meet her love her, and her goodness is rewarded.

The more I read, the more I sunk into self-loathing. I felt hot with shame, humiliation. How stupid I had been to think myself like this girl—to think that I might have a happy future. How foolish to think myself anything other than unwanted, unimportant.

It was as though the universe had drawn back a curtain and revealed a truth to me: only in fiction was there logic and sense. Good fortune and bad came in equal measure, the just were saved and the wicked punished. In real life, there was no limit to misfortune. You could fall and fall, and never reach the bottom. I had thought myself owed some happy twist of fate, some future good luck, but I knew now that it was only a dream. I was owed nothing. The ground beneath my feet was fragile and unstable, it could shift and break at any moment, no matter what I did.

I cried in soft silence, tears smudging the ink.

Aunt Daphne stirred, stowing away her glasses. "An early night, I think. I am too tired for anything more."

Either she did not notice my distress or did not care. I do not know which would be worse.

Once again, I found myself alone, watching the minutes tick down on the carriage clock, and listening to the church bells toll through the hours. The only way to endure it was to do my best not to exist. I had gone to bed at six the night before, drowsing myself back to sleep each time I woke, for it was easier to be unconscious than to be alive. Now, I was wrung out with tears, numb and dozy. It was too much to move my limbs or blink, my eyes growing dry and raw.

How frightening it would be to die, but how great a relief to sleep forever.

*

I am awake.

I am awake.

My mouth is dry and sour, my eyelids glued together with mucus. Fumbling towards the edge of the bed, I reach for water, anything on the bedside table, but my sleep-thick hands send something fragile crashing to the floorboards. I lick my index fingers instead and wipe the crust from my lashes, peeling first one then the next open.

I am naked, sprawled across a bed that is not my own, tangled in a sheet sticky with sweat. The air is humid and sultry, like a wave of pressure has descended on Nethershaw—for that is where I must still be, and this is Carmilla's bed. That much I remember.

But I am alone in it.

I am stretched diagonally across the mattress, and there is no one here with me.

No. I do not like that.

Where is Carmilla?

She must be here. I need her.

I peel myself from the sheets, slick and stiff, as though I sank into a bottle of claret last night. It is wet between my legs, and the first flickers of shame and ill-ease find me as I clean myself with a corner of the counterpane. A few red smears with the clear, and the pressure of Carmilla's teeth against my skin comes back to me in a sick rush.

There is no sign of her in the room.

Indeed, there is no sign she was ever here at all. The dressing table is neat, the clothes press empty save for the neatly folded pile of my dresses that she had borrowed. The whole room is perfectly clean and unlived in.

I look in drawers and under chairs for some sign of her, to no avail. We found her in nothing but a torn and sodden dress. She had *nothing*. What of hers would there be to leave?

Then, a small scrap of paper, slipped between the pillows, in a looping hand that I know at once is hers though I have never seen her writing.

Darling. Aren't you magnificent? You know now. Enjoy. I'll see you soon.

Distinctly uneasy, I go from her room to mine, as though we might have switched places.

How can she have left me so completely and utterly? It is inhumane, cruel, heartless. She takes me to pieces and leaves me to my ruin. I *need* her, and she has left me.

Coming back into the corridor, I encounter Cora, who gasps and spins to put her back to me.

"Lenore!" she says to the wall. "You have risen."

I frown. "Whatever are you doing?"

She coughs. "May I get you a robe?"

I realize then I am completely naked.

"No. I'll do it." I find one from my room, my cheeks burning. I feel stupid. Carmilla is gone, and instead I have Cora, and I am miserable.

I return to the corridor, stuffing my arms in the sleeves. "Don't look so shocked—I am sure you have shared many beds with your friends. You know what a woman looks like." I am angry at Carmilla, but she is not here for me to snap at, so Cora must do.

Cora peeps over her shoulder, and once she is assured of my modesty, she turns back to me and clasps my hands in hers.

"Thank goodness you are awake at last. I have been quite alone all morning, and this place is so unsettling."

I look at the cobwebs and twisted wood of Nethershaw and feel defensive.

"It's just a house, Cora." I focus on what she said. "Alone? Where is Henry?"

"I do not know. Neither came to breakfast. Carmilla sleeps in so late I thought you had joined her in the habit. Shall we wake her now?"

I step in front of Carmilla's door to stop Cora entering. I do not know what it is I wish to keep her from seeing, but I do not like the idea of her in this space where something so private occurred.

"She is gone."

"Gone? Did she disappear again?"

"No. It is as if she were never here."

"But where would she go?"

"I do not know," I snap. "Do you think me a clairvoyant? She is gone and told me nothing, and so nothing is what I know."

I realize I am about to cry, because it is all entirely true, and the betrayal has opened a wound in me I think could split me in half.

"I'm sorry," says Cora, cowed. Her face is a crumpled flower, and I meet it with guilt.

"Never mind," I say. She wants me to console her, and I would, but I feel spread so thin that there is nothing in me left to give. Who will console me? Who thinks of how I feel?

"I am glad she is gone. There was something wrong with her, Lenore—I did not like the way she looked at me. Her eyes were so dark it was as though she could eat me whole. Then today I woke up, and no one came to breakfast, and no one answered when I knocked on your doors."

"I am awake now. Go downstairs and ring for tea."

She does as I instruct, and I go to my room to dress, unable to find anything comfortable or easy to wear. All my gowns are like costumes, embarrassing reminders of my failed attempts to be different women.

Beneath it all, there is a low rumble of dread and the word *poisoned* whispered over and over.

Henry does not trust me. Henry has been keeping secrets from me.

Henry wants me dead.

In the drawing room, Cora and I take tea, the previous day's leaves rebrewed in order to save the best for the shooting party. Nethershaw feels tedious and mundane without Carmilla, and I

202

realize that I have never spent a night beneath its unsound roof without her. She is as integral to my sense of the place as the treacherous moorland and coarse limestone.

There are tartlets of jam and plum cake, digestive and garibaldi biscuits, some cold meats, tongue, bread and butter, and a slab of ripe cheese. I take a little of everything on my plate, but the idea of lifting it to my lips becomes quite repugnant.

Cora eats delicately as usual, placing nothing on her plate save a few strawberries and the lightest dusting of sugar. I want to eat to spite her restraint, but hungry though I am, I cannot do it.

As Cora prattles on, letters are brought to me, and a list of questions and problems form that I am expected to answer. Can no one think for themselves? It is quite maddening. I am in a house full of adults and not a single thing would get done if I did not urge it into being.

Very well—it is an excuse to leave Cora at least. She seems to have calmed to some pretense at normality and seems, if not content to be left with her needlework, willing to play her role in the day.

There is a great deal of correspondence on my desk, which I simply cannot face, so instead I ask the housekeeper to take me round the remaining works. Henry's guests will arrive in just five days, and I must take a view as to which room is suited to the men of which rank, whether to paint over the mold in the waterlogged dining-hall ceiling to disguise it in the short term, which flower arrangements to bring to which evening's dinner, and many other tasks I had once felt brilliant in assessing and dispensing with.

They have all lost their shine.

Did I want any of this? No. Why is this mine to deal with? Why have I worked myself tirelessly for someone who would rather have me dead?

I stand before the broad bay window in the dining hall, and brood across the heather to the drop of Hungerstone Edge, stiff and sticky in my day dress.

All of it, futile. Every year spent, every ounce of effort. I made a bargain in my youth, for safety, for survival, and it has all been for naught. I am not safe. I have never been safe.

So why have I tried so hard to create it? All I have made is a prison.

But perhaps if I have *never* been safe, that means fear has no purpose.

I am not safe if I obey and reduce and control, just as I am not safe if I rebel and shout and anger.

"My lady, the curtains." The housekeeper stands at my elbow, indicating the fabric swatches that have been sent by the haberdashery.

"Ask Henry."

"My lady?"

I do not glare at her, but neither am I capable of smiling. "Ask Mr. Crowther. This is his stage. Let him choose the dressing."

I go into the drawing room with my bureau and lock the door behind me.

The realization is maddening. All around me is Nethershaw, my marriage, the cold corpse of a life spent murdering myself.

Better be dead before anyone can come to kill you.

Only, it was all so stupid and meaningless, and now Henry truly means to kill me, and I do not know what to do about it.

It is easier to be angry than to be frightened. For I am so, so utterly terrified. How long has he been doing this to me? What damage has already been done? Am I too late to save myself?

Because Carmilla is right. I must do something.

I sit at my desk and piece through the stack of correspondence waiting for me. All the paper, from the creamy and thick, to the tissue thin and coarse cheap stuff, all the strokes of pen ink and licked stamps, all the people to whom I was nothing but a task on a list.

I sweep them up into my hand and toss them into the waste-paper basket.

I must think of what to do about Henry.

If I have been poisoned for many months, I must think first of my health. Perhaps I can arrange a visit to a doctor without Henry's knowing. It is not so unusual for a married woman of my age to consult a doctor if she has remained childless for so long, and even less so that I might wish to keep such a visit from my husband. There, my barrenness might come into use.

My second problem is how to avoid the pastilles. Of course, I could simply cease to eat them, but I must not fail to take the tins from Henry when he offers or I will risk arousing his suspicions. I can do as Carmilla did and throw them out of my window, grind them under foot—ensure no one takes a single bite. Then I can present Henry with ranks of emptied tins, and no dead wife to show for it.

Yes, I enjoy that thought. I want to watch him squirm.

Then there is the final necessity: bringing Henry down.

This is the hardest to establish my thoughts on.

As Carmilla knew, I am angry. I am furious. After everything I have done for him.

It is not enough that I thwart his plans.

I know what I want now.

I want him to pay.

Here, my cowardice rears up again.

Pay, but pay how? Do I truly have it in my nature to hurt him? To act against him? I am a passive, empty vessel at his side, and I do not know the language to articulate myself as something different.

I rise from my desk and pace before the window. The moor seems to mock me with its openness, beckoning me away from the narrow room of my life and out into its wildness. The sky is vast and blue, and the sun fierce where it hits the glass panes; the room is hotter than I realized; a rime of sweat appears around my collar.

Distantly, I think about closing the shutters to keep the rooms cool for our future guests.

There is also the matter of the poison. Henry still has possession of it, but until he returns from the works—I presume that is where he has gone—I have an opportunity to do with it as I will.

At first I think to dispose of it—then, hand on the doorknob, I stop myself. No. If I do that, he will know at once he has been found out. He will only move his plans to another method, given time. For once he has fixed his mind on eliminating me, what would make him stop?

Perhaps I can obtain a camera and make a record of this evidence? Or is that a mad thought? How would I even get one? What if he accuses me of staging it?

I could go to the police, but would they believe me? I could wait until he gives me another tin of sweets, and I could show them, but what irrefutable evidence is there that Henry has done it? It is all so impossible.

I return to my pacing.

There lies the issue. Whatever I do, it is too easy for Henry to deny it.

However the truth is exposed, my hand cannot be the one pointing to it. I must plant the seeds in another mind, bring others to this discovery as Carmilla brought me.

Carmilla. What has become of her?

I can barely think of our night together without a blush rising to my cheeks. It is like a fevered dream, some wild hallucination that could not truly have occurred—and yet I carry the marks on my own body to remember it by. What a strange, cruel gift she has given me: to truly know myself, to know pleasure, to know freedom—and to wake and find myself in Hell.

I bitterly wish for her aid in this, though I know she would never offer anything so uncomplicated as help.

I will search his study. Perhaps there is a receipt for the purchase of the poison or some other tool to build my case against him.

I head towards Henry's study, but I am stopped halfway along by the housekeeper turning the corner, her face as stony as the limestone edge.

"The police are here, my lady," she says. "They wish to speak with you."

*

Detective Inspector Lacey arrives in a plain coat and bowler hat, and scatters my thoughts to the four winds. I do not know what else to do but receive him in the muggy drawing room, a pot of tea ignored on the table between us, as though we are in London and I am receiving visitors. He is a fair man, with a snatch of freckles across his nose and forehead, and clear, blue eyes. I am sweating between my breasts and behind my knees.

What now? I hear Henry's voice in my head again: *no police.* Hah. I am such a fool. There is sense of a wave many times my height growing closer, the hush of anticipation and the sky darkening as the sun is blocked out.

"Is your husband home, my lady?"

"Not at present."

"Do you know when he might return?"

"No."

God. Is this my chance? Should I tell him of the poison?

Will he believe me, or will he think me mad? It is too outlandish a claim.

"We can leave this until he is present, if you would prefer."

"No—thank you. This time suits me adequately."

Perhaps I can try, if I sense him to be sympathetic.

"Very well." The detective takes his notebook from a pocket and positions himself ready to take notes. "This is not a formal interview, my lady, but I would appreciate if you can answer to the best of your ability."

I blink in confusion.

It comes to me in a rush: the injured man, the woman cooking on the range.

They want my testimony.

"Of course."

I am doing this all wrong. I should be welcoming and genial. I should take note of some aspect of his appearance to deduce a little of his personal history—a wife perhaps, or a hobby, some means to soften the tension that has caught me up.

"You were in the village of Hathersage yesterday?"

"Yes." Was it really only yesterday?

"What was the purpose of your visit?"

I falter, remembering Henry's anger.

I hold my hands still in my lap, though I want to scratch at the wooden arms of the chair. It is maddening. I must discuss some other woman and her desperation, when I want to leap up and drag Lacey upstairs, thrust the arsenic at him and wail for my tragedy.

But what real proof do I have? What good will accusations do me?

I want to tell him also that Carmilla, my only true friend, has vanished, but it has barely been a few hours without her, and I can say nothing of her past, her people. A strange woman appeared from nowhere, and then disappeared again—he will think me mad.

I feel dizzy. I have fought for mastery over myself and the hostilities of the world, and it has all been for naught.

"I was meeting a friend off the train," I say.

He asks me what brought me to the cottage in question.

"The commotion, I suppose."

What did draw me there? I fled the wife of the man my husband's industry had murdered—and came to a horror of my own. I had no need to enter, but I felt compelled to bear witness to whatever was inside. Like the girl with the chickens, it was as though there was some dark truth being spoken, and while any normal person would turn away from such monstrosity, I drew closer, as though the secret was being spoken just for my ear.

Carmilla, leading me there. Carmilla, who disappears at night and returns with muddy feet. Carmilla, seen walking the moors, leaving a terrible hunger in her wake.

Detective Inspector Lacey pauses, and an assessing eye roves over me, lingering on my neck. I remember the wound she marked into my skin with her teeth.

I shift, twisting to present my other side to him.

He clears his throat. "I understand this will be distressing, but can you recount for me exactly what you saw?"

I do as best as I can, reducing it to clinical detail. I do not tell him that it smelt like a banquet, that the dark light in the woman's eyes was like an invitation—like she looked into me and saw that we were the same.

I shudder, and Lacey pauses in his note-taking.

"Is there something wrong, my lady?"

I do not know what is wrong with me today. Snapping at Cora, harboring such dark thoughts.

"No. No."

His gaze drifts to my throat again, and reflexively I cover the mark with my hand.

Lacey puts down his pencil and speaks softly. "Is your husband often away from the house?"

I falter. I do not know what answer is expected, so I simply say the truth. "Yes. He has many business matters to attend to."

"I see. And when he is home . . . ?"

He leaves a space open for me to supply my own meaning. I feel alive with tension. Can I risk it? Will he listen to me if I tell him about Henry?

I know I should be cautious, but there is something ragged in me that cannot bear weight anymore. The words spill out of me before I have made a decision.

"Inspector, there is something—"

Before I can speak, the door opens in a clatter of bootsteps.

"Lenore? The housekeeper said the police are with you."

It is as though the ground drops out from beneath me, all the air thin and worthless.

I am too late.

Henry has returned.

16

DETECTIVE INSPECTOR LACEY STANDS and offers Henry his hand. He says something, but I cannot understand it. There is a ringing in my ears so loud I am sure others must hear it, too. Henry's mouth moves, a convivial smile on his handsome face, and Lacey does not return it.

". . . if you mean to interview my wife, I insist upon being present. I would know what business my family is drawn into."

"Of course. There is no need for a formal interview, though—I believe your wife has told me all she knows."

Lacey has folded away his notebook and speaks blandly to Henry, neither hostile nor ameliorating, and it causes Henry to be unsure of his footing. Here is a man with a pedigree not so far from his own, and so it is all the more important to make clear their different statuses, but Lacey will not accept the position Henry directs him into, and my husband is clearly unsettled.

As they speak, I am still pinned to the sofa, unable to move. Henry will sense I know his secret—I am sure of it. It is as though I have guilt written openly on my face, and the thought makes me laugh. I am not the one who should bear any guilt.

Henry and Lacey look at me, and I realize I have laughed out loud. I do not know what to say, so I only stare back at them. Once, I would have soothed and placated, but now, I look inside myself, and there is nothing to give. There is grave discomfort in my transgression, but it seems infinitesimally small against the pain of denying my own soul.

I want Carmilla here. She would be able to translate what is happening to me.

"I would thank you to take your leave, Inspector Lacey. Women are liable to lose their reason under pressure, and my wife has had a terrible experience, as you know."

Lacey bows his head, but at the doorway pauses, then takes a card from his inner pocket. "Should you remember anything else, my lady."

Henry takes it, but once the detective is out of sight, he crumples it and throws it onto a side table, before turning on me.

"What do you mean by entertaining male guests alone?"

I stare at him. "He was a police officer. I don't think it would have been a good idea to turn him away."

Henry comes up short. It is not the response he expected.

He takes another tack. "What did he ask you?"

"About the incident in Hathersage, of course."

"And?" He is frowning, lost in his own thoughts.

He will not discern that I have discovered his plan to murder me, because it does not enter into his understanding of the world that I might have my own agency, that I might set my will against his. I have not taught him to think any differently of me.

I am so incredibly tired—of Henry, of my life, of every response that comes to my lips. Why should I care about any of it? What consequences are there to anything I do?

"What else is there to say?" I say instead, setting my jaw.

"Did you say why you were there? You were foolish to take that letter and associate yourself with its contents—"

"Does it really matter whether I took the letter or a postman?" I cut in. "It will not change that a man died because of the greedy machine of your works."

Henry's disposition changes at once. It is as though an icy tide has washed through the room, a shock of force, cold, salt-rimmed, and dangerous. "The 'greedy machine'?" He speaks so quietly I must strain to hear, a pitch that promises danger.

But now I wade out through the shallows, braced to meet the waves. "Are you afraid you will be found cheating your workers? Is that why you fear me speaking to them? Or is there something else you fear exposed?"

I leave the taunt hanging, sure he will parse my meaning, but he is too wrapped up in his own turmoil.

"There is no culpability to be assigned. Accidents happen in all industries. A better man would have taken greater care of his workstation."

"A better man would take greater care of those in his employ."

Henry looks at me in resentment. "Where is this coming from, Lenore? Whose words are these?"

"My own," I say, and for the first time, I do not stumble over them.

"No. You do not have it in you."

He is so sure of himself, and I feel the first embers of a real anger ignite somewhere beneath my ribs.

"It is Carmilla." Henry strikes upon her name at the same moment it rises within my own mind.

Since Carmilla, something vital in me is changed. She found a crack within me and has levered me apart.

"She preyed on our hospitality." Henry's face narrows like a vice. "I knew we should have sent her on her way far sooner. She has poisoned your mind with alien ideas."

"My mind is my own." I rise, unsteady but sure. My heart races in my chest. This is new.

This is new.

"I think you have blood on your hands," I say, "and you should pay for what you have done in that factory."

It is as though I have slapped him. His mouth hangs open, slack, and then his fingers twitch by his side. Blood floods his cheeks until he is bright with controlled rage.

"Spare me your pious superiority," he snaps. "If I lost what my family has built, where would that leave you, Lenore? What would you have been without me? A penniless spinster trapped in your miserable aunt's miserable attic. You would be *nothing*."

I shrink from the blows. This is a step too far. I do not know this place, and I do not know how to travel through it—to induce ire, and weather its storms intact.

But I do know one thing.

Henry is wrong.

He draws back into himself, breathing a little too hard, and smooths down the golden curl of his forelock. "You have had a terrible shock," he states. "I will not entertain you when you let such a hysterical fit take hold of your senses." He yanks the door open and bellows into the hallway, "Cora? Cora!"

Later, I will remember this unexpected familiarity he has with her name.

My friend arrives a little too quickly, and I know she has been hiding nearby, listening to our argument. There is a flush to her cheeks that is not only from her girlish good health, and she looks at us both from under her pale lashes.

"Is anything the matter?"

I think, perhaps, I despise her.

"Lenore needs female company," says Henry. "Do something with her."

I sink onto a silk sofa once he has left, all the life draining from my limbs. I want Carmilla more than anything.

Instead, Cora sits behind me and pets my hair, as though I am her lap cat.

"There, there," she says blandly. "Let him calm down, and I am sure he will hear out your apology. It's all over now. I'm sure it was not so terrible a quarrel."

I laugh into the cupped mask of my hands.

Cora is so completely wrong.

It is as terrible as Hell itself.

And it is nowhere near over.

*

A sultry breeze tugs at the bonnet ribbon beneath my chin as the carriage draws past the gatehouse of the Bambury estate. Cora and I sit side by side, sweating in fawn and mint muslin, a picnic basket of lemonade and cold ham at our feet.

The ham is warm by now; I can smell its redolent odor through the waxed paper. We are late to a picnic that I had entirely forgotten about until Cora reminded me.

Yesterday, after Detective Inspector Lacey left, Cora slipped neatly into the role Henry asked of her, sending me back to my bed for my "shock," bringing up a tray of broth and bread, and reading to me from a book of Coleridge poems while I lay beneath the counterpane, unmanned. Cora went down to dine with Henry eventually, and I lay awake for a long time, tracing the bruises Carmilla had left at my throat. My life was over. Whether Henry killed me or not, this new knowing meant that the life I had lived until now was finished. It was as though a grief lay on me with such a great weight I could barely breathe. I remembered again curling into Carmilla's side and letting the anguish move through me, pain as old and deep as the stones of Nethershaw, a sorrow so vast I could be swept away upon its tides.

This morning, I rose late, unsure whether I could regain my composure. There was still no sign of Carmilla. Henry was not present, and I did not care to know where he was.

When Cora brought the picnic to my attention, I vaguely recalled responding to various invitations upon my arrival to Nethershaw, but the date and purpose of the picnic had escaped me. "Don't you recall me mentioning it? Here, I found the details on your bureau," she said, placing the invite before me at the breakfast table.

I refused anything to eat or drink, and allowed Molly to dress me in muslin, covering my neck with a high collar. I do not know what she thinks happened, and I cannot bring myself to ask.

Nethershaw has been Cora's household today: Cora marshaling the servants, and ordering the carriage brought around, and gifts brought from the kitchens. It is as though from the other side of a fogged glass, I see Cora execute the life I once intended for myself, and I remember the dinners I have planned for Henry's shooting party, the invitations I have issued to the local gentry to establish Henry and me as a foremost family in the area.

My God, it simply continues forever and ever. Dinners, balls, hunts, teas. And for what? What is any of it but animal survival?

"Lenore?" Cora presses her hand to my arm. "Lenore, we are here."

I come back to myself, unaware that I have slipped from the present for so long. Bambury house lies ahead of us, smart and bright in its white, neoclassical frontage and gently landscaped grounds. It is everything Henry wishes Nethershaw to be, and everything that is antithetical to its nature.

I cannot do it.

Before I have time to think, I lean forward to the driver and tap his shoulder. "I've changed my mind. Take us to the Botanical Gardens instead."

"My lady?"

"Do you have a question?"

He hesitates. "No, my lady."

He turns the carriage, and I sit back beneath the shade of the hood, fanning myself.

"Lenore, what are you doing?"

I shut my eyes. "I don't want to sit around with a crowd of women I barely know, let alone like, talking of the weather and hats and other nonsense."

"Oh, yes. I suppose it might have been tiresome," she says, though she does not seem convinced of her own words.

A quarter of an hour later, the carriage rattles over the cobbles as we turn into town, and I keep my eyes closed as we pass the cries of cress sellers, children laughing, dogs yapping, the rustle of wind in the trees.

Life. It is life.

"Do you ever think about how easily we die?" I ask.

"What on earth are you talking about?" Cora sounds a little nervous.

"Have I ever told you about my parents' death? We were in a carriage quite like this, and I remember how prettily the sun shone on my mother's hair. I tell people I don't remember the accident, but I do. I remember all of it. I remember being flung about like a flag in the wind—I remember the smell of the cows as they ran on all sides of us, like shit and grass—I remember the shattered glass that sliced through us all, like needles all over my skin—I remember the warm bath of my mother's blood as it ran down my eyelids, stuck my hair to my neck, and clogged under my fingernails. I felt her

217

body hot and limp, weighing me down. There was so much screaming, but I couldn't make a single sound. I think, in that moment,
I was pushed sideways out of the normal world that the rest of you
all live in, and I have been trapped here on my own behind a pane
of glass in some waking Hell."

I open my eyes and look straight at Cora.

"Do you ever have thoughts like that?"

The carriage draws up to the stone gate to the Botanical Gardens
on Clarkehouse Road. The gates are wide open, and families and
courting couples stroll in and out, dressed in white lawn and twirl-
ing parasols.

Cora smiles, tense and confused, the wary look of prey in her
eyes. "Whatever are you talking about? If this is a joke, I do not
think it in very good taste."

I see now why life is so kind to Cora. If it were cruel to her for
even a moment, she would not withstand it. She would crumple
and break with one blow.

How boring.

It is as though Carmilla is back with me, in that moment, and I
feel a great affinity to her clarity and candour.

I hop down from the carriage.

"Leave me alone," I tell Cora, and before she replies, I wander
into the gardens, past the glasshouses and fountains, the immaculate shrubbery and clipped lawns, and lose myself.

I hide beneath a parasol and take in this glorious day. I do
not know what to do with myself. I could do anything, and it is
almost paralyzing. I wish, deeply, that Carmilla was here to show
me how it is to live. I feel that I manage only a poor imitation
of her.

I follow first my desire for space, and move through the crowds
to more open areas, touching plants to feel their glossy leaves,

smelling each bloom to devour the abundance of the world around me. It is pleasing, but I am aware I am surrounded by so many happier people: those in love, with family, those who belong and know what it is they want in life.

I am so furious at anyone who is not alone.

Two women saunter just beside me, chattering about nothing. They are so easy together, so relaxed in their friendship and their own youth and beauty.

". . . ripped up the whole haberdasher's like a wild animal," says one in a conspiratorial whisper. Her bustle is too large for this year's fashions, and there is a speck of blood on her collar from where her hatpin has pierced her skin. "And did you know what she was doing with a length of Belgian lace?" she offers, leaning into her companion, who covers her mouth to giggle. "She was *eating* it."

I flick my foot sideways and catch the first woman with my heel, tripping her. She flies forward in a flurry of skirts, and her friend shrieks. Several people come to help her up, and with a flash of guilty glee, I see that she has hit her nose and a stream of beautiful red blood mars her lip.

The pleasure lasts only a moment. I can take out my anger on these unsuspecting people, but it is not their fault they have lived a different life than I.

How self-involved my pain makes me.

I continue to walk, hot and confused.

I know this is not what Carmilla meant for me. There has been too much revealed, and my mind cannot make sense of it all. I am a moth battering myself against the light, so easily burned in my desperation.

I spy Cora, laying out our picnic as though she can salvage some normality from our afternoon if only she follows every rule.

Part of me wishes to leave her sitting there alone, humiliated and exposed, to take my pleasure in her suffering—but it gives very little satisfaction.

What is the point of this cruelty?

I join Cora on the lawn.

"Oh! There you are. Did you have a pleasant walk?"

Sitting beside her, I spread my skirts around me. I cannot meet her eye. "Yes."

She gestures to the spread around us. "I thought you might still like to eat."

I eat a little, aware I am famished, but the food tastes bland, unsatisfying. First, a sandwich, then I stuff another in my mouth. I can see people watching me, the butter smeared on my fingers, the crumbs down the front of my dress. Let them look. I am a horror.

I take a madeleine and swallow it whole, then a fistful of grapes, a leg of chicken, a whole pie with its greasy pastry and thick gravy like slops on my tongue. I feel sick; I feel drowsy and numb. A reflex in me lifts my hand to my pocket to take a pastille, the bright, aggressive flavor to overwhelm my appetite.

But my fingers find nothing.

Poison or no, that no longer serves me. Its power is gone.

And all I am left with is my raw, untrammeled hunger.

I am a woman woken from thirty years slumber, and I would eat the world should it satisfy this empty, keening void where my heart should be. I would cry with grief over my life so unfulfilled, and drink down the salty tears, eat my worthless tongue and impotent fingers, skin this carcass and pick the bones clean.

Oh God.

There is something wrong with me.

I am so, so hungry.

Cora laughs again, bright and vital and pure as she tries to cover for my monstrousness, but I see the fear in her eyes—the fear that my taint will mark her, too. Other picnickers and passersby are looking. I look at the smooth curve of her neck, the unblemished pallor of her un-sun-kissed skin, and think about how I put my mouth on Carmilla and tasted the strangeness of another body under mine.

How powerful it felt to do exactly as I wanted.

I spit out a pear into my hands and drop it onto the grass.

I am hungry.

But there is nothing here to eat.

I stand abruptly, shaking a rain of crumbs from my dress.

"Lenore?" Cora's upturned face is so young and confused. She cannot understand this at all. Her appetite is welcomed and readily sated. She does not know what it is to starve.

"I'm leaving. Stay if you want. Or don't."

She gets up, blushing from the eyes on the both of us. "Of course I will go with you."

"Because Henry instructed you to watch me so I don't make a scene?"

She grows redder. "No."

For a moment, I wonder quite how much of Henry's thoughts Cora is privy to, then I dismiss it. Henry proved himself a coward at heart long ago. The only way he can kill me is if he does not even admit his plans to himself.

"Stop it," she says at last, once we are enclosed in the carriage. "You are behaving so strangely—it alarms me."

"I am feeling very strange. I keep thinking about death, Cora. How near it can be without us knowing. Perhaps we will both take food poisoning and die tonight. Perhaps you will be very old and in bed surrounded by a loving family. Perhaps I will throw myself off a railway bridge. Who can say?"

"Enough!" Cora's eyes are wet with tears, and I despise her. "I will not hear any more. You have been unspeakably cruel today, and I do not understand it. I must believe it is as Henry said: you are still recovering from shock. It was a mistake to come out today."

I lean back against the upholstery, jostled in my seat as we cross old cobbles. "It has all been a mistake," I say softly.

But it is all as it has ever been: I am alone. There is no one who will mourn my mistakes but me.

I am the only one who can right them.

17

CORA DELIVERS ME BACK to Nethershaw like a box of live snakes, writhing with latent danger barely contained.

That is a strange thought. I am thinking strangely.

Oh, enough—it is as much as I can do not to tear the hair from my head and smash every mirror I pass. I cannot do this anymore. I cannot. I cannot.

All the same, I am deposited in Nethershaw in a worse state than when I left, and Cora slinks away, grown wary of my madness.

Henry's study door is firmly shut, but I can smell fresh cigarette smoke. He is here. I imagine him on the other side of this simple piece of wood, leaned over his desk, examining some ledger or correspondence—or perhaps he likes to pleasure himself, looking over his vast piles of blood money, or—God—maybe he simply locks himself away to drink through the days and forget all the horrors he has assembled in his life.

I should have said something at the works, the moment the man was injured. I should have insisted Henry pay recompense in front of all his guests, to shame him into it. Henry is right: I have closed my eyes to so much for so long.

I am a coward, too.

I walk through the corridors of Nethershaw, hat trailing from one hand. There is evidence of industry everywhere, scaffolding and rolled up dust sheets, tools and timber, scuff marks from boots, and abandoned jam jars of tea. In the dining hall, I ease open the narrow door to the gallery stairs. I have never been up here, only given my commands from the floor. It is higher than I thought, a strange illusion of mastery over the hall below, as though from here I am God, observing all but set apart. The ceiling is freshly plastered and painted, the molding yet to be affixed.

I pick up my skirts in one hand and climb onto the carved banister, balancing against the wall with my other until I am stood high, high as angels, high as birds, high as the storm clouds. The parquet is so far below me I am dizzy.

It would be so simple to fall. My own weight would drag me down.

It could kill me.

Worse, it could not.

I look at the ceiling instead, drop my skirts so I can reach up and trace the blot of the water damage. It is damp again already. They have not done a good job. Or maybe they did the best job possible, and it still wasn't enough.

I dig my fingers into the soft plaster, and it comes away loose in my hands like dirt. A clot drops to the floor below. I claw another handful from the ceiling, as though I am digging into the earth, through the heather and the moss and the gorse, down to the bedrock of the timbers, as though I could climb inside this grave of a house and bury myself alive.

It is over. Whatever scaffolding I have constructed to hold my life up cannot disguise that I lie in ruins.

*

Sometimes, I think I died along with my parents in the carriage crash. They went to their own personal Hell, and I went to mine.

On the right sort of day or if the moon showed its right face, Aunt Daphne would become garrulous and pleasant. She would compliment the curl of my hair and the curve of my brow, talk articulately about whatever volume she was reading at the time, tell stories of her youth, of seeing the young queen crowned, the first railway carriages.

"Don't you want to hear about the Great Exhibition? You young people will never know a marvel like it." Aunt Daphne regarded me expectantly, long fingernails plucking at the faded muslin of her skirt. I knew this look too well, when there was something a little desperate, something a little hungry in the speed of her words.

I looked down at the copybook on the writing slope on my lap. I was teaching myself the order of precedence from an article in a ladies' magazine, copying out the lists of dukedoms and earldoms, and adding a delicate flower design beside the place at which my own father's rank would have fallen. I had found a very old edition of *Who's Who* and learned the nature of my lost status: if my father was the Earl of Dorset, it meant I had the right to be addressed as Lady Lenore, but that was all. The title had died with him.

"Yes, Aunt Daphne," I said. "It is very interesting—please continue."

"It *is* interesting, and everything within that shining palace was quite the most *interesting* specimen of its type. Do you know how many exhibits there were?"

Words were not money. I could not eat my title nor wear my rank. Before I was too old, Aunt Daphne would die, and I would be at the total mercy of an unkind world. I needed some other plan. I needed time to think.

"Lenore?"

"Yes?"

"I asked if you know how many exhibits there were."

"Oh. No, I don't."

"Over thirteen thousand! All in one place, something from every kind of art and industry, and from every country in the Empire . . ."

She took up her theme, and I returned to my list, dipping my nib in the ink to add some notes on patents and summons.

"Lenore." Her voice interrupted my thoughts. "You are not listening to me."

Irritation cut through me like a flash. "As you can see, I am writing at the moment, so perhaps you can tell me of the Great Fair—"

"The Great *Exhibition*."

"—another time."

We sat in stalemate, her eyes pleading, and my mouth an unforgiving line. Why should I offer her any scrap of generosity, when she swallowed my life as she did? What did I owe her in any of this?

I was struck, suddenly, by the fact that, without me, there would be no one to hear her stories—no one else at whom she could direct her spirit. It did not matter that it was me specifically; it was only that I was there, and I had nowhere else to go. I was a vessel, a figurehead, a carved saint to whom she could offer up her confessions.

Aunt Daphne's lips quivered, turning down at the corners. I knew the words that came next before she said them. "I'm not always the villain, you know." Her voice was tremulous.

I bit back the words I didn't dare say: if this was her defense each time, then she would never allow herself to be the one at fault. Her demands were allowed, mine unacceptable.

"I don't think you a villain," I replied, but it was too late.

She rose from her chair in huff and bluster. "You have no manners, Lenore. You have no softness. Your sharp tongue can cut."

What of *her* sharpness? Was it too much for me to want to think in peace about my own thorny future?

As always, she left for bed, though it was still daylight outside. I was alone. Again. As always. The sting of it was sudden and unexpected. I had thought I wanted the irritation of her gone, but it felt no better.

I had won a hollow victory.

Perhaps she was right.

I was a cold, calloused thing, unmeant for love.

*

Henry enters the dining hall with Cora. She stands close to him, her head bowed as she speaks softly.

Without thinking, I step down from the rail before they see me, drawing into the shadows.

". . . so strangely." Cora worries her delicate fingers together, and I feel a moment of empathy for this guileless girl.

"I am worried," she continues. "I think something is very wrong."

"It is Carmilla," says Henry without hesitation.

"Perhaps, but Carmilla is gone now, and Lenore herself seems changed—"

Henry speaks over her, running a hand through his hair. "It was madness to let a stranger into my home. I have lost control over matters, and I mean to take it back. I will not let the petty business of women undermine the success of this business that my father and grandfather gave to me to continue. I am on the cusp of greatness, and yet my household is in disarray because of some conniving woman who interferes in plans that have been months in the making."

Does he mean the shooting party—or poisoning me?

"Of course," says Cora, laying her hand briefly on Henry's arm. "I am sure all will be well. Perhaps Lenore—"

And then I can hear no more. They have passed through the hall and left by another door.

I feel sick, woozy, my heart racing too fast. The arsenic, I think, before I find the right word.

It is not only the arsenic that affects me so. It is my own rage.

I am *furious*.

The flagstones stretch far below me. If I wanted to end myself, there are so many options. I would rather it be by my own hand than by Henry's.

Perhaps, before Carmilla, I would have done it.

Henry is correct.

And he is a fool.

Carmilla started this, yes.

But I will be the one who ends it.

*

I dress for dinner, but I do not know why.

Ritual carries me through it. Molly places me at my dressing table and arranges my hair, buttons my dress, and clips my fingernails. I think about taking a hairpin and ramming it into the jelly of my eye.

"There, my lady—you look very well."

There are shadows beneath my eyes, and my beauty is lost behind misery.

I look like Hell.

Molly colors and hides her face, and I realize I have spoken out loud. The veil between my heart and the world grows thinner and thinner.

I do not have it in me to comfort her. She leaves, tension in her jaw.

The dress is too tight, the fabric abrasive and heavy.

I want it off. Now.

I struggle with the hook-and-eye fastenings of the bodice, tearing the fabric in my frustration. Once it is gone, it is easier work to pull the ties of my skirt, my bustle, let them fall to the floor like a curtain drops to the stage at the end of a performance. I bodily step out of them. In my corset and bloomers, I am lighter but not yet free. I am well able to remove my own corset after years with no maid at Aunt Daphne's, and I make short work of it, discarding my chemise and bloomers and stockings.

Naked, I stand amongst the ruin of myself, unsatisfied.

My stomach growls.

Even a condemned man must eat.

I throw on a fresh nightdress and dressing gown, and stalk around the now-familiar angles of the staircase, down to the drawing room where Henry and Cora await dinner. How stupid all of this is. All this formality and display—for what? Control. Mastery. Some sop of comfort, the idea that in this cold, loveless world we can overcome reality and impose our will upon it.

But we are masters of nothing.

Cora gives a squeak of shock as I enter. "Lenore! Is all well?"

I drop into a chair, fingers curling around the arms. "No."

She looks between me and Henry. "Should you be at dinner in . . . this state?"

"Do I not need to eat?"

"We can send up a tray—"

"This is my home. Why can I not come to dinner dressed as I please?"

Cora falters. "Of course. I am glad to see some of your spirits returned."

Henry, evidently, is not so glad. He watches me with caution, unsettled by the change in me.

Good. It is unsettling.

"Here." He stands and crosses to me, taking something from his pocket.

It is a tin of pastilles.

My stomach twists in a cramp—real or the memory of my past poisoning, I do not know. I feel hunted, like the hare exposed among the heather, a gun leveling on my soft animal body.

"An apology for my harsh words. It was ungentlemanly of me."

I do not know what to do with this. Is this a test? Does he suspect I know?

Or is it a challenge? He has taken the high ground, and he expects me to meet him on it, and deny the truth of what I said.

I could take the tin and stave his head in—smash the fragile bone of temple and jaw, flatten his nose and split his lip, crack him in two and find out if there is a heart in his body.

No. That is impractical. It would not be strong enough.

I shake myself, shocked at the tenor of my own thoughts.

What has Carmilla done to me?

Who am I becoming?

Myself, is the cold whisper that answers.

I take the tin, reckless, frightened.

"How thoughtful." I open it, looking at the rime of powder around the rim. "But where are my manners?" With a naive smile, I turn to Cora, who watches us nervously. "Won't you take one?"

It is the thrill of stepping off a cliff, the rush of weightlessness and the glee of transgression.

Henry's face turns waxy, a rictus of horror half-suppressed. "No—" he calls out before Cora's fingers touch the arsenic. "Not now. You will spoil your dinner."

She laughs, draws away. "That is exactly what my governess would say. How domestic you can be, Henry."

He laughs, too, faint and forced. When I meet his eye, I see fear. For the first time, I do not look away. My smile grows wider.

Cora keeps up a trill of conversation until the gong is rung, and we cross to the dining hall and its fraying plaster.

Henry and Cora take their seats, and I take mine as the servants bring in the first course of turbot in Dutch sauce. My hunger is strong enough that I eat before the dish touches the table, scooping flakes of fish into my mouth and licking the sauce from my fork.

Cora is watching me in horrid fascination, so I stick out my tongue with a masticated lump of fish on it, and she looks away quickly, color in her cheeks. The food is like dirt as I swallow it—tasteless and false. I choke it down, nausea rising.

We eat in silence, and I am done too soon, pushing the plate away in dissatisfaction. I have always eaten to numb myself, but now there is no blindfold thick enough to obscure my dissatisfaction.

God's teeth, I am starving.

I watch Cora eat, the flicker of muscle in her jaw as she chews, the fine column of her throat as she swallows, the delicate, tender skin. I lick my lips.

I wonder if her blood would give more satiation.

The thought brings memories of Carmilla, and I push it away before the pain in my abandonment cuts too sharp.

The fish is exchanged for veal cutlets, cold beef, beetroot, and mashed potatoes—a simple dinner constructed from the leftovers of previous meals. The kitchens have finished preparing for the grand dinners we will serve the shooting party. I have lost track of time. I do not know when these great men will arrive.

This food, too, is no sustenance to me. I throw down my cutlery in disgust.

You are feeding the wrong hunger.

231

The words come back to me as clear as though Carmilla is stood beside me.

I begin to laugh.

She understood it all, and I understood nothing.

I laugh so hard I shake in my seat, my eyes spilling tears and my jaw cracking wide.

Cora strikes up polite conversation with Henry as though I am not here. I understand. It is too much to look at suffering directly. We can only survive if we close our eyes; reality is not a thing to be experienced raw.

I despise them both.

I pick up a piece of beef and throw it across the table, its arc glistening in fat before it lands to the left of my husband's plate, splattering juice across his fingers.

Henry shivers with outrage. "What the Hell is the matter with you?"

I shove my plate away with a clatter of falling cutlery. "I am not hungry for this food."

"Do you want something else?" asks Cora nervously.

I lean forward, urgent. "Yes. Yes. That is the question. What *do* I want?"

A question for which I have no answer.

I thought it was the perfect mastery of myself and my world, to know and excel within any situation, to be impeachable, impervious.

To survive, at all costs.

But that is nothing but scraps of life.

I was starving and thought myself at a banquet.

Cora casts one eye to Henry, as though for permission, and opens her mouth to speak—but he cuts her off with a shake of his head.

"What?" I sit forward. "What is it you speak silently to one another?"

Cora cannot look me in the face. "Whatever do you mean?"

"Don't pretend to be stupid. You talk about me—I know it. What is it you have to talk about? What is it I have done that is so egregious?"

Cora is about to speak, but Henry shoots her another look.

"Enough!" I slam my palm on the table, and the cutlery rattles. "Tell me!"

"You are making a scene," says Henry quietly.

"Oh! A scene. How dreadful. Why, that's simply the worst thing any person could ever do."

"There is no point talking to you in such a state." Henry is cold, so assured of his superiority. "I suggest you excuse yourself until you are able to conduct yourself in a manner fitting for a woman of your age."

Oh. Oh, Henry has made a mistake.

"And how do you conduct yourself, husband? Are you proud of it?"

"For God's sake, is this still about the accident?"

"Accident?" asks Cora, but Henry disregards her.

"So many accidents happen around you, don't they?" I hiss.

He does not back down. "Women do not have the temperament to stomach harsh realities. I should never have brought you to the works. You are still only a woman, after all."

I slap a palm on the table. "Then why are you so concerned with what I do, if I am *only a woman*?"

"Don't pretend to be simple, Lenore—it is beneath you. A woman's behavior reflects on her husband. I thought I could trust you in that."

Perhaps I shall kill him. For a giddy, sick moment, I imagine it. Taking up the knife beside me, plunging it into his eye and ripping his face open.

No. His suffering would be too short.

"I wonder what else reflects on you, *husband*. Perhaps I shall tell Cora all about your *behavior*."

"What are you talking about?"

He is perfectly baffled, and for a moment it takes the wind from me. I can tell Cora that he once shot a man, and she will not believe me. I can tell everyone I am poisoned, and he will coolly deny it.

But then again, it will not occur to him that I might know about the poison. God, he thinks so very little of me that he cannot imagine I would see through his actions. He's right, though. I would not have unpicked that mystery without Carmilla.

Carmilla. I weep bitterly for the loss of her, folded over the table onto my arms, tears staining the sleeves of my nightgown.

There is a soft hand on my back, but I shake it off. "Go away."

The hand returns. Cora tries to draw me out.

"Get off. Get *off* me!" I yank back so violently she stumbles.

Henry advances on my other side, but I take up my wine glass and throw it at him. He ducks, and it shatters against the wall behind him.

"Jesus Christ, Lenore."

Before he can grab at me, I dash past, nightgown streaming behind me, and storm up the stairs to my bedroom, slamming the door shut and leaning against it.

I am lost. I am lost.

I do not know what will become of me now.

18

THEY HAVE LOCKED ME IN.

At some point while I sobbed into my pillow, someone came and turned the key. They would need to have gone to the housekeeper to obtain her heavy ring of keys and bring one to my door. I do not have another.

It is unacceptable. I would slap their shrewish faces if only I had my freedom.

No matter how hard I hammer my fists, no one comes.

This is *my* house. They do not rule here.

As I pound the door, it only rattles in its twisted frame, as solid as the day it was hung, however many centuries before. This is a castle. A prison.

Little demons inside my house come to count my sins and cut them from me pound by pound.

I must calm myself. These are not rational thoughts.

I will sleep.

I do, I think, sleep in a fevered manner, tangled in my sweat-drenched sheets, kicking my way free then burrowing under when the cold comes.

What is happening to me?

I think I hear voices at my door, and I rise to press my ear against the wood to listen to them. It is Cora and my husband, discussing me as though I am a distasteful specimen left upon their doorstep by a house cat, and now they must dispose of me. They talk about sending for a doctor. They say I am not sane.

I rattle the doorknob in my rage, and the voices go.

How dare they. How *dare* they.

If I am mad, it is only because they have made me so.

*

I am on the floor.

I do not know when this happened.

Dinner seems so long ago.

There is soft wood and rough fabric beneath me, the scratch of thick weave and nail. It is a little peaceful down here. It is not a usual place. I am unusual.

I remember returning to bed, sweating through the sheets despite the empty grate, then slithering to the floor, snaking across to the door, and scratching at the gap between the frame with my fingernails. Above me, the vines on the wallpaper coil and stretch, weaving an intricate pattern of shadow and light.

My skin burns.

It is like I am flayed by a thousand needles. A fever ripples through me in waves of hot and cold, my hands tingling, my eyes sweaty and glued together.

Am I ill? I must be ill. There is a fever raging inside me—of that I am sure.

Something has caught.

Is this Henry's poison? Am I dying?

I have spent these heartless days since my discovery drowning in self-pity. It as though, in this awful truth being revealed, every lie I have ever crafted to survive has come undone. The truth is rancid and unpalatable, a meal I have been unable to digest for the last twenty years. I am not safe. I have not saved myself. I escaped Aunt Daphne and the mausoleum of my youthful grief for a new prison of my own making.

I am dying, whether Henry poisons me or not.

I heave my aching body onto my front, pressing my dry mouth into the rug, breathing stale must, damp, dust, decay. If I am smothered, what of it? I touch my tongue to the fibers, lapping at it as though it is the dinner I abandoned.

My stomach rolls. I want something.

I think of the crucible that sits within the Ajax Works, as high as the roof of Nethershaw, an angry sore of molten pig iron crusting and boiling over, the impurities oxidating into slag and gas.

Carmilla is the coke burning below me. She has changed me.

And I am *hungry*.

I hook my nail beneath the wallpaper, tear off a strip and roll it into a ball, then put it into my mouth. The paper is sour, chalky. It is a struggle to get it down, but there is something in swallowing that satisfies for a moment. It is fleeting. I eat another strip but choke on it this time, retching onto the boards in a string of bile and saliva. Now that I have begun, it is impossible to stop. It is like those moments when I forced pastille after pastille into my mouth, gorging myself on the sugar, past the point of enjoyment, past the sweetness, past tears and loathing, into that calm, distant plane where I can no longer feel a thing.

But now I feel everything.

*

I sleep again for a while. There is morning at some point, thin and insipid, and I think of Henry's unpleasant little smile. How did I ever long for his attention? It is humiliating.

There is a tray of food waiting for me on the dresser. The room has been unlocked and opened while I slept, and I feel a pang of horror to think I have missed my chance of escape. The tray contains a small bowl of cold beef tea and some bread that is curling at the corners.

I wonder when the doctor will come. We are far enough from town here that it may take a little time. Or perhaps he is downstairs, making plans to declare me hysterical. Lock me up, kill me—Henry will get his way one way or another.

I am sick with hunger.

I swallow the tea in two gulps and tear through the bread, but it sits like a stone in my stomach.

No one comes, so I rove the room, looking for more to eat. I am dizzy and weak. My hands tremble as I overturn books and empty drawers, crawling on my hands and knees between my dresser, my clothes press, my trunk. Carmilla threw out all the pastilles, so there is nothing, not a crumb.

I scrape the ends of a rose oil lotion with my thumb and lick it off; it is acrid and harsh against my tongue. I go through the rest of my potions, scooping thick gobs of cold cream, slivers of lip rouge. I slump to the floor again, inching over the rug, looking for any dropped crumb. Nothing. I come to a chair leg, and it is as thick and solid as a joint of beef. My mouth waters.

I think of Molly with a fist of Carmilla's hair in her mouth. The girl with her mouth red with chicken blood. The woman spearing the meat of her husband's arm and tearing off strips with her teeth.

I understand them perfectly.

I take a bite, clamping my jaws around the wood, gnawing at it for splinters. I want more. I *need* more.

But nothing will fill this void inside me.

I pull the sheets from my bed and chew them like bread, crunch through dried flowers, the leather of my shoe. None of it is enough, and I am crying again, the rich salt of tears coating my lips. Carmilla was right.

Poor sad dead girl.

*

It is dark. A day has passed, and it is evening again, black paint daubed onto the window glass. An oblivion, a blinding.

The tray has gone from my door, and another one has replaced it. No doctor has come. Will I languish here forever? I think back through my time with Aunt Daphne, meeting and marrying Henry—all the ways I have survived. And for what?

I roll over and bury my face in my pillow. My throat is ragged from crying. I am empty of it now.

There comes a tapping at my window. At first I dismiss it as a tree—in London, the branches hang so closely they drop leaves inside my room when the sash is open.

But this is not London.

I sit up, head swimming.

The tapping comes again.

It is so dark and so cold.

Trembling, I slip from my bed and pad towards the window and the open shutters.

There is a smear of white, something moving beyond. A pale oval draws nearer and resolves itself into a face.

It is Carmilla.

*

"Come to me, my pretty darling."

She curls a finger against the glass, nail scraping down it.

I do not know how she is here. My room is on the first floor. Has she climbed up? Is this all some fevered imagining?

I press my hand against the glass over hers, a sheet of ice between us.

"Carmilla?" I whisper.

She comes closer, her red mouth a few inches from mine, and I remember the feeling of her lips, a wet heat that shocked me. Her face is as perfect as I remember, a pale heart and pointed chin, the chestnut waves of her hair, and the moon behind the crown of her head like a halo.

Her nail drags along the glass again, scratching a high note. "What have they done to you?"

"You came."

I pull at the latch, the painted shut frame of the window. I am still trapped.

"You are not," says Carmilla, as though she can hear my thoughts. "You simply have to do what you want, not what you think is safe."

I understand her.

Now, I truly hear her.

Perhaps I might experiment with a little violence.

I turn back to my room, pacing round to find something of the right size. There is a heavy pot of pins on my dressing table, and I weigh it in my hands. It feels good. Carmilla draws to one side, and I wrap a shawl over my hand holding the pot, then slam it through the glass.

A wretched, beautiful sound. Glass shimmering onto the floor. The cold bite of the moor air. My heart a bell, ringing clear and clean.

"Magnificent." Carmilla breathes softly over the jagged edge, her face no longer muted by the windowpane.

I pull out the final shards, leaving a clear path out.

Then I stop.

"You left me," I say, and it is an accusation as strong as I have ever managed.

Carmilla is delighted. "Ah, at last we can speak as two honest creatures."

"There is nothing honest about you."

"Nonsense. In what way do I dissemble? It is all of you who string lies together like a net, closing yourself in."

I cannot deny the pull I feel towards her, like honey and wine, sharp vinegar and the prick of rose thorns. I do not want her to leave me again.

"I do not believe your carriage crashed. I do not believe you have people waiting for you," I say, studying her face. "I trusted you once."

And you took me to pieces. I do not know yet how to say this, but I think she knows all too well.

She cocks her head. "Those are surface things, of no real meaning. They are only appearances. My heart is true, my dear Lenore." She takes my hand and places it over her cool chest, over the soft swell of her breast above her dress. "Don't you feel it?"

I swallow. "Yes."

I relish the touch of her breath on my mouth, the feeling of her skin beneath mine. She is so cold it is as if she is hardly human. These days without her have felt like a lifetime.

"I needed you," I say, like a child. I think of this madness that has consumed me, this hunger. I think of the girl with the chickens, the woman at the stove, the dark light in their eyes. "I think I am losing my mind."

With her other hand, Carmilla strokes my hair from my face, tucks it behind my ear in a gesture so gentle and small it seems unlike her. "No, my dear one. I think you have found it."

She holds me there for a second, and then she turns, quick and sharp like the flick of a blade, and draws me out into the night so fast that I fall against the windowsill, hips slamming painfully against the ledge. At least I miss the ragged glass, but the drop below lurches towards me.

"Come with me."

"Where?"

The night is dark like tar, no light but that from the lamp in my room. Carmilla is flush against the wall, but I cannot understand what it is she stands upon.

"Does it matter?"

"Maybe."

I see her tire of my hesitance, as though I am a poor student.

"Do you want to stay here?" she asks.

"No."

"So, what do you want?"

That question again. Before, it held me at the brink, an edge over which I thought it might kill me to fall. It is terrifying now, but tonight I recognize fear and excitement as two names for the same sensation. Something in me is provoked.

"I want . . . I want to feel free. I am like a hand that has been grasped so tightly around something that it has gone numb." I close my eyes, letting the tears that need to come spill over and pass away. "I want to let go. I want to *feel*."

"How wonderfully exciting." Carmilla's smile spreads wide and sharp. "Now, let's have some *real* fun," she says and yanks me through the window.

*

There is a moment in suspension, hung above the drop below, where the world flattens out—no, spreads out all around like a shell opening. There is no doubt, no confusion. I can see all. Before, I stood on the banister of the balcony above the dining hall and thought the solution to the burden of myself was to end it all. How foolish that seems now. How futile. I could go, and no one would care.

How much better to make them all regret knowing me.

Then, the lurch, the raised fist of my stomach rising inside my ribcage as we drop, drop, and the impact, blunt and immediate.

I have done it.

I am free.

Carmilla is somehow standing beside me, pristine in a claret evening dress, extending one manicured hand as though she was not just clinging to the wall outside my window. I allow her to pull me up, measuring the ache in my hips and the smear of cold mud along my leg. It was long enough a way to fall, but the heather is soft and giving; it cradled me in my landing.

In the darkness, we steal like thieves across the moor, wet ground sucking at my bare feet. Over the crest of the hill, there is a fine carriage waiting at a turn in the road, lamps lit at all four corners. From within, Carmilla draws out a green satin dress, the twin of her own, green as arsenic. She smiles at her joke.

"Where did you get this?"

"You should not hide your beauty from the world. It is something to be enjoyed."

It is warm, thank God, as I strip in the wild. The air is fresh and strange on the soft skin of my belly and my breasts. Carmilla does not turn away. I am as vulnerable as I have ever been, so it seems no great thing to ask the questions in my mind.

"Why did you leave me?"

"There was no need for me to stay. You needed to do the rest on your own."

"You are wrong. This was almost too much to bear. What have you done to me?"

"*Almost*. But you are here, are you not? And now, you know your appetites are your own. Not mine. Not Henry's."

I fasten the skirt behind me and slip on the bodice, turning so that Carmilla can fix the hook and eyes along the back.

I think about what she has said.

"Does this mean you will leave again after tonight?"

When she does not reply, I try another tack.

"Where did you get the money for all this?"

"I am a woman of means."

"That is no sort of answer."

"Do you truly need one?"

Yes. Some part of me does. There is a deep, old anxiety in me that cannot abide uncertainty, that cannot rest without all facts and knowledge within my command. To be so wholly in another's hands is unbearable.

But so what? What would I do with the knowledge if I had it? From what do I believe I am protecting myself?

The fear and hurt I have striven to master is pain over a life already lived. Mastery only muted my pain; it could not heal it. There are wounds I carry with me, and there is no way for me to unmake them.

Turning back to Carmilla, I am clear in my answer.

"No."

We mount the carriage together. The dress fits me well; there is a neat pair of satin slippers waiting inside, and with a few pins, my hair is up.

There is some heat in my blood that feels new and unnerving.

I have spent a year or more watching Cora move through the world as though she expects it to mete out gifts for each desire she names.

That is not the world I have lived in. But perhaps I built that world with my silence. Perhaps there is another unfurling, somewhere entirely unknown to me, terrifying and enticing all the same.

Who would I be if I was someone who wanted things?

Carmilla leans up to talk to a driver I did not notice before, and then we are moving, down the snaking road from the peaks and into the smoky crucible of the city.

It is a different beast by night, the light from the steelworks never dimming, a bonfire of red and gold from every building. The smog is hidden by nightfall, and there is only a moody haze across the gas lamps that burn low from lack of clean air.

Carmilla takes my hand and licks a line across the back, up to where our fingers are interlaced. I feel the sharp scratch of her teeth, and I flush hot with the memory of our night together.

"I dreamed of you, you know."

"Oh?" she raises one eyebrow and I sense she knows what it is I am about to say.

"In London, before I ever met you. I dreamed you came into my room and into my bed."

"How curious."

"Was it a dream?" I press.

She stretches, languorous and wanton, drapes herself across me, breath tickling my neck. "What do you think?"

I smile, and do not answer.

"What will you do first?" she asks me when we come to the city.

I look away, unsure.

This hunger that has risen inside me—I hardly know how to parse it. I can eat and eat and will never be satisfied. I want *more*. I want—I want to scream, I want to dance, I want to slap Carmilla for leaving me, I want to kill Henry for what he has done, but in the same breath, he is so beautiful that the animal part of me wants to fuck him, take the pleasure that is owed me. I want to rule Nethershaw, I want to bring only those I like into my home. I want to have money and spend it as I wish. I want to travel, I want to sing, I want to see the world, I want to rule it.

I want to be free.

I want not to analyze every decision that lies before me. I want to act on whim. I want to follow each passing curiosity. I want to make mistakes. I want to ruin things. I want to lay down the vigilant watch I have kept over myself and my life.

So. Start there.

We are passing the long blank wall of a factory, which has been thickly papered with music hall bills and advertisements. I see one—a play at the Grand Varieties Theatre. The poster is red and black with lurid lettering picking out the word *murder*.

"That." I point to it. "I want to see that."

It is only a play, hardly some grand rebellion. But this is instinct. Impulse. I can test the ground with this one small step.

Let me state what I want and watch the sky as it fails to fall.

Carmilla kisses my hand. "At once, my lady."

She converses with the driver, and we rattle over the cobbles along Division Street, onto Surrey Street then left onto Tudor Street where it meets the downward slope of Arundel Gate. The theater sits on the corner, its name painted in gold along the red canopy sheltering the entrance.

There is a crowd already, bunching around the main doors. I am amazed to see so many people out so late. Perhaps it is my ignorance; shifts are long in the steelworks, and I am too used to the quiet residential streets of Kensington.

Carmilla loops her arm through mine, and we join the press, edging towards the ticket booth. We take our seats, which I am not sure I saw Carmilla pay for, just as the curtain begins to rise. The play is *Maria Marten, or The Murder in the Red Barn*. It is an old tale, done to death and known by even someone with as reclusive an upbringing as mine. It is not the respectable sort of production I would be willing to be seen at in London, too close to the music hall and the penny dreadfuls sold by the fistful. A salacious tale of betrayal, murder, and supernatural intervention.

The production is mediocre, but I do not mind. I like the brightness of the costumes and the soft gas lamps in their wine-colored shades, the gild molding of the boxes and balconies above us, the high, ornate arch of the roof, painted like an Italian chapel. It is frivolous and charming and *fun*.

The story, despite its tired narrative, draws me in. Maria, betrayed by her lover, shot and buried in a shallow grave. I am hot with injustice, sick with my own impotence. Maria appears to her stepmother in a vision, and the law is brought to act upon her killer.

Who do I have who would pursue a reckoning for Henry's crimes were I to die? How could I ever convince the police of what has been happening?

But I cannot go quietly. I cannot let him get away with what he has done.

The seed of something grows within me. It is not enough that I stop Henry from poisoning me.

I want revenge.

19

REVENGE.

From the old French, *revengier*, and ultimately the Latin, *vindi-care*. To lay claim to, avenge, punish.

Lessons at Aunt Daphne's knee come back to me, the old, old schoolbooks with languages from dead tongues, speaking back a thousand, two thousand years before, of human feeling, human suffering.

Vindicare. To set free, protect, defend.

Vindication.

Is this what I truly mean? To take my vengeance would be to be vindicated in my grievance, to be proven right about my mistreatment.

It is a difficult, complicated thought. How far back does this mistreatment go? Henry, yes, but Aunt Daphne also bears some blame for the way I have suffered.

Does it mean anything, to blame them? One is dead and the other is blind to his own shortcomings. Will I gain anything in vengeance?

Carmilla and I spill out of the theater, and I let her lead me through the soft streets, our carriage following a little way behind. There is the rich sound of voices around us, the flash of a bright dress or vivid smile, and above, rooftops, shuttered windowpanes. The night is lively and fresh. This is a city for the taking.

We fetch up in something like a supper and song club, though this is nothing so salubrious. A series of rooms above closed shop fronts, tables set out around a stage where a sweet young girl in fawn silk sings songs that seem at first sentimental but with each verse lean further into the bawdy. Carmilla and I are placed at a table of our own, ushered in with little word, despite our being in the minority as women. There are men, finely dressed, packed into paneled booths and around tables, playing cards and smoking and yelling over the performance. Among them are women who I do not believe are their wives.

I did not know this side of Sheffield existed. I have been naive.

We eat robustly: chicken ballotine, boiled salmon with mousseline sauce, cauliflowers à la crème, potato dauphinoise, then a smart charlotte russe, bavarois aux pêches, cheese, heaped bowls of cherries and strawberries, delicate raspberries and thin slivers of pear and apple. A bottle of red wine is followed by a bottle of sherry, my glass forever full and my plate forever teeming.

I eat gladly, but only until I grow bored. I feel compelled neither to restraint nor to self-abuse. There is joy in food, tonight, but that is all—a simple pleasure that need serve no other purpose.

Around us, events lurch from debauchery to depravity. A woman is singing now with her corsets undone to display her fine breasts; there is dancing between the tables; someone, somewhere, is reading poetry; a pipe is passed, sticky and sweet.

"How is it that this place exists in the same world as Nethershaw?" I say, fingers tight around my crystal glass.

Carmilla is in her element, gaslight glinting on her jewel eyes.

"Did you know, the Duchess of Devonshire would play cards until two in the morning when she was nine months pregnant? She was *so* much fun."

The act changes, the singer replaced by a comic turn, telling a story I can't follow but for the vulgar gestures. I am too hot. We have raced so fast through the city; I feel a little sick. The room rolls around me like a ship, my hands slipping on the chair back as I stand. Carmilla bucks with laughter, licking sugar from her fingers. Her mouth is all sharp teeth and wet red tongue. The places where she once bit me ache in pain and want.

Perhaps this has been too much too soon.

I stumble through the supper room, looking for the way we came in; all the doors have been concealed by heavy red curtains, and I yank them open in turn.

A peal of familiar laughter stills my hand.

A table away—is Henry.

He has his back to me, but I know the curl of his golden hair and the broad strength of his shoulders and narrow waist.

On his lap sits some unknown woman, dark hair coiled atop her head, with her arms around his shoulder, her face pressed against his.

A punch of humiliation knocks the air from me. I scramble away, pulling a final curtain that gives up the way out. I stumble downstairs and into the street, sucking down the sultry summer air. I cannot bear for anyone to witness this moment of humiliation, least of all Henry.

There is a church opposite, and I stumble into the graveyard, touching the moss of the stones, sinking to the loamy earth.

It would be stupid to be shocked.

I went into my marriage with no naive notions of fidelity or honor. When Henry approached me at that bazaar all those years ago, I knew the nature of the contract drawn up between us. There was a trade: new money for old blood. He had kept his side of the bargain. I had not kept mine: with no child, Henry's ascent to the establishment would stop with him.

I think of the diamonds that were not given to *me*.

A hand on my shoulder.

I start, but it is only Carmilla, who has slipped through the grass noiselessly.

"Lenore. Why are you in this hateful place?" She lifts her skirts to avoid the gravestones and wrinkles her nose. "Come away at once."

I shake my head, unable to speak. I think I will cry if I open my mouth, and I am far too angry to cry.

She takes my hands and sits before me; we are two ghosts in the darkness. "Tell me."

After a moment to gather myself, I tell her.

Henry, his adultery proven. A life thrown away on a deal for my safety but not my happiness. My parents' carriage crash. Aunt Daphne and the cold tomb of her house, the quiet, dead hours in the same four walls, kept pinned by her constant observation. The babies that have not come, the regret I do not feel over it. There was never a path for me in this world where I could be someone who wanted those things.

"I have been so foolish for so long," I say. "I have let life control me when I thought I was mastering it."

Carmilla presses hot kisses to my hands. "Yes. Yes. But you know now."

I do not want my life to be over.

I have stopped Henry and his poison, but he has sickened me in body and mind. I have nowhere to go, no friends, no money of my own. I am free, and I am doomed. I have nothing.

"He has won," I say, eyes closed. I am exhausted by my own existence. "He takes whatever he wants."

I feel Carmilla's cold hands push the stray strands of hair from my face, brushing tears from my eyes.

But my face is dry. I am not crying.

I have nothing, except myself.

"I want him to *pay*," I say. "What if Henry was the one to find arsenic in his food? A rich widow could do whatever she liked."

There are so many accidents a man could have in a remote place like Nethershaw or somewhere as dangerous as the Ajax Works. It would not be so hard to do.

The idea is all too real in my mind, and some small, old part of me is frightened.

Carmilla cocks her head. "You could do that. But you would still be playing the game on terms he has set."

"So?"

"So, is he worth risking arrest? Hanging? Why bring so much danger upon your head when it is he who should bear the suffering? Stop allowing him to control the board. Play your own game."

I like that.

I must consider the hand I hold, for there must be some power in it.

I think of the blood spray across the grinding room at the works. Blood pooling on the kitchen table in Hathersage. Smeared on the mouth of the girl in the farm.

I do not need to contain my appetites.

What is a monster but a creature of agency?

*

There is a memory, as pure and clean as rainwater, that rises up within me so often.

If I could will my past to disappear, it would have done so already, so much have I longed to pare its rotten meat from my flesh.

I passed eight long and silent years with Aunt Daphne, and it was, I suppose, inevitable that some sort of bond would grow between us, from prolonged exposure and the natural human instinct to become attached. We were fraught, and both of us damaged, but still we were not without love.

When I told her of my engagement to Henry, she cried. I thought then it was in happiness, but later, once the marriage turned, I thought perhaps she cried *for* me, sensing something of my fate. Now, I think she cried as much for herself. I was leaving her, and she knew she would not survive it.

We had no money for wedding clothes, so she went to the camphor trunks to retrieve an old gown of her own, only a little moth-eaten. The bell skirts gave plenty of spare silk and tulle and lace for me to cut my own wedding dress. I ran my hand across the fabric and felt a rush of something unnameable. Fear? Hope? Care?

I worked at the table in her drawing room, unpicking each seam and laying out the pieces to match against my new pattern. Aunt Daphne watched me from her chair, silent but attentive.

"You have a very steady hand," she said as I ran the scissors along the new shape of the fabric. "I have always been far too clumsy. I could never make such neat work."

I stopped my cutting. *You do not have to put yourself down to compliment me*, I meant to say but I did not know how.

"Thank you. I hope it will look passable."

"You are beautiful, Lenore. People will not like you for it."

"Henry likes it well enough."

"My own mother was so beautiful," she said, as if not hearing me. "Hair like corn. Everyone in town would stop to watch her."

I had never asked Aunt Daphne about her past, and she offered up little of it. I wondered then if I had been thoughtless in not inquiring more. To my child's mind, her isolation in this house had seemed a fixed point; it had not occurred to me to look for a reason for it. Now, as a fledgling, my curiosity came. I would ask her after the wedding, I thought. Maybe with Henry's money I could make her rooms a little warmer, bring in a companion for her now that I would be leaving her alone.

How strange that loneliness was the thing we traded between each other. In another life, perhaps we could have brought each other closeness. Perhaps.

Outside the church where I was to be married in my white silk, I lowered the lace veil over my face so that it was as though the world had been lost in a snowstorm. There were white roses in my hair, and in gloved hands I held a posy of white hothouse blooms. I had seen Aunt Daphne delivered inside to a pew. I did not know when she had last left the house, not since my early days out in society, and I was shocked by the gesture.

Henry was keen for the deal to be done as swiftly as possible, as though I was a fish that will wriggle off his hook. I had no father whose permission he must seek. Aunt Daphne had refused his visit but made no objections to the marriage. On the matter of my future, there was no one else but me to consult, and I had signed it over to Henry. There was only the paperwork left to complete.

I could not afford the common license, so I would take whatever path Henry set us on gladly. I had no sister to play bridesmaid, no mother whose tastes I must satisfy, and no money to do any such thing should I desire it. Henry paid for my trousseau, and the shame of it lay hot in my throat. A school friend of Henry's was both his best man and witness. This friend was dropped a few years after, when Henry felt he had risen into smarter circles.

Outside, stood fatherless in the porch, it was all before me. I would walk the aisle alone, and for the first time in many years, I felt the deep humiliation of my situation. A friendless child in a friendless world makes life a job of survival. The dreams and joys of my early years were so long lost I could barely taste them, and their remains were bitter, rotten. What had I once dreamed of for my wedding day, when had I been so naive as to think I could make choices for my happiness?

Aunt Daphne had known.

The memory will not leave me: I stand alone at the church doors, the air chill around my throat, and I do not think to run for even a moment. I have sunk so far that I know there is no hope for anything more than this.

It is not possible, even in my imagination.

And then, a matter of days later, the last person left to me was gone. Aunt Daphne died, and in her I lost the only person who needed me. Henry, no—he has never needed me. He wanted what I could give him and knew how to wield the tool that I was. Cora has well used me, too, to perform her own social elevation.

Aunt Daphne, in her own hurtful, desperate way, needed me.

There is not a single soul alive who cares what happens to me, now.

*

My husband has always been a mystery to me. Husband seems such a warm, familiar word for someone with whom I have occupied similar spaces yet entirely separate lives. At first, I hoped we might grow to truly love each other, over time, over shared burdens and joys. But this seemed impossible. I found myself eternally tense in his presence, watching him carefully to spy his moods and divine his need from the auguries of the set of his mouth or the tone of his voice. I was alert to threat at every moment, a woman living inside a tiger cage.

I wish I could say he was a monster from the start, but it was not so. He was far from a perfect man, but he was no painted devil. I think perhaps I carried some poison with me, a crack in my foundation that made me distrustful, defensive, on guard. There was too great a wound running through me to live any other way.

It was not until Carmilla came that I could see clearly. Henry's very presence was the threat, as Aunt Daphne's had been in my years of forced confinement. Another I believed held total power over me, to force my own soul into silence and replace it with their own.

I was a tool, not a person.

Only, for Henry, I was a poor one. And I, a failure in my own mind.

As we take the carriage back through the river valley towards the moorland tops, each moment of hurt rushes over me. So much acute loneliness. So much want, starvation.

In the first year of our marriage, he would ask more months than not whether I had news for him. After my first twelve failures to fulfill my role, he stopped asking. He traveled more for business, stayed out late, and I learned not to ask where or why. Our Holland Park house became a second enactment of Aunt Daphne's house, only now, I was completely alone. I had a phalanx of staff, and not a single soul who saw my heart. I entertained, yes, took calls and paid visits, made precise schedules for Henry to appear at the social occasions necessary, made charitable donations, patronized the arts, even found a few protégées like Cora who saw me as a useful stepping stone to their own desires.

But Carmilla was right.

I was dead.

I have been dead for so many years.

*

The road breaks through the forest to a stretch of river sheltered by trees but canopied by bright starlight. The clouds have shifted, and the world is silvered and unreal.

I knock on the carriage roof to stop and climb out to look at the spread of constellations overhead. It is overwhelmingly beautiful, and I begin to cry.

I have made so many mistakes. I grieve so deeply for myself.

All I have is the hope Carmilla has brought me. And this truth: I cannot master the world and hope to fix everything in its place. This cannot bring fulfillment.

All we can hope for in life is to know one's own desires in order to be able to act on them. To *want* is to surrender to uncertainty. To step into the unknown. To expose ourselves to all possible outcomes and trust we will not be destroyed by disappointment.

Oh, how powerful that fear has been.

But the things I feared have already happened. I have lost my parents. I have lost my youth and joy to Aunt Daphne. My marriage to Henry. I am so alone and so unsatisfied.

What have I left to lose?

I turn to Carmilla, who has joined me, and pull her mouth to mine.

"Ah." She smiles against my lips. "There you are."

"Make me feel something," I say. "Tell me I am alive."

Our kiss is hot and sharp, fingers tangled in hair and nails on skin. My dress comes off first, hers after as I trail my lips and tongue across her, feeling the soft curve of her breast and the flesh of her thighs. I am a drowning woman clinging to a wreckage, but I will sing so loud as I go down.

The night air is sultry and thick, so I lead us to the river and down the banks into its diamond dark water. Carmilla swims out and rolls onto her back, letting her hair fan around her. I follow, but she darts away, and I chase, a game between us that riles my desire higher each time I am bested. At last, I catch her along a stretch of rock, pinning her in place, this strange marvel mine to contain.

I go to kiss her again, but she catches my hand instead, and draws it down. But I do not touch flesh. She has pressed my palm against the rock behind her.

"Do you know what a hunger stone is?" she asks, breath warm against my skin.

I shake my head.

"In times of drought, there are stones that are only exposed when the river runs so low. People mark them, so that, next time, they will know when they are to starve. Their appetite will go unfilled." She runs my fingers over a cut in the stone. "It is a death marker."

I dip my mouth to hers but again she moves, and I raise my eyebrow in question.

"You see the river now, though. This stone is long drowned. The water is free and powerful and raging." This time, she brings my hand to her lips and sucks the length of one finger into her mouth, before releasing it with a wet sound. "It is unleashed."

With a growl, I catch her hair to hold her still and kiss the column of her throat, the peaks of her breasts, biting and nipping at her skin. Her hands claw my back, her body arching in pleasure, and we fall into each other in hunger and delight. We feast upon each other, chasing desire and satisfaction. My body is all animal: I am nothing but want.

I will starve myself no longer.

"Take me back," I say, when we are done and panting on the shore. "I have unfinished business."

20

WITH CARMILLA'S HELP, I scale the wall and return to my bedroom the way I exited. We have concealed the shattered glass as best we could beneath the flowers in their beds, and after a final kiss, I close the shutters to hide the broken pane.

Alone and still, I wait for dawn.

There is much to think about.

I want justice. I cannot poison Henry in return; there is too much risk for my own future. I cannot reliably prove his guilt; I have already done too much to paint myself a hysteric.

But perhaps there is another way.

I want to see him taken apart. I want him exposed—under my control and releasing me from fear.

I have an appetite for revenge.

What did Carmilla say? I must play the hand I hold.

Henry and Cora believe me mad. They have sent for a doctor. There is danger there—but Henry is not without his vulnerabilities. He does not know Cora has divulged his secrets to me. His anger betrayed him when he found that I had read the letter I delivered to Hathersage. His business is not so neatly sewn up as he would have us all believe. His temper would not be fraying if it was. That he risks reigniting memories of the shooting party *accident* nine years ago shows that he is desperate. And that he thinks he has me to heel.

That is something in my power: he will not move against me before the party. There is too much riding on it. I can see now how it would play out in his plans: a display of his arrival into high society, but a visibly ailing wife witnessed by all—a wife with little surviving family and no ability to conceive. There must be weak blood; it would be no surprise when I died. He would be free to remarry, having safely inserted himself into the establishment.

What a delight it will be to deprive him of it all.

*

There is a knock on the door in the early morning, when the rosy light has warmed the curling vines of my walls. I know what must be coming. I have folded back one shutter to let in the light, tided the room as best I can, brushed and pinned my hair, and put on a clean day dress. I have left the dark circles beneath my eyes and the pallor in my cheeks. I am the very picture of the tired, dutiful wife: polite, good, gentle, only the nerves a little taxed, feeling the strain as a new mistress of a grand house. What doctor would not understand that?

Cora comes in first, cautious as a little mouse, nose twitching and hands twisting together. She does not know what to do, finding me sat by my dresser, so nicely presented.

"You're awake!" she says, and I pity her. How I must be ruining her plans, too.

The doctor comes in behind her, and she remembers herself.

"Lenore, this is Dr. Foxfield. He has come to see if you are quite all right after . . ."

She trails off, that unsettling dinner lying unspoken between us.

This is a different doctor than the one that came to treat Carmilla. They do not think this a malady of the body.

I lower my eyes, a little smile of embarrassment playing upon my lips. "Oh yes. I made quite a spectacle—I do not know how I can excuse myself."

Dr. Foxfield seems pleased by this—I wonder if he has already offered such a conclusion to Henry, said that I have merely had a turn, as women are wont to do. Here I am, to prove all his cleverness right.

He comes to my side and makes a small bow. "My lady, your husband and friend have asked me here to check on your health as you have caused them both quite a deal of worry. You are lucky to have such dear people to look out for your well-being."

Now I look up at him through my lashes, all earnestness and hope. "You are entirely right. I feel quite ashamed." I look at Cora and then to the doctor. "May we speak privately?"

"Of course."

Cora reluctantly leaves. I am sure she will be waiting outside with her ear pressed to the door.

"What is it you wished to tell me?" asks the doctor.

"I am so very embarrassed to admit it," I say carefully, "but I have never been mistress of a house such as this before. It is quite the task to be responsible for, and I have been so terribly worried that I have not risen to it. My husband counts on me, and I am so afraid I have let him down." It is too easy to let a tear fall.

"Oh dear." He pats my hand perfunctorily. "How you women do let your burdens fall upon your spirit so heavily. Heavens, look around you. What a fine house and a fine welcome I have been met with. A little less time spent with books and solitary thoughts, I'd suggest, and a little more in lively, wholesome activities. I am sure your young friend is more than keen to have you show her the ropes, if you will excuse the rough language."

He softens his voice and turns to me, and I anticipate his next words with a sudden clarity.

"When a marriage is not blessed by children, there is a natural vulnerability to a woman's sensibilities—a maternal energy that cannot be appropriately placed. Do you understand what I am saying?"

I nod sharply, my discomfort not feigned this time. "I do."

"In such circumstances, one must find other outlets, or it is possible to become destabilized."

"Destabilized." I latch on to the word. "Do you think that is what I am?"

For a moment, I wonder if he is correct. Has this all simply been the effect of my fickle female physiology? Am I simply a predictable woman, undone by the matter of my maddened flesh and blood?

I watch Dr. Foxfield closely. Have I done enough to convince him?

He leans back in his seat, appraising me. "Ah. Well. Perhaps for a short time, but I think you are a bright woman, and you have listened well to everything I've had to say. Your dedication to your husband is admirable—but leave the worrying to him. Your prettiness and good cheer is the greatest boon you can offer him."

He goes to the door and directs Cora to bring Henry.

My palms sweat. I am frightened to face my husband after how I behaved. I revealed too much of myself, and I am sure it was a mistake.

Henry appears in shirtsleeves, a curl of hair falling in his face, and I hate that he has only become more handsome with each year.

"Well?" he says, glancing at me warily.

I hold my breath.

Dr. Foxfield waits for him to step into my room.

"Nothing to worry about," he says, and Henry does not relax. "I don't suspect a full-blown case of hysteria—far from it."

Henry looks around the room as though he might find some evidence of my insanity. "Did Cora give you a full account? The girl can be skittish—she may have missed some of the . . . gorier details."

"No, no, she was quite forthcoming."

"Oh." Henry looks at me as though I have cast some sort of spell over the doctor. "So then you think . . ."

"A moment of fragility of the nerves, which is not unusual among women in your wife's position. Hysteria is too often the result of an active, bright mind in an enfeebled body that is ill-suited to the functions for which it was made, easily disordered and prone to react abnormally to the ordinary stimuli of life. But your wife seems a robust woman, and with the right mental direction will quickly recover her former spirits."

I hold Henry's gaze. "I can only apologize for causing you and Cora such distress," I say sweetly. "I am embarrassed that you saw me in such a state. A husband should not have to worry about his wife in such a way."

Dr. Foxfield appears quite pleased by my speech. "There we are." He scrawls a note onto a piece of paper. "It is understandable to worry. Valerian and asafetida may be of some help. Your housekeeper should be more than capable of preparing anything required."

He waits, paper in hand, until Henry remembers himself and takes out some coins.

Dr. Foxfield turns back to me with a smile. "And remember what we discussed. A better outlet."

"Yes, Doctor."

He goes, and Henry and I are left alone with the detente constructed between us.

"That was very expensive," he says, and I almost laugh. Of all the things to care about.

I don't say anything, and that unnerves him even more.

He shuts the door on me, and at last, I breathe out.

I rise, smoothing down the rumpled silk of my day dress, and press my hands against my rolling stomach.

Now, my work must begin.

*

I descend to luncheon dressed for war.

My hair is immaculate, my dress neat and stylish, each ornament at throat or wrist perfectly chosen. I am unassailable.

I join Henry and Cora as they arrive in the conservatory from disparate parts of the house. It is the newest portion of the building, a structure of wrought iron and glass affixed to the outside wall of the morning room, with double doors that open onto the rolling heathland. The sun is strong today, and blinds have been drawn across the glass to protect us from its wrath. A sweet breeze blows, carrying the scent of ling and bell heather, and the sound of bees drowsing between blossoms. Great banana leaf palms and monstera reach towards the ceiling, bringing with them a humidity in strange contrast to the fresh moorland.

"Lenore." Cora greets me with a kiss on each cheek in the continental style, and I wonder from whom she has adopted this affected habit. "How good it is to see you looking well."

"Thanks to your care," I say, returning the kisses.

We sit, Henry stiff as a fence post, to a luncheon spread of risotto, cold veal and ham pie, salad, then blancmange and stewed fruit, butter, cheese, bread, and biscuits. I take a little of each and eat thoughtfully.

I have been turning over Henry's weaknesses in my mind, and a plan is forming. I know better than any the places where his soft underbelly shows, but I will need a measure of privacy to achieve my aim.

"Cora," I begin, turning to my increasingly nervous friend, "I must ask a favor of you."

"Of course."

The color has much left her cheeks since she came to stay with us; there is a bruised look about her eyes suggesting lost sleep. It is something to know that she, like all of us, succumbs to human frailty. Perhaps in time it may allow me to feel a little more generous towards her.

"I have placed orders for several new hats at a milliner's in town, along with quite a sizeable order at the haberdasher's for all sorts of things. I daren't tax my strength to fetch them myself, but I would so appreciate your keen eye on each item before they are delivered. You have such fine taste—I feel assured that any faults or short-comings could be resolved by your good sense."

She breaks out in an entirely genuine smile. "I would be glad to offer my assistance. If you are quite sure—"

"I am entirely convinced of it."

Henry watches our exchange in brooding silence. Good. I will let him stew a little longer.

Cora and I talk on, discussing menus for the shooting party, place settings, and what sort of flowers to put in the guest rooms, seating plans and entertainment for the wives who will be staying.

Henry interrupts only to insist on sitting next to some lord with a hand in the colonial service in order to solicit mass orders for the cutlery coming out of the Ajax Works.

Sweetly, I correct him that the order of precedence dictates otherwise.

"What on earth do you mean? They're both earls—don't I get some say in this arrangement?"

"English peers come before Scottish peers, I'm afraid. Unless you would like this to be a more . . . informal gathering?"

He is embarrassed by this gap in his knowledge, fingers twitching around his knife. I almost feel a little guilty for pressing upon the bruise of his parentage. I have fallen low enough in this life to know not to judge anybody upon their circumstances; it is not I who thinks Henry's background shameful, but him. But if he will wear his sensitivity so plainly, then I will use all the weapons at my disposal.

"No." He is sullen as a schoolboy. "Sit me next to the damn English earl then. I want this done properly, Lenore."

"It will be, but you will have to trust me on that, won't you?"

There is a thick cord between us, the tension held evenly at present, but both of us primed for a pull, for something that will throw us off-balance.

Cora refills her glass and takes a quick sip. "Perhaps it would be better if I returned to London before the guests arrive," she offers. "I must be something of a distraction."

"Of course you must stay, Cora," I say, pressing her hand. "Mustn't she, Henry?"

He makes a gruff noise I take as assent, and saws at a tranche of pie.

When the meal is over, Cora readies herself for her trip to town.

"Won't you drive her?" I say to Henry, as casually as I can manage.

The three of us stand in the entrance hall, Cora pinning her hat and Henry with his hand on his study doorknob.

"What?"

"I thought you said you had business at the works?"

He said nothing of the sort, but it is a fair gamble.

"As it happens, yes, I do. But I have work to do here first—"

"Well, if Cora takes the carriage, then how are you to get there? You aren't planning on *riding*, are you?" I glance down at the dust already on his shoes. "Riding is a fine pastime for a gentleman, but I cannot imagine wanting to arrive at one's place of business head to toe in mud and sweat. I certainly never saw you do so in London."

"What do you know of business?" he snaps.

"Oh, nothing at all. But I know a great deal about the behavior expected of a gentleman."

I have won. He does not give me a reply, but with a grunt, he takes his coat and hat, and marches from the hall, Cora hurrying behind him.

I stand at the doorway, watching as the coach is readied. Cora takes her seat, Henry holding the reins. It is the image of the day she arrived at Nethershaw, but now they are both placed there by my hand. I wait until the carriage is out of sight—and a little longer, to be sure they are not returning.

Then, I set to work.

*

My first task should be simple.

I go to the kitchens with a sheaf of menu cards covered in notes and adjustments. The cook meets me, resigned, and takes the set to review with a couple of maids. As they debate, I casually mention that I want to check on the speciality confectionary I ordered in. With the shooting party guests arriving in only two days, of course it is to be expected that I am anxiously monitoring every aspect of the event.

In the pantry, I locate a paper bag of icing sugar stamped with the name of the pâtissier on the smart side of town and take it out with me, providing vague claims of dissatisfaction.

No one questions me. This is my house.

I feel Nethershaw fold around me, a great mantle of stone and rot. From the birds' nests in its rafters to the moss on the flagstones, it guards me.

I thought it an infinitely sad place, maligned, unwanted. Henry has bad instincts in women and houses.

Again, I sense his net closing around me. He means to kill me and find a better wife who knows how to turn lead into gold. Hate burns through me like acid. I hold the bag of sugar tight to my chest, breathing coming hard. The passion and violence I felt in my confinement sweep through me again, a burst of unfamiliar emotion that threatens to take me down.

I press a hand to the twisted wood of the banister, feel the cool, ancient grain against my hot, living flesh. Nethershaw has stood for five hundred years and may stand another five hundred more, whatever comes through its walls. I, too, am solid—unmovable. I will do exactly as I please.

Upstairs in Henry's room, I take the trunk from its hiding place and open it, breath held. For a moment, I think it will be empty—that I imagined the pastilles and poison.

But I did not.

The bag of arsenic is so innocuous, only a simple packet like any other, and if I saw it in the scullery beside the cleaning vinegar and camphor, it would be nothing but rat poison, a household staple.

My hand goes to my stomach reflexively. It is impossible to imagine I have been consuming it unknowing for so long. The nights of sickness, the cramping and blood and headaches have all passed now that I have gone several days without exposure.

It seems unreal, something from a melodrama or a Newgate trial. It cannot have happened to such a nobody as me.

It would make me far more important than I have ever considered myself, to be the target of such a plot.

Perhaps I am not the ghost I thought myself. Perhaps I have always had substance.

If, then, I am allowed a story, perhaps I can become the author of it.

It is short work to empty the arsenic into an empty pot of shaving cream from Henry's dresser, but more delicate a job to transfer the powdered sugar into its place. A fine white mist clouds around me, sweetening the air. There will be a residue of poison within the bag, but at such small ratio, I must believe it safe.

I restore the trunk with its new contents, return the remainder of the icing sugar to the pantry, then contemplate what to do with the arsenic. It is dangerous to be left open to discovery, but I cannot bring myself to dispose of it entirely. There may come a time when it is useful.

In the end, I bury the pot whole, sealed with its lid, among the roses beneath my smashed bedroom window. There: another task I must dispense with before Henry notices.

It is done.

Let Henry try his best. I have rendered him impotent.

Again.

No seed of his in my womb, and no poison in my belly. I am whole.

My next move is more complicated.

Henry's study is unlocked—of course, he does not think me capable of subterfuge. In London, he kept me as securely restrained through words as with any key. It is a pleasant transgression to be here, among his private things. It looks much like the London study, only a little more sparse. There are boxes of paperwork and leather folders across the desk and stacked on chairs beside it. I do not remember these coming with us from London; he must have brought documents here from the works.

I leaf through the material, unsure what I am looking for. Most of the documents are dull or impenetrable: orders and accounts, employment and board minutes—but there among them, a letter to Henry from another board member. I read it with interest, then search through for the same name, unpicking a trail of correspondence. In the boxes around me, I find the same names again, the same words, the same agreements.

Cora's father. The journalists. The man in the grinding room, the shards of wheel punching themselves through his mouth and jaw. The man's fault, the letter said. Poorly maintained tools. No money due.

Finished, I sit surrounded by papers, arranged by date and name. The details of Henry's conspiracy are all here—a story played out over years.

I am hot with injustice, and turn to the window, resting my forehead against its pearly glass. Beyond the moorland, flowers dance coyly in the breeze, the smell of peat reaching even here. Henry has been colluding to defraud workers and their families of the compensation due following death or injury at the works. He has put pressure on Cora's father at the Home Office to discredit the journalists investigating him. It is all true: everything Cora told me—and more.

The same lies each time, from the aging men to the smallest children. An accident. Blood spilled. An internal review finding the worker at fault. Compensation denied.

In the five years of records I have found, not a single case was granted.

When I close my eyes, all I can see is the splash of blood across the floorboards, the smoke and dirt of the foundry.

It recalls another moment: blood wet on my cheek nine years ago, the smell of gunpowder and leaf mulch and the gristle of human meat and bone. Henry's wide eyes.

An appetite untrammelled.

I know now what I must do.

From his desk I take paper and pen and blotter, and write a short letter. If Henry is ever put on trial, I would not be considered fit to stand witness against my own husband. But I can provide insurance against my own future.

I tidy the desk, covering my tracks, then sign the letter and enclose it within an envelope, alongside as much of the evidence as I can fit, enough to paint a full and damning picture.

On its face, I write one line.

To be opened in the event of my untimely death.

21

THE LETTER IS LIKE a magnet, a pole around which my mind turns.

I need to get it to someone safe, someone authoritative but also sympathetic to my cause.

My list of allies, unfortunately, runs slim.

The problem worries me all day, through a plain dinner with Henry and Cora, sweat creeping between my shoulder blades as though they can see what I have done. Henry does not offer me any more pastilles, and I worry I have aroused his suspicion too far. Should I have made up a benign tin of sweets to demonstrate my gullibility?

I am thinking too much.

The solution comes to me at night, as I lie in the empty space of my bed, longing for Carmilla or some other warm body.

Detective Inspector Lacey.

He gave my husband little deference, and he is familiar with our household. Who else is there?

It was a mistake to have insisted to Cora that I could not leave Nethershaw on account of my health. How, now, can I reach Lacey and deliver my precious charge into his hands? I have his card, smoothed out after Henry crumpled it and threw it out of his sight, but I do not dare risk my letter in the post. I must know it is delivered and every solemn vow made to obey its instructions.

*

I am still turning this challenge over in my mind the next morning at breakfast. The guests are to arrive tomorrow; Nethershaw is alive with activity. The last of the workmen are folding up dust sheets and carrying out ladders. Wood is polished. Floors are mopped, grates scrubbed. The paintings return from their repair and are rehung; carts from the butcher's and grocer's rumble up the long approach from the valley, and everywhere rooms are aired, linen changed, silverware polished, and stables mucked.

I should be at the heart of it, busy from dawn to dusk, but I have done my job too well. Nethershaw operates smoothly and efficiently; each soldier in my army knows their role and executes it perfectly. I have made myself redundant.

If Carmilla were here, I think she would laugh at me, low and sweet and mocking.

This marshaled, mastered life I have created, and no place for me in it.

Cora puts down her book where we are cloistered in the drawing room. "The weather is so fine, we simply must take the air, dear Lenore."

I am struck by a sudden anger at the epithet. That is Carmilla's word for me. It is hateful and perverse from any other mouth.

"We can take watercolors and paint this charming landscape—I am quite captivated by every vista, are you not? And a picnic, like rustics! Oh, do say yes."

I am too slow to think of a reason to decline, and the staff are more than happy to see us gone, so the plan is arranged around me, baskets of art supplies and food packed for each of us. Then I am chivvied into my lawn dress and a broad-brimmed hat to protect my aristocratic skin. Henry would choke if I were to host his precious guests with a sunburn.

Cora is too lively, and I curse myself for my praise of her yesterday. I have no patience for her when my very life lies in the balance of action. Perhaps we can walk through Hathersage. Was Detective Inspector Lacey stationed there, or in the city? His card is safe in my bureau, but I have been foolish enough not to commit its contents to memory.

Cora is quite correct: it is a fine day with a broad, azure sky striped with cirrus clouds and a golden sovereign of a sun. We cross the moorland towards Stanage Pole, and then along to the edge, where a jumbled path continues for miles unabated. We walk for a long while, Nethershaw vanishing behind the horizon, only a few sheep for company.

It is too hot. My shoes rub, and my dress pinches at the armpits, and the sun is a sharp knife against my skin and in my eyes.

I am not made for this, but Cora is. She skips lightly from stone to stone, vivacious and bright and so unencumbered. Jealousy is not an emotion I have easily tolerated in myself before, but it spills out now, raw and vicious, a blade turned against my own heart. I am jealous of Cora's passion and carelessness, but most of all I am jealous that she can experience all these things at an age when I held myself under such rigid control, when I was a creature made only from fear and survival. I am jealous that anybody has the gift of growing up differently.

We set up in a spot overlooking the valley, down Derwent moors to the village of Derwent itself. Cora takes out her watercolors and a sketchbook and frames the passage of the river, the pale scar of moorland, and beyond, the high table of Kinder Scout. She has a fine, delicate hand that moves deftly to capture the angles and textures of our view. She is talented.

I sit nearby, fanning myself and stewing in self-pity.

We take the picnic out, bottles of lemonade sticky and warm from the sun, apple tartlets and roast chicken, cheese and biscuits, grapes wrapped in paper, and cold potatoes.

Cora talks about her drawing master in Italy, about light and color with words I do not know and an ease I can only imagine. In my pocket, the letter jabs into my thigh, a constant reminder that I am not safe. I cannot yet turn my eye to the trivial and banal. I can have what I want, but only if I hold my nerve. Only if I can steel myself to create change.

The more I understand my own appetite, the more I understand how far I am from satiating it. It is as though it spills out from me in every direction. I want to be desired; I want to travel, to paint or write, to be listened to and respected, needed; I want true family—whether that be children or not—I want, I want, I want.

My appetite is vast, and I am in agony knowing myself to be unsatisfied.

When we are finished eating, we repack the baskets and wander onward. Cora wishes to go closer to the edge, to feel the breeze on her face, and if we dare, sit with our legs over the side like heroines in a sensation novel. She drops the basket and picks her way up the larger stones to the precipitous drop.

I follow, struggling over the uneven ground.

Right as she reaches the crest, Cora turns, the sunlight catching on her shining hair, and something bright glints at her throat.

I frown.

It is a necklace, slipped from beneath her collar.

Diamonds.

Far too valuable to be worn casually, but perhaps it is something precious she cannot bear to be parted from.

They are familiar stones in a familiar setting. A necklace I searched for and never found again.

"Cora?" My voice is flat as water. "Where did you get that necklace?"

Her hand flies to her throat, and her face drains of color. "What? Oh. These are nothing." She pushes them out of sight.

"They don't look like nothing—let me see."

I close the gap between us, reaching for the jewels, but Cora backs away, encroaching on the edge behind her.

"They were a gift," she says, "from—my mother."

"Strange, you have not shown them to me before. You show off every little trinket."

Cora laughs, but it is dead in the air. "Not everything."

"No. Apparently not."

I dart out a hand to grasp it again, and Cora takes another stumbling step back. The cliff edge breaks beneath her shoe. Behind her, the whole of the Derwent Valley opens like a book: rangy forest and hilltop, glistening river, dark smudges across the fields, shadows of the clouds passing before the sun.

"Lenore, stop this. It is too much."

"Do you know what I think is too much?"

My question frightens her. She wraps her hand around the diamonds as if invoking Henry's gift might summon some measure of protection.

"I think fucking my husband for jewelery is *too much*, Cora, don't you?"

On instinct, she takes another step back, away from my snarling face, but there is no more ground below her.

She is out of luck.

Her arms wheel, comical as a musical hall act, the slapstick of death as her eyes widen and her body hangs in a moment.

"Lenore—"

Shock runs cold through me, and I grab for her, fist closing on her shirt. It pulls tight as I take the weight of her. For a moment, she looks relieved—until I do not pull her to safety.

Her body is the heaviest thing I have ever held, my arm straining. In a minute, I will lose my strength, and she will go over, perhaps taking me along with her.

I should save her. That is the thing to do—the human thing.

But in that moment, I hate her so completely. She lied to me, when I came to her in my vulnerability and fear. I asked her for the truth, and she lied. I have been so powerless for so long.

Not anymore.

All the power is now in my hands, and with the flex of a muscle, this could all be over. Henry thwarted. My enemies punished. I can paint my will across existence with an indelible brush.

It all seems so perfectly clear.

"He wants to kill me," I say, seeing each puzzle piece slot into place, "and replace me with you."

I will not have it.

There is only a moment of doubt, when I see the confusion cross Cora's face at the mention of my murder.

But it is too late.

My grip has failed. The thin cotton of Cora's blouse slips from between my fingers.

She drops slowly, like a pebble over the side of a bridge, vanishing down, down, small and unreal, until her splayed limbs meet the rocks below.

*

Cora is an English rose. This was the first impression I had of her at her maiden assembly after coming out, when I was a little shy of my twenty-eighth birthday and firmly in the ranks of the older women who gathered at the sides to judge who was dancing with whom, and whose dress was newly made and whose altered from the season before. Long married and childless, I was something to be feared, like a portent of bad luck, and the courting girls avoided me as though by doing so they could avoid my fate. I looked on them with disdain. They might fear my fate, but worse awaited them if they could not do what I had done. I might not have made a love match, but I was one of the richest women there, and my safety was of my own engineering.

Cora was the sole exception.

She arrived in a vision of lilac that offset her silky brown hair and the pink flush of her cheeks. She danced neatly, made pretty conversation with a number of notable bachelors, and set society alight by making it known that she wished to spend a season or two at leisure before receiving a proposal. Towards the end of the night, on the arm of the hostess, an acquaintance of mine from charitable circles, Cora steered them both towards me so that our mutual friend was forced to make introductions.

Cora lost no time covering me with flattery; she had heard of my reputation for the most charming dinners and for the card nights I held a few times during each season for the wives left behind by their husbands attending events at White's or the Reform Club. Though Cora was unmarried, it felt churlish not to invite her when she seemed so keen, and after a few minutes' conversation, she had inserted herself into half of my social engagements for the month.

She got exactly what she had come for.

I confess I was a little distracted by her youth and beauty, the way her hair was arranged so carelessly and yet at the height of style, the neat nip of her narrow waist and the delicate curve of her lips. It felt special to have been singled out by someone who could command the attention of anyone in the room, and it had been some time since I was the darling of society.

At a card evening held by Lady Harlow, Cora hovered near my table until a seat became free, then joined our four for whist. She was a lively conversationalist, which came as little surprise, but I was taken by the genuine warmth behind her words, an enthusiasm that was infectious. She lost little time creating an audience in us, listing her various achievements and successes of the season, whom she had danced with, who complimented her looks, who invited her to an exclusive private salon, who had called on her and what invitations she had for country stays. It was quite dizzying, and on anyone else it would have seemed rank arrogance, but her charm was difficult to deny, like the warmth of the sun that turns your face to it even as you know you will be burned.

We were all examined in turn, mined for our conquests and talents, and she received intelligence of each with wonder and enthusiasm. She was brilliant, according to her own assessment, and she liked us all; therefore we were brilliant, too.

It was hard not to enjoy being in her orbit. For all her self-involvement, she had the beauty and breeding to back up her claims. It was clear she would go far, and I could see my companions at whist assessing her as a potential ally.

I saw her next at the opera—I forget which—when Henry and I encountered her in the foyer, seeming a little lost. She made a beeline for me as soon as our eyes met and clasped her hands around my arm.

"Oh, thank goodness I found you. I was supposed to meet a friend here, but I've just heard she's unwell today, and I must have left before the news arrived. Papa let me take the carriage alone only on assurance that I was meeting my friend and her parents as soon as I stepped out, and now I'm entirely on my own, and I don't even have the tickets for our seats. I'm utterly stranded."

I could see where this was headed. I would have suspected the story fabricated, if not for the fact that she was the kind of fortunate girl who didn't need to construct opportunities for herself.

I invited her to join us in our box.

I had been making the same calculations as the other women. Far better to join myself to Cora's rising star than to be left surplus.

I had not considered, then, that my husband might have been making his own calculations. How naive I was.

From that evening on, Cora made a pet of me. She came to me first at any dance or dinner, dashed across roads to greet me when we were both out shopping, and paid so many calls that I was obliged to rearrange my schedule in order to make room for anyone else. She solicited my opinion on fashion plates in magazines, which invitations to accept and which to spurn, how to manage pushy mamas and their awkward sons, whether to dance every dance or make herself frustratingly unavailable.

She rejected suitors, confident in her belief that there could only be good things coming. An opportunity spurned now meant nothing when life was a banquet that would only give more. She admitted to me, conspiratorially, that she had told more than one young man he must wait at *least* a season or two for her to accept his proposal, to prove that he loved only her and was not simply chasing the prize of the day. The sheer self-belief astounded me. I was dazzled.

I gladly poured forth my advice, buoyed by being needed, respected. I felt secure and masterful, a skillful player in the complex games of society. Cora paid me so many compliments I became half-drunk on them. The truth was, I was so unbearably lonely, I lapped it up, a light-starved plant pressing its leaves against a windowpane, keening for the sun.

I wanted to be near her light, even though she cast me in shadow. I must have been so obvious to her, an easy mark. I was ashamed of wearing my want so nakedly, when I never quite got what I needed in return. But it was closer than anything else on offer.

But it did not last. Though I craved her attention, it left me feeling sour and melancholy, full of my own failings and inadequacies. Something was punctured, my self-image crumpled under her careless handling. My humiliation laid me low. I hated her, and I loved her. I wanted to be her, and I wanted to destroy her.

The worse I felt, the less I wanted her company, but it was too late. She was a part of my life now, and I could not snub her without consequences. And it would be cruel. She had done nothing wrong and thought herself my friend.

What a naive fool I was.

It was intolerable to see someone else live all that I was denied. I hated her, because I did not understand what it was I had lost before I saw it in her.

Now she is ended.

Cora is dead, and I am free.

22

WHAT HAVE I DONE?

Oh God, what have I done?

I am sick onto the heather, splashing my shoes and the hem of my dress. I retch until there is only acid and water.

When I peer over the cliff edge, Cora lies unmoving. There is a shadow below her. Maybe just a shadow—maybe blood—

Oh God. I can't do this—I can't do this.

Our picnic things are spilled around the moor like an accident, and I repack it all to keep my hands from scratching at my face in horror.

I am a *murderer*.

Just like Henry.

It is impossible to pace over the uneven, rocky formation of the cliff edge, but I cannot stay still. My chest is tight, and lightning streaks of energy rush from my heart to my stomach and throat. It is unbearable. I have known anxiety before, but this is something so severe I think I might grow mad from it. I strike my hands against a boulder, trying to force the energy from my body, to exhaust myself enough that I can think.

Cora is dead.

There is nothing I can do to change that. If I am to survive this, I must go on with absolute precision.

I sink into the shade of a rock, the early afternoon sun casting a blessed pool of shadow into which I can crawl.

Should I survive this?

Is this not a moment that should mean the end? I have crossed some unforeseen Rubicon, a threshold I had not known lay so close. The last few minutes play out over and over in my mind's eye. The memory of my anger is as bright as it was then. The precise feeling of Cora's blouse between my fingers. The burning in my arm as the weight of her took its toll.

It was an accident. I did not mean to let her fall.

I grind the heels of my palm into my eyes until bright stars burn and die in turn and my head aches.

An accident.

Yes.

I have survived this far. I cannot allow myself to take the blame. I know of my appetite for violence, but I do not need to share it. Who is to say what really happened here today? I am not sure even I know.

I saved Henry before. Now, I must save myself.

I think of what Carmilla would say, imagine her curled against my side, running her cold fingers through my hair.

My imagination fails me. I cannot replicate her assurance, her greedy confidence. I have only my own small soul to turn to.

I weep then, for Cora, for myself. Cora did not deserve this, but then I have not deserved all I have suffered. None of us deserve our bad fortune, but that does not stop it from coming.

All I know is this: I will not end here.

The sun has traveled far across the sky by the time I find my way back to Nethershaw. I have lost our picnic baskets somewhere, and the paints. I am not sure if that was before or after Cora. There is a tear in my sleeve, and my elbow smarts with a graze. My hat has come loose from its pins and dangles from my throat like an anchor.

The walk has been interminable.

I am going to the gallows. I am going to Judgment Day. The sun mocks me with its perfect shape and unbothered rays.

My story is straight.

Most of it is true.

Cora and I walked until she found a spot to paint—there are spatters of color on the rocks still—then we ate, and on the return, Cora danced along the edge like a sprite, glorying in the wind and hostile expanse.

I stopped to tie my shoe, carrying most of the baskets. Cora ventured too close to the cliff, turned to wave—and lost her footing. I was too far away to do more than grab at her before it was too late.

Cora's small body lies at the foot of the cliff, a smear of red and cream against the heather. I cannot say exactly where; this inhumane moorland is a monolith of heather and peat.

Nethershaw rises above the gorse like standing stones; still, ancient, sacrosanct. There is some commotion afoot, and I wonder just how long we have been gone.

How long *I* have been gone.

A cry goes up at the sight of me, a cluster of servants dashing forward, and I remember our fruitless search for Carmilla on her first disappearance.

Henry hurries from the house, his face twisted in worry.

When he sees me alone, his expression goes cold.

"There's been an accident," I whisper.

He can see it in my face—I know it. He fears me and how I could undo all his careful work.

I think again of Cora's confusion when I spoke of my murder. Did she truly not know? Did Henry act alone?

Damn him. He has done this. It is all his fault.

Cora would be alive if it were not for him.

He is yelling to the butler now.

Fetch the police.

My stomach roils with fear and hope. The letter still lies in my pocket.

I am close. I am so close.

*

Detective Inspector Lacey comes to me in the same room as before, but this time I have nothing left in me. I am worn through. Still in my torn lawn dress, I recline on a couch with my eyes closed. I have refused to speak to anyone in more than the most basic terms, pushing Henry away when he tried to touch me. I cannot bear it. I know he does not mean this softness; he wants to work his fingers between my gaps and prize me open.

The couch is my respite. My corset is loosened, my brow pressed with a cold flannel, and beside me are smelling salts and a glass of water with half a teaspoonful of spirit of *sal volatile*. The police have sent a telegram to inform Cora's family. The maids do not know if they should cover the mirrors or take out the black dye. There has been a death, but did Cora belong to us?

Henry waits with me in silence, unable to speak, as I know he must wish to, due to the to-ing and fro-ing of the maid turned nurse. He watches my performance closely. A ghost. A nightmare. The shadow in the corner of my room as I slept, the weight on my chest.

I open my eyes a crack, looking at my beautiful husband, the downturn of his pretty mouth.

I have made sure that Cora belongs to no one.

Lacey comes with a soft voice into the hushed halls of Nethershaw. The shutters are half closed, casting us in dim light, dust motes dancing in the evening sun. I take a little water, allow myself to be wrapped in a light shawl as Lacey positions a chair close by, his notebook ready for my testimony.

Henry discharges formal pleasantries, then Lacey turns to me, pencil against paper.

"What happened?"

It is not so hard to cry.

I let tears fall into my cupped hands, and I lay out my story.

The painting. The picnic. The wicked edge, death running for miles in the sharp limestone fault. Cora, painted in a streak of white against the August blue sky.

The sound of stones shifting. The soft "oh" of shock.

Cora, gone. Nothing but unending air and the ragged horizon.

"I could not get to her," I say, covering my face with my hands. My nails are torn, and my palms grazed. "I could not find a way down. I tried, but I feared I might fall, too. So I left her."

This much was true. I did not need to go to her body to know she was dead. Her glassy eyes stared up at me from where her twisted limbs fanned out around her corpse. But I tried. I did.

Lacey's eyes are gentle with sympathy. "That must have been very difficult."

I look up at him. He is regarding me, if not with sympathy, then at least with a lack of suspicion.

"I keep thinking, there must have been something I could have done. There should have been some way to stop this."

"An accident in a place like that has only a few endings," he says, though he does not fold away his notebook. "I have seen more than one poor soul come afoul of land they weren't familiar with."

Before he can speak again, there is a knock on the door, and another policeman comes in, summoning Lacey to deliver a message quietly into his ear. I hear the words *body* and *found*.

Cold panic flushes through me again, but I force myself limp, placid.

Lacey returns, notebook in hand, pen tapping against it.

Did I leave some sort of evidence on Cora's body? Is the way she landed proof she could not have fallen the way I said she did?

Lacey paces a moment, then crooks his finger at Henry. "Walk with me a moment. Your wife can be spared this."

When the door closes, I sit up, push the loose hair from my face. He is telling Henry about Cora's body in private. He is either sparing my sensibilities or breaking the news to Henry that his wife is a murderer. In my stockinged feet, I pad closer to the door to listen.

". . . it will take several men to move the body. I would not recommend leaving her overnight. If you have an icehouse, the coroner can collect her tomorrow."

"I understand. We will spare everyone willing to go."

There is a catch in Henry's voice, some true emotion.

I feel sick. Cora in the icehouse. It is too much.

When their voices retreat, I slip out, thinking to retreat to my room, but Lacey appears from the shadows as though he has been waiting for me.

"Lady Lenore."

"Detective." I clasp a hand to my throat, and his eyes follow the movement.

"You seem a little recovered from our conversation."

I nod, unsure of the ground between us.

He pauses, deliberating his words. "I wonder, is there somewhere in the grounds where you are free to think your private thoughts?"

I do not understand him for a moment; my mind too jumbled. Then I see what he is asking.

"Yes—there is a private courtyard to the west of the house that is little used."

He makes his formal goodbyes, and I hover at the top of the stairs, waiting for him to be gone. When he is, I tell Henry that I will rest in my room. There is a grunt in response, then the sound of his study door opening and closing. With my skirts lifted in one hand, I descend the stairs, careful to step on the outside of the tread to avoid the wood betraying my movements.

Lacey waits for me under a thick canopy of ivy, smoking a pipe in short, uneasy bursts.

"Detective Inspector," I say, drawing my shawl closer around my shoulders. "This is quite unusual."

"Forgive me. I wanted the opportunity to speak to you privately. *Absolutely* privately."

My nerves shift from expecting cold iron around my wrists to curious anticipation. He does not want Henry to know that he is talking to me.

He takes a deep pull on the pipe, the smoke clouding between us tinged blue. I have come out in my stockings without thinking. The cobbles beneath my soles are hot from the sun.

"Did she fall?"

I tense—perhaps I made my assumptions too soon—but then he speaks again.

"Sometimes it is too difficult to contemplate that a person we loved might have had a hand in their own passing."

My shock must be plain on my face, because Lacey, for all his professionalism, seems uncomfortable, finger tapping on his pipe.

"I have upset you," he says.

"No—I—"

My mind races. I look at the cobbles, where my dress brushes the dirt. I see Cora tumbling over the edge of the cliff, but now the picture shifts. Different possibilities open up—ones that keep me safe and push Henry into position.

I raise my eyes to Lacey meaningfully. "I am not so sure it was an accident."

He gives a small nod of acknowledgment but leaves me the floor. I imagine Carmilla behind me, whispering the right words in my ear.

"I think Cora came here for something my husband was unwilling to give her."

I let him fill in my meaning.

"I see. And how long . . ."

"I have had my suspicions for a while."

If only.

Lacey nods again. "I will need to take a new statement, if you're willing."

"Not here," I say quickly. "I do not want anyone to know what Cora did. She does not deserve to be thought of that way."

"Of course." His eyes flicker to my wrist, where my sleeve has slipped back. A ring of finger marks from Carmilla are dark smudges against the pallor of my skin. "Is there anything else you want to tell me?" he asks softly.

I make a show of pulling my sleeve down.

"My husband is a man who gets what he wants," I say, looking at Lacey darkly. "No matter the cost."

It is time. I must do it now.

"There is something I must ask of you." I draw the letter from my pocket and hold it out, hand trembling. "Take this. I am too late to save Cora's life, but I ask you to save mine."

23

WE ARE DOWN TO TWO.

A team of men brought a handcart covered in sacking from the moors to Nethershaw and over to the icehouse. The coroner will come for the body early tomorrow, before the guests arrive. I saw Henry slip a palm full of coins to a policeman to ensure it.

The police are all gone now, and Molly has helped me change into a simple housedress, braiding my hair into a thick rope. I am saving all my fine evening gowns for the shooting party. Henry does not warrant them.

We sit at either end of the dining table in silence as a short meal of tinned lobster, cold roast beef, and salad is presented, followed by cherry tartlets, cheese, and biscuits. As soon as the lobster is placed before me, I feel sick to my stomach, pushing a small morsel around my plate.

Henry is mulish and unsettled. I have found him watching me from a distance since Detective Inspector Lacey left, though there have always been too many servants and workmen between us for anything to happen. Around Nethershaw, dust sheets are being folded up, ladders carried out, paintbrushes and hammers packed away, floors swept and beds freshly made.

The guests arrive tomorrow. We are to be exposed to the world, each dark corner and forgotten blemish.

Carmilla is gone for now. Cora is dead.

I can barely recognize myself as the woman who left London only a few weeks ago. She is as distant and alien to me as Cora's easy confidence was. I cannot take a full breath; it is as though my chest is stoppered, bound tight with tension.

The letter is with Detective Inspector Lacey now. My fate is quite literally out of my hands. I must trust him—and trust myself.

All that is left is to tell Henry what I have done.

We retire early, and I send Molly to draw me a bath. Despite the heat, I feel cold. It is the thought of Cora in the icehouse, only feet away from my bedroom. I can see the edge of it from my window, a sunken outbuilding converted from some earlier martial use when Nethershaw still stood in defense.

I am alone in my room, stripped to my shift, brushing the golden weight of my hair, when Henry's hand closes around my bruised wrist.

"I know you're lying," he hisses, eyes bright. He has been drinking alone; I can smell it on his breath.

"What are you talking about?" I whisper.

I should tell him now.

But my nerve fails me.

He shakes me, and I drop my brush to the floor. "You monstrous bitch."

There is a soft gasp from the doorway—so soft Henry does not hear. There's a smudge of red hair in the open gap: Molly.

I have an audience again, as with Lacey. Good.

I go limp, eyes wide.

"Please," I say, breathy. "You're hurting me."

"You've been a sly little cunt since the day you tricked me into marrying you."

He raises his hand to slap me, but Molly, God bless her, clatters into the room.

"Are you still wanting a bath, my lady?"

Henry drops me rapidly, and I lose my balance, collapsing against my dressing table. He wipes his hands on his clothes as though cleaning himself of my transgression. As he strides past Molly, I feel dread sink deeper into my stomach.

There is no veil of politeness between us now.

There are two of us left.

And only one can survive.

*

It is a long, black night.

There is something stirring inside me, something impatient and hungry. In my mind, I replay my encounter with Henry and curse my cowardice. He will not escape me again. But I have done well. Lacey thinks me a vulnerable woman at the mercy of a cruel man, whose coldness has already driven one woman to suicide. Molly will corroborate this now.

I have killed Cora, and I will get away with it.

I do not know what to do with this unnatural mix of guilt and power. My bed is a prison cot, too hard and narrow, and I cannot take any comfort from rest.

I should be solely wracked with misery, abject from the horror I have wrought upon the world.

But I am not.

Perhaps I could have saved Cora if I had wanted to; perhaps not. It is done now, and it is a relief. I know the truth of her and of Henry.

And now he knows to fear me.

Still, I cannot sleep.

I rise, stretching my back and working the muscles of my shoulders and legs, sore from the day's adventures. I want Carmilla. I want to tell her what I have done, have her be proud of me. I want to bite her red lips and touch the base curves of her flesh. I *want*. It is a new and thrilling revelation. I can *want*, and it will not destroy me.

I wonder what else I will want. The world opens before me like some pleasure ground of old, an unending vista of appetite and glory, if only I am brave enough. Perhaps I shall usurp Cora's dreams of painting in Italy, or I could return to the Paris of my short-lived honeymoon, and remake the city for my own desires.

I go to the washstand to splash the last of yesterday's water onto my face and neck. The shutters are folded back, and the broken window lies exposed, letting in a soft heather-scented wind. Tonight, the sky belongs to the stars, cloudless and rampant, so thick it is as though I could scoop them up between my cupped palms and drink down their brilliance.

I feel a little mad.

A flutter of movement, white against the dark moorland.

I still, hands at the fast-beating pulse in my throat.

I think of Carmilla and her night-walking. Could it be her?

No—it is near the low outbuilding.

The icehouse.

In the wind, a white shift is flaring and snapping against the legs of a figure. She is luminously pale, ashen face with dark, hollow eyes, a smear of something dark around her mouth that could be blood.

There is something wrong with her neck. It is twisted too far to one side, unnatural where it snapped on impact.

Cora lifts one broken arm, beckoning to me.

I jerk back in shock, catch my foot on the rug and go crashing to the ground, a jumble of smashed elbows and swallowed cries.

I wake when I hit the floor, sweat-drenched and tangled in my sheets. I have fallen from the bed in my nightmare. My heart is racing so fast it is painful, my chest a squeezed fist. At first, I cannot move. I lie, stiff as a corpse where I have fallen. The shadows grow darker in the corners of the room, and again I think of Carmilla, and the dark weight on my chest.

Slowly, I furl and unfurl the fingers of my right hand, then my left, then my feet, then my legs, until I can sit up and shakily light the candle by my bed.

At the window, the shutters are folded back, and a path of stars pulls across the sky.

When I have steadied my breathing, I force myself up, to look out.

The icehouse is dark and silent. No tracks in the grass nor footprints.

There is nothing.

Only a worm of grief in my thoughts.

*

I rise early with a hunger that churns inside me like a sickness. I go down to the kitchens and nose among the maids, eating handfuls of grapes, a piece of pie, two slices of bread and butter, a boiled egg, cold ham, a block of cheese, soft scoops of blancmange, potato salad, a whole tomato, the head of a cooked fish left for the stockpot. It sits like a stone in my stomach, indigestible, and I only make it back to my room and the chamber pot in time to bring it all back up.

I clean my mouth out with water, and take the pot down to the scullery maids, pink with humiliation. They both look at me with their wary, doe eyes, scuttling prey shivering around the movement of a fox, a hunter.

The dogs bay in their kennels as I pass, frothing against the gates with rolling eyes and lolling tongues. They are hungry, too.

By the icehouse, a gang of men I do not recognize have positioned a hearse by the door, concealing the interior from view. It is not the delicate, elegant coach of a London undertaker: this has large, solid wheels for country use, and the men hoist the body into it like a sack of grain. They have put her in a cheap coffin for transport. It is too early for the telegram boy to have traveled up to us yet with any word from her family. There will be a burial, of course, likely in London, in Brompton or Highgate.

We will be expected to attend.

From my toes to scalp, I am drawn taut like a bow, bent almost to snapping. The future mapped out before me is not one I want. I refuse to follow its path. They cannot make me.

I am done with all this.

I am *done*.

I turn on my heel and stalk back to the house, skin prickling with the static of an oncoming storm.

I am hungry.

In my room, I find Henry, placing a tin of pastilles by my bed.

Warm delight spreads through me like honey.

Oh, how wonderful of him.

I shut the door forcefully, and he startles, fumbling with the box, then smoothing back his oiled hair with his other hand. He has dressed very carefully today, in the new shirt I ordered for him and an expensive and purposefully casual sack suit, ready to meet his guests.

"Here." He proffers the tin. "A gift, to apologize for last night."

"How thoughtful." I take it and prize off the lid to see a fan of jewel tones, thickly dusted over with white powder. I reach to select one, then pause, taking in Henry's hungry gaze as it follows my movements. Instead, I extend the tin to him. "Will you not have one?"

"No, no. They're for you." He is casual at first, but I hold his eye with an expression that makes his face fall.

I take a step towards him, like advancing on Cora at the cliff edge, and shake the tin.

"Won't you try? Perhaps you will like them."

He glances down at the white powder then back up at me, his Adam's apple bobbing as he swallows. "No, thank you."

"Come to think of it, I've never seen you eat one of these. Hmm. I wonder why?"

I regard the sweets contemplatively, then pluck one at random and pop it into my mouth.

Henry's eyes widen a fraction. We are close enough that I can see the pores in his nose and the fine lines around his eyes.

I suck the sugar from the pastille, then delicately take it from my tongue and look at it again.

"The only reason I can think of is that you know there's something wrong with them. But that's silly," I say, holding his gaze, a smile on my lips. "Because it's only sugar."

Without warning, I blow into the tin, and a cloud of white dust bursts into the air, filling my nostrils and coating my tongue in sweetness. Henry yells and scrambles back—then stills, licks his lips.

His mouth falls open in horror and confusion.

"I've disposed of it," I say, in answer to his silent question. "Leaving arsenic around the place could be quite dangerous."

I snap the lid back on the tin and toss it onto my bed.

"I have written up an account of everything and passed it to Detective Inspector Lacey, along with several documents about the

Ajax Works injury compensation scheme that people might find quite interesting. Cora was ever so helpful in telling me all about the trouble you've been having with journalists."

"What have you done?" he whispers, ashen and weak.

"Nothing. Yet. That is in your hands, you see. The letter is only to be opened in the event that something unfortunate happens to me. All you must do, dear husband, is make sure I live a long and healthy life."

I lean in and plant a kiss on his cheek.

"There now. That's done."

I go to the door and open it for him, then return to take out a day dress and other things for my toilet. I stand among the trappings of my beauty, mouth bright with sugar and triumph, Henry dismantled to pieces before me.

"Your guests are arriving, Henry. We mustn't be late to greet them."

He scurries out, and I turn to my dress, running my hand over its pretty stripe and the lace at its cuffs. I hum a tune to myself.

I like this new world.

It is going to be so much fun.

*

I am mistress of Nethershaw, and my world is exquisite.

My guests are greeted warmly and installed in each freshly cleaned and made bedroom, the rooms bright and well aired, smart servants acting quickly and quietly, just as I have worked for these past weeks. There is a casual luncheon served in the conservatory with the doors thrown open to the shimmering heat of the summer grouse moors. Wives kiss my cheeks and tell me what magnificent work I have made of this strange old place, how the crooked, moldering corridors and dank rooms have been made charming and quaint.

The dining hall is my masterpiece. Lit by candlelight, the damage in the ceiling is invisible; there is only the vast table laden with course after course. Crayfish soup, stewed trout and turbot in hollandaise sauce, salami of grouse, minced veal and béchamel sauce, saddle of mutton, black game, salad, potatoes and haricots verts, followed by greengage compote, raspberry and currant tarts with vanilla cream, and a parmesan soufflé.

The conversation is convivial, the wine pouring as I hold court. Henry sits at the other end of the table, deep into his cups, cheeks high pink points and eyes glassy. Let him stew. This is what I excel at. I am charming, pretty, an elegant and witty hostess, so enticing that the men stay with the port only for a short while before we are all together again in the drawing room, and I take up the piano. Wine spilling over glasses, I switch from Chopin to a popular song, remembering the lyrics as best I can. One woman claps her hands in delight; a man toasts. Soon they are singing with me, hair uncoiling from pins, jackets discarded over chair backs.

The mistake Henry makes is that the society he so desperately wants admittance to is one he has created in his mind. The rules and formality are the dressing, the habits of generations. No one here fears making a mistake. They know they belong. They know that whatever they want is theirs. If he were a little more like he was at the Ajax Works, they would recognize him at once.

It is a mistake I have made, too. I thought controlling myself completely would gain me Henry's respect. I thought it would keep me safe—my lack carefully concealed.

Damn control. Damn mastery. I want, I lack, I *hunger*.

I will die like all mortal things.

At least let me taste a little life before I go.

The night runs late, and at some point, Henry has slipped away, though I do not know when. I am drunk and have been flirting with a cavalry officer in the Queen's Royal Lancers who I am surprised to find myself attracted to. What a strange and dangerous thing, attraction.

Henry is not here. Stupid, handsome monster.

I stumble upright, swaying, and push the officer away.

Henry cannot hide from this. I have endured ten years of his rule; he will endure mine.

My shoes are not on my feet. No matter. I leave the singing, a bottle of brandy being passed around like water, and stumble towards his study.

He is not there either.

The front door is open, the cold night air a balm on my sweat slick skin. I pad onto the gravel outside, relishing the sharp prickle of stone against the soles of my feet and the wheel of stars above, like delicate gifts handed to me by the heavens.

Soft voices come from the direction of the stables.

In the shadows, I follow them, holding on to the walls for support.

I hear Henry first.

". . . directly. I know it is late but wake them—tell them to come tomorrow."

"What if I cannot rouse them, sir?" A groom, holding the reins of Henry's prized chestnut, set to ride. He slides a letter into his pocket.

"It's a damn asylum—their staff don't sleep through the night."

"Yes, sir."

The groom mounts and takes off at a trot, holding a lantern above him, horseshoes crunching along the drive and then softer on the moor road.

I press myself against the stones of Nethershaw, the world spinning.

Henry has sent a summons to an asylum.

Oh, you clever, dangerous monster.

Closing my eyes, I feel the buoyant hope of the evening stream out of me with each trembling breath.

So close. So close.

But this is not over yet.

24

IT IS AN OUTRAGE. It is monstrous.

Henry has outflanked me. How could I not have foreseen this?

I cannot bear it. I do not sleep; it is impossible. Pacing my room, I hunt for another way forward, but I cannot see it. I cannot see it. Damn Carmilla—damn her for opening my eyes. Damn my own stupid self for being so cowardly, for not leaving already. Damn this cursed, cruel world for laying such burdens upon my shoulders.

I will not give in. I will not break. I will not give anyone the satisfaction of seeing me cowed again. If I cannot have what I want, then no one can.

As dawn creeps through the limestone outcrops and bristling gorse, I see a carriage approaching in the distance. The headache that has been brewing cracks through my temples like a shot. The air is too close, too heavy.

From the landing, I hear the quiet squeak of the front door opening, the tread of stealthy footsteps. Henry's voice, and another man's. It is Dr. Foxfield again. What a scummy, weaselly little man. I thought I had charmed him, but Henry will work his power again, turn him against me. Men conspiring in dark little holes like vermin, chittering their spiteful thoughts to one another, make the world like this, hurt people like that. I hate them I hate them I hate them.

I am at Henry's study door, though I do not remember moving here. No matter. I press my ear to the door. I must know. Like the telephone conversation about those nasty diamonds back at the London house, when I still thought Henry might care for me. Like listening to Henry with the groom last night. I am endlessly crouched outside doors, squirming into corners, picking at scraps to make something from, these offcuts of men who toss power around carelessly. I want them to choke on it.

"Worse?" This is Foxfield, eating up Henry's story, no doubt.

"I don't know how else to describe it. She can playact the part at times, but she is consumed by delusions, convinced I am poisoning her. I fear she is a danger to herself, and God forgive me for saying this, but perhaps to others, too."

A long pause.

Then Foxfield speaks. "I heard there had been an accident . . ."

"She has become entirely irrational. I have some very important guests staying, and if she were to misbehave in front of them . . ."

"I understand. I have been able to assist in many cases where discretion is required."

A hand pulls me away, and I turn to snap at it with my teeth.

"My lady?" Molly is beside me, wary but loyal.

I straighten, ashamed of my behavior. "I . . . I haven't slept."

She takes my arm. "That's all right. We'll get you straightened out."

I hesitate—I want to listen longer.

"The guests will be down for breakfast soon," she reminds me. "It is the shoot today."

"Yes. Yes. Of course."

She leads me to my room and begins to wash the sleep from my face. Then she dresses me and my hair. I am shaking with anger and ball my fists in my skirt, though of course Molly notices. Poor Molly, who has seen everything.

Impulsively, I grab her hand and pull her close.

"You have family, don't you?"

"Yes, my lady." She is overtly uncomfortable, but she does not attempt to remove her hand. I am her mistress, and if I want her hand, she must give it to me. How sick and wrong this all is. This little pantomime of a life, each of us miserable and none allowed their own appetites.

I release her hand. "I think you should go to them. Take a holiday. A month, more."

She clasps my hairbrush to her chest like a shield, face puckering. "Have I done something wrong?"

"No. Nothing. Here." I dig in the drawers of my dressing table and find a five-pound note, crisp from the bank. "Take this. Go and do something that you really want to. Whatever it is. However frightening. *Do* something."

"I don't understand. Are you . . . letting me go?"

"The job is yours for however long you want it. But so is this." I prize the hairbrush from her fingers and replace it with the note.

God, maybe this is worse. I am only making Molly feel uncomfortable for my own selfish reasons.

*

Breakfast is a grand affair. Half the guests are down already, ranged around the table and sideboard, the men in their Norfolk jackets with pleated backs and belted waists, knee breeches, and thick socks and boots, the women in lighter day dresses, suited for a lunch outside but little more. A lady may ride with a hunt, but she does not shoot a gun.

My head throbs in rhythm with the racing beat of my heart. I take a little coffee, black with sugar.

It is all coming apart.

I do not see Henry until the open carriages are drawing up in front of Nethershaw. The ladies climb into a number of fine landaus while the men scramble onto the narrow benches of the dog carts. The dogs themselves have already been loaded into their boxes, yelping and scratching at the wood. Henry is at the driver's seat of the lead cart, looking rigidly ahead.

While the men start the shooting, I take the women to our lunching place, where the house servants have already set up a number of tables and chairs. In the distance comes the volley of guns, and as a pall of smoke rises from over the moorland, the world fills up with the clatter of china, overlapping voices, and the barking of dogs, the puncture wounds of gunshots and cries. It is dizzying.

The men tramp back to us over the peat and heather, guns snapped open over their arms, limp like the birds tied in braces that swing from the leathery hands of the groundskeeper. The smell of blood mingles with gunpowder, rich and metallic.

Luncheon covers every inch of table. Fillets of sole in mayonnaise, iced lobster soufflé, braised beef with savory jelly, dressed ox tongue, and fillets of duckling with goose liver farce, a dish of braised stuffed quails, and a roast pheasant in crust, plates of salad, rice, stewed prunes and pound cake, savory cheese fingers, bread and butter, mounds of peaches and nectarines and glossy cherries, bottles of lemonade and claret, champagne, and coffee and tea. The party descends on the table, pulling apart birds and scraping meat from the bone, fingers slick with grease and lips bright with sugar.

When the shooting recommences, half the women take a landau back to Nethershaw, but I stay with the rest who wish to watch the sport. We follow the men up and over a hill to the sprawling grouse moor where beaters are working through the undergrowth to shoo birds into the sky. The sun beats down on the back of my neck as hot as the Ajax Works. I cannot think; it is all too loud, too much for my tortured senses. Foxfield is waiting for me at Nethershaw, I know it. I cannot return there—but what can I do?

In a line, the men fire and reload, fire and reload, speckled brown feathers bursting like dandelion seeds, drifting away on the wind as the birds plunge to earth. Blood seeps through runnels between knots of heather, staining the earth red. I ease myself away from the women who have gathered in an audience, commenting on the aim and poise of each hunter in turn. There is not much time before we return; even now, I see the landau making its way towards us in the distance.

I am out of time.

Why did Carmilla think I could do this alone? I close my eyes, breathing in blood and blossom, summoning her voice to my mind.

I know what Carmilla would tell me.

Settle the score.

Get what I want.

Give Henry what he deserves.

For a moment, she is so clear to me it is like a vision, as though I can feel her stood behind me, her cold tongue licking a line along my neck as her teeth brush my skin.

When I open my eyes, Henry is coming towards me. Around him, several dogs bound and bite at the birds he holds by their tail feathers; he kicks them away and, whining, they spring backwards. They chase after the grouse as soon as they drop to the ground, evading the keepers' call to heal, one or two tearing into the flesh in a spray of blood.

"Not a well-trained gun dog among them," says Lord Berrington, gun broken across the crook of his arm. "Damn fool has got himself a pack of hunting dogs."

"My husband can't resist a bargain," I say. "He's a terribly talented businessman."

Laughter.

Henry flushes red, and I know he has heard us.

It is a delight to be cruel.

The men ready to return to Nethershaw.

Henry snatches up my wrist hard enough to grind the bones together. "I must talk to you."

My heart races, light and giddy and agonizing. "Very well."

"I'm consulting my wife about a few things—finish up without me," he calls back to the party, but no one is listening. He is disposable. The dog carts are packed and ready to leave, beaters making the final passes.

Henry hauls me away around the bulk of a tor so that we are hidden from view.

"I do not know what is wrong with you, but I will not stand for it any longer."

I say nothing.

"You shame yourself and me."

"Perhaps I do shame myself. But your shame is all your own doing."

He runs a hand through his hair, tugging at the roots. "God knows why I married you. Christ."

"You know why you married me," I hiss. "And I you. It was a pact, an understanding."

"Fuck an *understanding*. You were a cheap little con artist when I met you, tricking everyone into thinking you were any better than the whores at Covent Garden. You'd sell yourself for anything. I was the damn fool who bought you, and you never delivered the goods."

"Never? What has this life been? Who has built your household, established your name, brought you *every* introduction into society and painted a gloss of civility over your violent empire that is drenched in *blood*? Who has kept your secret for a decade? I have done everything you asked of me. Everything."

"Oh? Then where the fuck is my son?"

That blow lands too well, and I cannot speak.

He tosses the birds to the ground to scrub his hands over his face with a hollow laugh. "I really thought you weren't like other women. I was wrong. You're worse."

I am choked with rage, lost for the words that will do justice to my feeling.

"Yes," I spit. "I am so much worse. You cannot begin to imagine. You pathetic, aggrieved man. You preferred to unsex me, put me apart from womanhood and deny my emotions in the same breath as insulting all my kind. How dare you lay this blame on me when you wanted to *kill* me. I know what you are capable of."

He blanches, but he holds his ground. "You have no proof."

"Of which crime? So many stain your hands."

"And Cora's blood is on yours."

"I don't know what you're talking about."

"You're a poor liar, Lenore. Don't kid yourself." He flexes his hand, first into a fist, then fingers outstretched as if to slap me. "I am a good man. I will offer you this one last favor. Agree to a divorce, and we can both be free of each other."

I laugh. There is only one legal ground for divorce. "Now you confess your adultery? I *know*, Henry. Cora let it slip."

He frowns. "Cora?"

"I saw the diamonds. I know you took her to your bed. You wanted to marry her once I was dead and gone—once you had murdered me."

Henry has gone pale. "Is that why you . . . ?"

"Do you deny it?" I hiss.

"She would have made a better wife than you, there is no question. I saw a future for myself with a woman like her. But she was innocent in this."

It is as though I have missed a step, the world lurching. "No. You were having an affair. I saw you together."

"You have lost your mind." He is frightened of me. Truly frightened.

"But the diamonds," I falter.

"A gift. For her assistance in the Ajax matter."

"You're lying again." He must be. This cannot be true.

Cora. Oh God, Cora.

"I want a divorce," he says again. "You will agree to an uncontested divorce with you at fault for adultery."

My eyes narrow. "Will I, now?"

"Yes. Or you will live out your days locked in an asylum."

*

I know the moment hope died.

I can pull it up like a photograph even now, a detailed scene in my mind's eye, a living tableau.

It was perhaps a year after coming to Aunt Daphne. One evening, much like the others, alone, so breath-stealingly alone, it was too much. I felt myself dying, every silent part of me, rotting from the inside out.

My life stretched before me, three score years or more to endure, with nothing but my room, the door shutting, and the deep smothering solitude so vast my heart began to race, my stomach seethe. The dread that filled me was so great that if I could have climbed out of my own skin, I would have.

I could not stay. It was intolerable.

So I left.

I gathered up no things, packed no bags. I simply walked from my room, down the corridor, down the servants' backstairs to the entrance hall, where I opened the front door and walked out into the London night. The paving stones were cold beneath my stockinged feet, and at once a chill wind whipped my hair across my face. I walked perhaps a hundred yards beneath the gas lamps in no particular direction, only driven by a need to be away. If I kept walking in one direction and never stopped, perhaps I would come to the sea, and I could find a boat and sail away even farther. That was as far as my child's mind could think.

At the end of the street, a larger road ran in two directions. I would have to choose one. I stood on the curb, watching the carriages and dray carts rolling past. I did not know what to do. Perhaps someone like that man before would come and take me, and I would let him. Perhaps I would walk into the street and die, like my parents, in a splinter of wood and hooves. I was too hopeless to fear either end.

There were infinite options before me, but they all led nowhere. The only guarantee was death, perhaps slower, perhaps faster. But nowhere love. Nowhere home. There was no safety waiting, no welcoming arms. There was no one to help me, no one to worry for my absence. No one to see me.

There was nothing.

The world held nothing for me.

I was nothing.

Something within me broke. Something small, something vital.

All that was left to me was a will to survive.

And my best path to survival, however bleak, however deathly, was with Aunt Daphne.

I turned back, went to my room, and climbed under my covers.

I knew then that I could die, and no one would care. There was only me to care about myself. So I would not let my mortal body die; I would keep it alive and propel it forward by the only means possible. Instead, to survive, I must die inside; I must shut down every sense of self, every dream, every weakness.

I killed hope, to live.

Now I must find a way to live again.

Even if it means I must kill.

25

I KNEW IT WAS COMING. I knew what his threat would be.

But to pretend to offer me a choice is another cruelty on top of cruelty.

No.

I will not take his terms.

A shiver ripples through me, cold and prickling like needles across my skin, and my vision clouds.

I am hungry.

His clean white throat bobs as he swallows, waiting for my answer. A pulse point flutters beneath the skin, anxious and fragile. A fragile little man making demands of *me*.

No. I do not think so.

"I will not divorce you," I say, voice calm. It would ruin my reputation and leave me penniless; I have not given Henry ten years of my life to lose it all now. "You cannot do this. I told you. I have insurance."

Henry looks so pleased with himself. "Oh yes—your long and healthy life. I've heard excellent things about Dr. Foxfield's asylum. And well, perhaps I'll pay Lacey a visit and explain to him that my poor wife has been found to be suffering delusions of persecution. Get back my sensitive business information. I'm sure a sensible man like him will understand."

He is right. Of course he is right. Lacey is an astute man, but he is a man all the same. Henry's side is so much closer to his own. My pretty house of cards is knocked down again.

I should be scared, but somehow, I am not. My anger is like a cloak that wraps around me. I feel my fingers long and my nails sharp as I flex my hands. My teeth scrape against my full and rosy lips. I am hungry, and here is the man who has starved me for years.

I slash my hand across his face, drawing blood in four sharp lines.

Henry gapes in shock. Blood trickles into his eye, matting his eyebrow. "What the fuck are you—?"

I slash again, this time towards his throat, but he minds me now, dancing back more elegantly than I thought him capable of. It is as though I am a match that has been struck. I burn with the heat of the sun and the song in my veins. My senses sharpen. I can smell the sweat and fear on Henry, and the tinny, penny bright, salt-rich smell of his blood.

I want it.

I dart forward, hands crooked to claws, and he skitters back.

In the distance, a volley of shots rings out from behind me, and I lunge.

Henry bolts, and I chase him, feet swift over my moorland. It is wild and barren out here; he cannot hide from me. I fly across the ground, pure and perfect in the hunt, lungs and muscles in glorious harmony. He trips, and I am on him at once, scraping my nails along his jaw, but his knee catches my stomach, and he bucks me off, scrambling to his feet and running again before I am up.

The distance between us closes, springy heather giving way to limestone, and when he falls again, I am ready, bounding upon him teeth bared.

But Henry has also prepared. He swings his hand at my head, a rock clenched in his fist, and I dodge it narrowly, feeling it graze my thick knot of hair that has come loose from its pins. He smashes the rock into my shoulder, but it only drives me closer to him, his wet breath panting against my cheek, his eyes wild and rolling like a doe. His throat is there before me, a column of white and blue veins.

I stretch my jaw and bite.

Teeth sinking into the meat of his neck. The crunch of larynx and spurt of arterial blood into my mouth. I tear, rending his flesh, fingers digging beneath his collarbones, ripping and yanking and wrenching until the gurgling of his breath fades and his body's twitching stills beneath me.

I sit back, breathing hard, slick with blood and blazing with triumph. Somewhere, the guns still ring out and the dogs yelp. A breeze pulls at the hair stuck to my cheek.

I am alive.

In my mind, as clear as a bell, I see Carmilla, the heart of her face and the sharp snag of her teeth as she smiles, hear her cold, inhuman laughter.

26

It ends with blood.

Henry is a smear of flesh and bone across the heather where I have torn him apart. It is strange how little a human life is made from. The flaps of skin, bunched fibrous muscle, hair and jellied eyes, lolling tongue, blunt ribs and ribbons of gut.

I have unmade him.

There is a blanket wrapped around me, coarse and scratchy. A policeman placed it around my shoulders as the sun fell.

We were found, of course.

The blood had dried on my face and hands when the shooting party came across us. The dogs had found us long before then, following the scent of carnage and descending eagerly. When the men with their guns finally arrived, the dogs had bloody mouths and paws, but they moved sluggishly, satiated and docile.

I think there was a great deal of screaming before the police came.

It is all over for me. I cannot see a way out.

Detective Inspector Lacey crouches beside me, as Henry's body is covered by a sheet, and asks me to tell a story.

I am lost for words.

Then one of the men says something, almost thrown away: "Fool of a man quite literally couldn't train a dog to save his life."

Ah. There. The smallest light in the dark.

The dogs, I explain softly. The dogs attacked him. I give out the story of the mauled servant when we first arrived, the dogs wild at the shoot, stealing birds and biting at shins. Yes. The dogs with their stained snouts and fat bellies.

What other explanation is there?

Who could look at me and think I have done this to my husband?

The men nod and look at one another. Yes, this is right. A lone woman of good breeding and impeccable taste, and a grasping, vulgar man with his sly business affairs and naked ambition.

I do not quite believe it, but it happens. Ranks close around me. Lacey is edged away, and I have a blanket and tea, a wet cloth for the blood smeared across my face. Lacey makes his way around the men, asking questions, and piece by piece, the story stitches together. It is a gruesome story, but simple. Someone jokes that whoever marries me next will be a rich man. No one laughs.

Is this it? Am I free?

The knot in my chest eases a little, and my fingers grow warm around the tea. I close my eyes and feel the honey-scented dusk breeze on my skin. Perhaps I am crying; I can no longer tell.

As the light fails and the police disperse the crowd, a fine carriage draws up, as unlikely in this place as a brutal crime, but there all the same, with shining black lacquer paint and gold at the windows.

The footman jumps down and opens the door to let out the impeccably dressed woman inside. She is elegant in red silk, her glossy chestnut hair piled atop her head and a delicate, high-brimmed hat.

Carmilla lifts her skirts and crosses the moor, hem brushing yellow-flowered bog asphodel, fruiting bilberry plants, and sphagnum moss. The crowd parts around her reverentially, dazed by her radiant beauty. Even Lacey takes off his hat in respect.

She comes all the way to my side, cooing in sympathy at my terrible state.

"Gentlemen, thank you for taking care of my dear friend. You must allow her to come with me now. After such great shock, a person must be cared for with the greatest tenderness."

The men nod in agreement. This is correct; Carmilla is a fine woman.

I look up to her and see that terrible dark light in her eyes, as I know it now shines in mine.

We are the same.

Carmilla smiles, extends her hand to me. "Come, my dear. You must be so terribly hungry."

Historical note

I have taken a few liberties with the geography of Sheffield and the Peaks where I felt narrative flow trumped pinpoint historical accuracy. Mostly notably, the station at Hathersage wasn't built until 1894 but I have brought it forward a little in order to make travel a little more feasible for what were still remote locations that required crossing stretches of open moorland.

Several resources were invaluable in the research for this novel. This is not a bibliography, more a collection of interesting books and resources I am indebted to, or that I think readers might find interesting.

To map and conjure Sheffield and the Peak District of the late nineteenth century, I particularly owe a debt to the travel guides and trade directories of the era. The 1879 *Illustrated Guide to Sheffield* gave particular detail of the daily life of the city, including the new and old routes from the city to Hathersage and other destinations. *Murray's Handbook for Travellers in Yorkshire* was also helpful, as were a number of trades directories for the city. The National Library of Scotland provides an extremely helpful database of interactive historical Ordinance Survey maps that helped me navigate Lenore around a city that has been half lost to history. Finally, *A History of the Peak District Moors* by David Hey provided much helpful background.

Henry's Ajax Works is loosely inspired by real steelworks like the Atlas Works and the Cyclopse Works. The steel industry was spread throughout Sheffield from major smelting operations to piecework done in private homes to the smaller grinding hulls speckled along the city's rivers. You can see evidence of this heritage wherever you go in the city, following routes up the Rivlin and Don, where waterwheels, industrial buildings, and abandoned grindstones are grown over by ivy and ferns, like the ruins of some mythical past. Kelham Island museum is particularly worth a visit, as is the Abbeydale industrial hamlet museum. Go and see the Bessemer converter on Kelham Island; it is truly a frightful and wonderous thing. I have never felt more small and vulnerable than I have standing beneath it.

Sheffield has also been at the heart of the trades union movements throughout its history. The "Outrages" Lenore references were a conflict between trade unionists and factory bosses that took place in Sheffield in the 1860s. Much has been written on the episode, but I found particularly helpful as a starting point a study guide created by the Sheffield City Council Libraries Archives and Information team and available online.

I am grateful to the museums of Sheffield for their thorough research and detailed displays that I was able to access online and in person. There are countless resources on the history of working conditions in the steel industry, but I found particularly interesting a series of articles published in the *Illustrated London News* in 1866, entitled "The Trades of Sheffield." The strange knife statue Henry presents to his guests at the Ajax Works is based on a real object called the Year Knife, made by Joseph Rodgers and Sons in 1821, and you can see it on display at the Kelham Island Museum.

To create the material world of the period, I turned to a number of books, particularly Judith Flanders's very accessible works on the Victorian City and the Victorian Home, and *The Victorian Girl and the Feminine Ideal* by Deborah Gorham. All the meals eaten are taken from menus supplied in *Mrs. Beeton's Book of Household Management*, as well as much advice and detail from a number of contemporary etiquette guides too numerous to mention. I looked to fashion plates from the era for inspiration for Lenore, Cora, Carmilla, and Henry's dress, as well as items from the collections at the V&A in London and the Met in New York City.

Hungerstone owes, of course, a huge debt to *Carmilla* by Sheridan Le Fanu, but it also takes inspiration from Coleridge's *Christabel* (the inspiration for Carmilla), Miss Havisham and Estella in *Great Expectations*, Keats's *Lamia*, Bram Stoker's *Dracula*, and Wilkie Collins's *The Woman in White* and *The Moonstone*—and a huge number of other Victorian sensation novels. Texts such as *The Invention of Murder* by Judith Flanders, *The Arsenic Century* by James C. Whorton, as well as *Victorian Sensation* by Michael Diamond, *Violent Women and Sensation Fiction* by Andrew Mangham, and *Studies in Scarlet* by John West provided invaluable context.

I am grateful also to Tim Neal for his extensive knowledge of the natural world of the Peak District, and the endless walks we have taken together, where he has kindly educated me on the plants, rocks, and animals of this land, as well as the human history marked across it.

Acknowledgments

I wrote *Hungerstone* in a great deal of anger and confusion, at a strange inflection point in my life where some tragedies had come to pass and I was left in the aftermath, wondering what it had all been for, the life I had exhausted myself building, the extreme vigilance with which I held myself. I became interested in the idea of appetite in its most expansive sense, in the world of desire, and why it is that for so many of us it is a world fraught and tentative. I was interested in our relationship with demand and dependency, and what injuries here can do to our own sense of our right to want, to need. The figure of the vampire is a sinister one, and one of pure want, need, of monstrous appetite. Rereading *Carmilla* pushed a door open, gave root to my thinking, and narrative shape to my own confused appetite. There was a book in here somewhere, and consumed by my own rage and frustration I poured it out onto the page, whether more or less successfully, that is for you to decide.

My previous novel, *Bitterthorn*, was just as personal, but I am quite nervous to share this darker, less palatable story, to find out whether anyone else will recognize these feelings. I hope you do and I hope you don't. I hope you know your own hunger, and how to feed it well.

I am grateful to the teams at Manilla Press/Bonnier and Zando, to my editors Sophie and Erin, Nicole Otto, Ellie Pilcher, Beth

Whitelaw, Nikki Mander, Justine Taylor, Zoe Yang, Natalia Cacciatore, Sophie Raoufi, Misha Manani, Vincent Kelleher, Stuart Finglass, Mark Williams, Kevin Hawkins, Jeff Jamieson, Jennie Harwood, Robyn Haque, Alan Scollan, Andrea Tome, Stacey Hamilton, Laura Makela, Jenny Richards, and Nick Stearn.

To Hellie Ogden for her continued support and confidence in me and my work, you have taught me so much. And to Caitlin Mahoney, for finding the perfect home in the US. I am very lucky to work with such wonderful, clever, and incisive women.

To my friends within the industry, who know exactly how mad it can make you, and my friends outside it, who remind me it's only books. To my family, particularly Tim, Saskia, and Coco, to whom the book is dedicated. Thank you for welcoming me in, and introducing me to a landscape that has profoundly changed me. Thank you for listening to me ramble about book ideas, and your patience with my frequent emotional struggles.

Thinking of the dead who have so shaped me, but did not get to see where it was all going.

Kat Dunn grew up in London and has lived in Japan, Australia, and France. She has a BA in Japanese from SOAS and an MA in English from Warwick. She's written about mental health for Mind and the *Guardian*, and worked as a translator for Japanese television. Her YA has been published by Head of Zeus and Andersen Press and has been nominated for the Carnegie Medal for Writing and shortlisted for the Nero Book Award.